Red DIAMOND
PRIVATE EYE

MARK SCHORR

St. Martin's Press   New York

Design by Kingsley Parker

Library of Congress Cataloging in Publication Data

Schorr, Mark.
  Red Diamond, private eye.

  I. Title.
PS3537.G598R4 1983   813'.52   82-21534
ISBN 0-312-66645-4

First Edition

10 9 8 7 6 5 4 3 2 1

To B. V. D. & K

Red
DIAMOND

1

I hit the floor in the darkened room as the slug from the big .45 whistled past my head like a truck driver ogling a pretty girl. There were two more whistles, followed by thuds, as the lead burrowed into the cracked plaster behind me.

The rotgut I'd soaked up at the Arab's place in the Tenderloin was making me slow. I fumbled under my trenchcoat for my roscoe. The butt felt like a royal flush at a hot poker game as it slipped into my hand.

My eyes were just getting used to the dark when the door opened and a bucketful of light was thrown in. A woman's shape filled the doorway.

"Red?" she asked.

"Get down," I yelled, jumping up and letting go two rounds where I'd last seen the muzzle flash.

There was a male grunt as my .38 earned its keep again.

Fifi had frozen in the doorway, the light behind her giving her blond hair a halo. Her big blue eyes were trying to take in the scene that her brain didn't want to know about.

"It's all right, angel," I said, walking slowly to where she stood quivering. "Everything's taken care of."

"I knew I'd find you here," the woman's voice said. It was harsh, sarcastic, not like Fifi's usual throaty caress. It cut through the fantasy, and Simon set the book down on the parson's table next to his chair.

Milly had padded up soundlessly on puffy pink slippers and found him in his ratty but comfortable overstuffed chair in the unfinished basement. He leaned back and braced himself for the inevitable tirade.

"You and your damn books," she began. "Other men have serious hobbies. Like woodworking, so maybe you could fix up this dump. Or coin collecting. Do you know Jasper Murdock's collection is worth over twenty thousand dollars?"

She waited until he acknowledged her question with a properly surprised "hmmm."

"He only spent about three thousand dollars, she told me, and now it's worth nearly seven times that," Milly continued. "They had a good offer just the other day, they can sell it and buy . . . ."

Even as she berated him, he couldn't help but admire her. Without make-up, a slumbery bleariness clinging to her eyes, she still seemed too good for him.

At forty, she had come into a mature beauty, better even than when he had married her, nineteen years earlier. Nineteen years. It was hard to believe.

She had gained a few pounds over the years, but they were well distributed. Thick auburn hair framed her face well, and she knew it. When Simon had met her at the diner where she was waitressing she'd been a frisky colt, influenced by her high school-aged co-workers. Now, she was a thoroughbred.

". . . or a second job," she was saying. "Annie was telling me Peter makes three hundred and fifty a week moonlighting at the deli. They're buying a new car next week. Are you listening to me?"

"Annie and Peter are getting a new car," Simon repeated dutifully.

"That's right. I hope you heard what I said. I'm fed up. Now it's after eight-thirty and you better start getting ready."

He watched her walk away, admiring her shape as the nightgown curved around her hips. Maybe there was time for . . . no, he decided without finishing the thought. He'd have to get going. And she just didn't feel the same way about him that he did about her.

Simon got out of the chair and walked to the bookcase at the far wall. He'd made it in high school, his final project. He'd been an average student, except for shop, where he was terrible. He still had the scars on his hands from slipped chisels to prove it.

The six-foot-high bookcase, with gaping joints and mismatched stain, held his most prized possessions.

Simon had several thousand books and magazines. Others may have had larger libraries, but no one loved their collection as much. He had read all of them, most of them at least twice. He could open them instinctively to his favorite scenes.

The shelves were packed with the classics. Only the best were on display, with a dozen or so cartons tucked away in the garage.

As he stepped up to the bookshelves, the unfinished room around him blurred. His fingers tingled as he reached out and made contact with his passports to a better world.

It was a world where men were men, and women were available. Simon had lived in the city all his life, and westerns had no appeal. Science fiction was ridiculous. Nonfiction was like reading a textbook. Simon's library was devoted to tough-guy literature, where tommy guns were described as musical, and the hero could take it on the jaw and give it back in spades.

There were the *Black Mask, Dime Detective, Crime Busters, Gang Worlds, Spicy Detective, Thrilling Detective* and *Detective Fiction Weekly* pulps.

Most were so fragile he couldn't open them without doing damage to the brittle yellow pages. But just gazing at the covers, he could see Race Williams pulling the trigger, or the Continental Op dodging a bullet, or Max Latin outfoxing the cops.

Then there were the paperbacks and the hardcovers,

about an even mix, many continuing the adventures of friends he'd first met in the pulps. The hard-boiled dicks.

When he'd first found his passion, he'd tried other mysteries. But Erle Stanley Gardner's Perry Mason was no match for his Lester Leith. Ngaio Marsh's Roderick Alleyn was too much of a gentleman. That was the problem with the British. From Sherlock Holmes to Nayland Smith to James Bond. They drank French wine that cost more than a good meal. And they took time out from fistfights to drink tea.

John Dalmas, Cellini Smith, Race Williams, Mike Hammer, Mike Shayne, Lew Archer, Jo Gar, Dick Donahue, Pete Wennick, Oscar Sail, Chester Drum. And, of course, the kings. The Continental Op, Sam Spade, Travis McGee, Philip Marlowe and Red Diamond. Sagas of guns, girls and guts.

It was Red Diamond he'd been with that morning. Diamond didn't waste his time talking. He was eloquent in several calibers. He always got his man, the girl, a couple of knocks in the head, and his fee. Red Diamond was the last person in the world you'd want to mess with. What a guy!

He stepped back from the bookcase and scanned some of the titles. *Trigger Happy, Blood on My Fists, My Job Is Murder, Terror Is My Trade, The Crimson Corpse, Killer at the Beach, The Lady in the Lake.* He could almost smell the cordite.

Another step back, and his bleary surroundings came into focus. An unfinished, sparsely furnished basement in Hicksville.

He was feeling every day of his forty-two years as he began walking upstairs to prepare for another day. Each ounce of his 225 pounds seemed to beg to go back to his chair, to relax and read how Diamond would explain what happened to Fifi.

Not that there was any suspense. He'd read the book fourteen times. If he dropped it, which he was careful not

4

to do, it would automatically open to the best parts, the scenes he'd read again and again.

As he climbed the stairs, each step rattled under his foot, reminding him of his bulk and the flimsiness of the house.

It was one of twenty identical tract houses set on six acres of former Long Island marsh. The land was gradually returning to its primordial state. The houses were sinking, some at a rate of an inch a year.

Simon's house was going down the quickest, so fast his neighbors kidded him about when he'd convert the attic to a basement. It wasn't that funny, but aside from the weather, and the deterioration of the property, there wasn't much for him to talk with them about.

The house itself was a seven-room ranch-style structure, made of the cheapest materials possible. So cheap that the contractor had been indicted by a federal grand jury investigating organized crime and shoddy practices in the construction industry. Two witnesses had been murdered, and the third suddenly forgot everything he knew about construction and moved to Canada.

After reading in the newspapers about what had happened to the witnesses, the homeowners decided they could live with cracking plaster, walls as thin as crepe and houses that creaked when the wind blew.

Actually, there were only fourteen houses left in the group. Six had burned down because of electrical fires caused by substandard wiring installed by the contractor's unlicensed cousin. The cousin's company had gone out of business, and through microscopically fine clauses in the contract, repairs became the responsibility of the homeowner.

It had cost Simon nine thousand dollars to have the house rewired. Then there'd been the money for the plumber to find out why Simon had an indoor swimming pool in his basement; the carpenter to shore up sagging beams in the attic; the exterminator who subdued the

5

termite swarm that was nibbling the house into oblivion; and the assorted handymen who had done to his bankbook what the termites were doing to his wood.

The house was seven years old.

"Good morning, Dad," Sean said as Simon reached the top of the stairs. The teenager's eyes twinkled, his smile was warm, his lean eighteen-year-old body held perfectly erect as he walked to the kitchen. He had the same soft tread as his mother.

"How are you?" he asked Simon.

"Fine, Sean. And you?"

"Just fine. Looks like it's going to be a nice day," Sean said. "Well, got to hurry up and make myself a sandwich. Don't want to bother Mom. I have a computer club meeting before classes today, but I don't want to skip breakfast."

"Have a good day," Simon said.

"Thanks. You too." Sean hurried off.

Their conversations were always so stiff, like dialogue out of a bad TV commercial. His own son, and there seemed to be nothing to talk about. What could Simon say to someone who was perfect?

Well, maybe not perfect. But damn close. The kid was brilliant. He'd already been offered jobs by a couple of *Fortune* 500 corporations. Starting pay fifty thou a year. He ranked fifth in chess on the East Coast, spoke fluent French and Spanish and had a patent on some electronic gadget that Simon didn't really understand. Simon had grunted knowingly when Sean, in a mere three hours, explained the concept and how he'd worked it out.

But Sean wasn't just some bright egghead in an ivory tower. He was also the pitcher on the baseball team, and second-string quarterback for the college football team. He was an inch taller than Simon at six feet two inches, and about twenty pounds lighter. He moved with the lithe grace of a natural athlete.

He was popular with the guys, successful with the girls,

6

charismatic, healthy and disgustingly happy. Simon wondered how something so perfect could spring from his
meager loins.

What did Sean think of his father, the cabbie? Did his
son think about him at all?

As Simon passed through the living room, the pop-eyed
Keene paintings on the wall smirked at him. Milly
boasted how she'd decorated the house herself. Simon
thought she'd done a terrible job, but he dared not complain, or Milly would smoothly segue into how if she had
more money, she could decorate better.

He made it to the bathroom on the second floor and
began to shave.

"Are you almost done in there?" Milly shouted through
the flimsy bathroom door.

The safety razor slipped on his lathered jowl. It lifted
the flesh and nipped out a thin slice, leaving a red line
that leaked a few droplets of blood onto Simon's green
robe.

"Are you in a hurry?" he yelled back to her as he
pressed a nubbin of toilet tissue on his cut.

"I don't have all day," she shouted back.

It didn't pay to argue with her about bathroom time,
and how even he was entitled to some. Milly inevitably
turned it into an economic discussion, how if they had a
bigger house, with more facilities, etc. etc.

Like an attacking snake, her complaints would then
twist and turn to how little Simon made, how everyone
else his age was making more, the successful men she
could've married, how ashamed she was of her wardrobe,
and on and on.

He preferred to retreat to the unfinished bathroom in
the unfinished basement.

It was always easier going down. He was that much
closer to his library.

The book was lying where he'd left it, folded open to the
page he'd been reading. He was glad he'd come back

7

down. How could he be so careless, leaving the opus with its spine being stretched like a heretic on the rack?

He pressed it shut and gave the book a squeeze as he walked into the small bathroom. He closed the toilet cover, sat down, and studied the illustration on the paperback's cover.

Under the blood-red letters *Diamond in the Rough* was a bosomy blonde with knowing blue eyes. Red Diamond had his arm around her, his strong hand gripping her shoulder. The other hand held a smoking .38. Diamond was smiling, a grim grin that exposed teeth as hard as his eyes.

Simon caressed the book again, extending the foreplay, as he blotted out his surroundings and began to read.

I wanted to wipe my feet on the hood's face, but the sawed-off shotgun in his hand ruled out using him for a welcome mat. At least for the moment, it was his show.

"Against the wall," he said, gesturing with the ugly double-barreled weapon.

I did as I was told. I looked at the wall, figuring it might be the last thing I saw. There was a framed picture of FDR nailed onto the beige painted surface.

It wasn't a swell place to die, a Bowery flophouse with hot and cold running roaches. Then again, when the boys from the morgue are scraping you off the wall, it don't matter if you're in a flophouse or a mansion.

I turned to face the punk with the gun. A couple of beads of sweat clung to a mustache as thick as a pauper's sole.

"Turn around," he barked.

"What are you going to do, shoot me?"

He looked the way I felt.

"You better step back when you pull the trigger."

There was a twitch at the youthful gunman's mouth.

"Why's that?"

"Because when you pull that trigger, it's going to look

like someone threw two hundred pounds of chopmeat into a fan."

The barrel began to shiver a little.

"And you wouldn't want to get my brains and eyeballs and guts all over that fancy suit. What would your girlfriend say if she saw you looking like—"

"Stop it!" the gunman yelled. The gun was shaking now, and he was gnawing his upper lip.

"Hit him now," I yelled over the hood's shoulder. It was an old gag, but the punk was shaken enough to go for it.

As he turned his head, I grabbed FDR's picture off the wall, and smashed it down on his head. The heavy wooden frame pinned his arms to his side.

I only hit him twice. He was just a kid with a gun trying to do a man's job. He looked even younger after I put him to sleep.

The torn picture of FDR lay on the floor. I guessed he didn't mind getting ripped up for a good cause.

And it's not many guys can say they got saved by the president himself.

The doorbell upstairs chimed "Raindrops Keep Falling on My Head." It lifted him out of his reverie. He tried to ignore it, but by the third trill he knew he'd have to answer it.

"I'm coming, I'm coming," he yelled as he set the book down on the toilet-tank cover.

It wasn't so much the break in the story, he thought as he trudged up the stairs again. It was the whole mood. He knew the plots by heart, and still didn't understand many of them. Everybody had a perfectly good motive for killing all the people they did, which Spade or Marlowe could explain neatly in the end. But who knew what was going on? Who cared? It was the scent of jacarandas that Chandler could shove up your nose, or the sound of the Fat Man's laugh that Hammett could make familiar. It was

9

a world he could slip into. Who cared if it made sense?

Melonie was at the door. He remembered her as a pig-tailed, fresh-faced young girl, always hopping on his lap and asking to hear a story.

No one could've matched the sixteen-year-old at the door with the innocent of his memories.

Her eyes were half-closed, with bags under them the size of overnight luggage. Make-up that looked like it was laid on with a trowel did little to add to her charm. There was a streak of green in her long, greasy brown hair.

She was wearing a white silk blouse that had a couple of stains on it, and was so low cut he couldn't avoid gazing at his daughter's cleavage. The feeling revolted him.

"This is Roger," she said, pointing to a young man standing behind her. "He's into Rolfing."

"Are you a professional golfer?" Simon asked.

Roger didn't look like much of an athlete. He had a pudgy, debauched face, with pale and pitted skin. His head reminded Simon of a golf ball.

"Not golfing, Rolfing," Roger said in a condescending whine as unpleasant as his features. "It puts you in touch with your body." Roger reached over and squeezed Melonie's behind.

Simon felt like snapping the scrawny neck under the golf ball head. But he'd been through it before. All he'd gotten were ugly scenes, with Milly supporting Melonie. He guessed Milly took some sort of secret pleasure in watching their daughter's escapades.

Roger was just the latest in a long parade of oddballs who promised to raise her consciousness if she dropped her drawers. Yogurt yogis, EST espousers, scientology scholars and supposed practitioners of religions formerly restricted to the upper Alps. They were drawn to Melo-nie's mecca, her bedroom, where they closed the door and made noises of religious ecstasy.

"What happened to your key, young lady?" Simon asked, trying to gain control as Melonie stepped into the house.

She stood close to him, pelvis outstretched. He stepped back.

"I met this guy at the club, and, you know he was going to take me home, and like I gave him the key, but you know, later, after we spent some time together, our karmas didn't like click."

Time to change the locks again, Simon thought. He looked over at Roger, who was smirking off into space.

"So this prize is a second fiddle guru," Simon said.

"Oh Daddy," Melonie said, reaching for Roger's hand and pulling him past her father into the house.

The couple headed upstairs, Melonie leading, and Roger staring at the jeans stretched skintight on her rump.

Simon slammed the door and the house shook.

Milly's dog, a Pekingese who wore a yellow ribbon in her hair, came charging out from under the couch and ran yipping straight to the door. Seeing there were no intruders to attack, she turned to Simon's ankle and began a feverish assault on the bluish vein that swelled on his bare foot.

"What did you do to get Vossie so upset," Milly hollered from the top of the stairs.

"Nothing," he said, bending over to fend off the crazed Pekingese's attack. She nipped at his fingers. They were like two old boxers who had fought each other so many times they could anticipate their adversary's every move.

He reached for the scruff of her neck, she danced backwards, then darted to his left ankle and nipped. He grabbed her hair and she screamed as if he'd stabbed her.

Milly bounded down the stairs and lifted Vossie to her bosom while glaring at Simon.

"You disgusting animal! You bully! You creep!" she said, adding more venom to each word. The dog nestled in her arms and sneered at Simon.

Milly went back to the bedroom and snuggled under the covers with the dog. Simon finished preparing for the day in the upstairs bathroom.

He dressed in the bedroom without saying a word to Milly, who was making cooing noises in the dog's ear. He put on a red- and black-checked flannel shirt, blue slacks that were too tight, and stretched-out nylon socks. A small hole was beginning to grow in the bottom of his Navy surplus oxfords. He laced them up and wrapped a belt around his girth.

He looked back to say goodbye, but Milly ignored him as she rubbed noses with the little beast.

The door to Melonie's room was shut as he walked past.

He walked down to the basement, giving his library a wistful look as he passed, and went through the basement door directly into the garage.

There were two cars parked inside—Milly's three-year-old, gas-guzzling station wagon, and Simon's cab.

It was the bright yellow mandated by New York City: smile button yellow with a dab of orange to it. The cab had 123,000 miles on it. It was five years old. Every part had been replaced at least once.

Simon was an owner-driver, one of the 5,000 among New York City's medallion fleet of 11,787 cabs. The medallion, which had cost him $56,000, entitled him to cruise the streets for fares.

For fifteen some-odd years, Simon had been one of the other 6,787, a driver for the fleets, an employee, busting his chops and his kidneys for ten hours a day to pay the bills. Three years earlier, he'd scraped together enough to buy the medallion, and a used cab. He was able to just barely make the payments, but at last he was his own boss.

He cranked the engine over six times before it caught. He pulled on the windbreaker he kept on the front seat, adjusted his clipboard, got out, and opened the garage door.

Milly always nagged him about opening the door before he started the engine.

"You'll die someday of carbon monoxide poisoning and leave me a stack of bills," she said in her usual affectionate way.

She didn't understand that Simon didn't like being seen in his cab by his neighbors. Many of them were pompous low-level executives. Others made even more, as used car salesmen and television repairmen. They didn't understand that an owner-driver was not just another cabbie.

He pulled out into the street, leaving the garage door open. Milly hated that too. Maybe Vossie would run away. Simon should be so lucky.

He drove quickly, eager to put distance between himself and his home and neighbors. Maybe it would be a good day. No one saw him leave.

What was a good day? A fare to the airport? A pretty, flirtatious customer? A big tip? No drunks throwing up in the back seat? No other cabbie cutting him off and stealing a fare? A rider who treated him with respect?

The cab took to the Long Island Expressway like a faithful old horse, knowing the way to the city without so much as a giddyap. But it was a tired old horse, stumbling with every pothole and gasping bluish smoke every time he jabbed down on the accelerator.

He rolled down the window and let the air rush across his face. The speed was an unusual pleasure on the road nicknamed "The World's Biggest Parking Lot." It was one of Simon's few joys—he could make his own hours, and not fight rush-hour traffic like ordinary Joes.

No one but another cabbie would understand. He was free to go where he wanted. Hell, he could even go to Brooklyn if he wanted.

Damn, he thought, I forgot to bring a book. A hard-boiled dick to keep him company made the day more tolerable. Sometimes he'd just pull over under the West Side Highway and read. One day, he'd actually only spent a couple of hours on the road. Milly had been furious when he'd come home with twenty-three dollars and change.

He knew she had a point. He just didn't care about money. When he'd hit thirty-five, he'd realized that there was no pot of gold at the end of the rainbow. Just gallstones. He'd stopped going out weekends to play ball with the guys. He'd stopped going dancing once a week with Milly. A passing interest in tough-guy literature had become an addiction.

He had a choice. Either get an ulcer, or accept what he had. He hadn't done so bad. A house, a family, a marriage that, while it was far from blissful, had lasted. It just hadn't turned out the way he planned.

2

He took the Midtown Tunnel into the city, leaving his on-duty light off as he headed south. He parked his cab in the long line of yellow outside the Balmoral Cafe on Fourteenth Street.

The usual raucous sounds of human, mostly male voices, rattling trays and silverware and assorted movement hit him as soon as he pushed through the revolving doors. The cloud of cigar and cigarette smoke was beginning to grow.

He spotted a few of the regulars as he made his way to the counter. A couple of bag ladies nursing coffees while the manager glared at them, old men who slept in the shelter nearby and spent their days hanging out in the café, bookies, cabbies, cops, a few office workers, and assorted city flotsam filled out the crew.

There were shouts of greeting, lost amid the clatter, as cabbies recognized and hailed each other. It was an axiom of city life that on a rainy day, the only place to find a cabbie in New York was inside the Balmoral.

He picked up a scuffed and stained plastic tray and got on the line moving slowly past the glass and stainless-steel counter.

"Hey Sy, how you doing?" Benny asked, smoothly sliding in front of him on line.

In his barely five-foot-tall body, Benny had managed to incorporate every ailment known to man, and some as yet unknown. In the two dozen years Simon had known him, Benny had never missed a day's work, or a chance to complain.

Without waiting for Simon's answer, he began his recitation. "Me, I'm not so good. These hemorrhoids, you wouldn't wish on your worst enemy. The pain, I can't describe. I went to a doctor, he looked at my kidneys, he said he's amazed I'm still alive. And my heart—"

"Excuse me," Simon said, cutting Benny off and jumping ahead on the line. He wanted to get away before Benny launched into his enthusiastic description of his bowel movements.

The portly man in front of Simon grabbed the piece of cheesecake Simon had his eye on. The last piece. Simon didn't bother asking the surly, white-aproned men behind the counter if they'd be putting out a fresh piece. The Balmoral help were legendary for their invective if they felt put upon, like if a patron asked for help.

Simon wound up with a cup of strong coffee and an insipid apple Danish.

"Hey, hey Sy! C'mon, take a load off your feet," he heard as he paid the cashier.

He made his way through the crowded restaurant, spilling most of his coffee on his tray as he was bumped and jostled by the currents of humanity that passed through the narrow spaces between the tables.

Nick the Greek, Pedro, Alex and Eddie Fong were seated at a table near a giant artificial potted plant. Their talk halted briefly as Simon pulled up a chair and they greeted him. Eddie, the thinnest of the men even though he had the most on his plate, was eager to continue his spiel.

"So like I was saying, this baby is running in the fifth

at Aqueduct. She could walk past the rest of those nags. The last time she was with this jockey at Belmont, she did the track in just under—"

Pedro let out a resounding belch and the men laughed. Eddie was such an astute judge of horseflesh that everything he owned had been hocked to keep his bookie from having Eddie's legs broken.

The bookie, a fat man known as Dirty Dom, was holding court on the other side of the cafeteria. Applicants and supplicants would come up to him and bet their souls away. Dirty Dom lived on a twenty-five-acre estate on the north shore of Long Island. The cabbies lived in apartments and small houses with big mortgages. Simon recognized a losing proposition, and gambling was one vice that had no allure for him.

"You know Sy, there's gonna be an opening in my radio group next month," Pedro said.

"Yeah?" Simon said, sipping his coffee.

"For ten Gs it's a bargain," Pedro said. "We're the second busiest group in town. You get good calls from our dispatchers, not the pukin' winos. Wall Street types."

"Who don't tip worth a shit," Nick the Greek said.

Pedro ignored him. "You're all alone out in the street," he said. "With a radio you can call for help. What would you do if some junkie puts a shiv in your neck?"

"I know what I'd do," Nick said. "I'd crap in my pants and give him the money."

Alex, at sixty-one, the oldest member of the group, mumbled. His talking was such an unusual event that everyone around the table quieted down.

"I got stuck up again last week," Alex said, his words barely audible. "A white guy. Can you believe it? At the end of my shift. He got eighty-seven dollars." He returned to silence and sipped his tea.

The men took turns telling stories of how they'd been robbed. Nick and Pedro were smug. They had bulletproof partitions and felt safe.

"Makes me feel like I'm in a prison," Eddie said. "I'm carrying instead."

"What?" Simon asked.

"I got me a .38 off this guy I picked up over by the docks last week. Cost me seventy-five bucks, but the next time some bastard tries to rip me off, I'm gonna punch his ticket."

"Louie tried that," Nick said. Louie had been stuck up six times before he'd gotten his gun. The seventh time, he tried fighting back. His funeral had been three months ago.

Simon broke the silence that ensued as they mourned their companion.

"You know, we don't get enough respect," Simon said.

"What are you, Rodney Dangerfield?" Nick asked.

"I mean it. They had this big fuss with the kids in the country," Simon continued. "Talking about how great truckers and construction workers are. And what do we get?"

A wisecrack was forming on Nick's lips and Simon cut him off. "I tell you what we get. A movie about some nut case who goes around shooting people. And some song about a guy wants to fly an airplane. And a TV sitcom. Big deal!"

"We heard this before, Sy," Eddie said. "So what are you going to do about it? Make the fares sign a petition? Run for president?"

"It just don't seem right," Simon said. "Like in the old days, we had a mystique."

"Sounds like a type of perfume," Nick said.

The men laughed, but Simon persisted.

"Bootlegging. Knocking around. Like Steve Midnight. And all the private eyes had a cabbie they used to—"

Pedro belched, and the men laughed again. Simon sulked.

The conversation drifted through sports, politics and the economy. Simon tried to regain control, but didn't get any support.

17

Then Pedro, at thirty-one the youngest and already twice divorced, began regaling the men with a semipornographic tale about his latest girlfriend and her taste for whipped cream.

Simon finished his breakfast and headed out.

His first fare was a businessman who nervously tapped his attaché case as they headed crosstown; then an elderly matron, taking her Yorkie to the vet; then two businessmen going to a chichi restaurant for a long lunch.

A little excitement when he picked up a model in the garment center, and drove her up to an East Side town house. She was frigid and aloof as he tried to make conversation, and stiffed him on the tip.

"Bitch," he muttered as she strode away from the cab.

Cruising the Upper East Side, he picked up a flagrantly gay man who boasted of being a coke dealer. Simon took him to the lower West Side, to the meat market where the leather bars were. Although the man wanted to talk, Simon kept conversation to a minimum. Homosexuals made him feel uncomfortable.

"Instead of cash, you want a little blow as payment?" the man asked as they pulled to a stop in front of The Gay Blade bar.

"I ain't no fag," Simon snapped, realizing he was probably ruining whatever chance he had for a tip.

"I can tell that," the man said disapprovingly, fingering a small gold spoon on a chain around his neck. "A blow is coke, you silly, provincial fool."

"The meter says nine fifty. That's cash. American."

The man threw a ten-dollar bill at Simon and got out.

A few more dull fares: a conservative man who wanted to discuss politics; a woman who talked to herself, but tipped him two dollars on a three-dollar ride; and then it was time for his midafternoon break.

More chatting with a couple of cabbie cronies at a West Side hamburger joint. Again, someone brought up the idea of buying into a radio group. Simon argued that he liked his freedom, though he knew that wasn't really much of an argument. He just couldn't afford it.

Traffic was beginning to thicken with the evening rush hour impending when he spotted the fare standing on the corner of Forty-second Street and Second Avenue. It was a good spot—diplomats from the United Nations, reporters from the *Daily News*, assorted Upper-East-Side types—and he cut across two lanes of traffic to make his pickup.

"You're a loser, just like me," the man said as he slid into the back seat of the cab. He had the nondescript appearance of a good spy—he could disappear in a phone booth.

Simon shifted in his seat so he could study him in his rearview mirror. He wasn't in the mood for a crazy.

The man looked sane. Middle-aged, medium build, cleanshaven, thinning brown hair. A dark-colored suit that was clean, but out of fashion. Simon felt himself forgetting the face as soon as he shifted his eyes back to the roadway.

"You wanna go somewhere or you just wanna talk? You wanna talk, I know a good shrink," Simon said, putting on his toughest tones. The best way to deal with loonies was to show them who's boss right away, even if the words sounded hollow.

"Fourteenth and Broadway. Near the Balmoral," the man said.

As he pulled out into traffic, Simon regretted snapping at the stranger. He seemed harmless as he sat silently in the back seat, gazing out the window.

"What'd you mean by that crack?" he asked the man several blocks later.

The nondescript man hesitated briefly. "I recognize a kindred spirit. No offense meant. You know, a guy who is looking for a better place, but who doesn't know where to look, who sorta . . ." He paused in his verbal fit, as his mind struggled to catch up with his mouth.

"Who is, who is, afraid to look. Sort of content with things in the rut. Maybe watch TV all the time. Just leave it on and let the voices keep talking." The stranger's words were spilling out, banging into each other like Coney Island bumper cars.

"Everyone wants green grass. Crab grass. Doesn't work. Deodorant. Foot odor. Sit com. Shit com. All the pressure. Building up. Falling down. No way out. Change the channel. Ticking. Friends die with nothing. Less than nothing. You and me."

Simon studied the stranger again in the mirror. He could just drop him off at Bellevue. He had had fares before who told how the networks were jamming their brainwaves. But the man looked strangely sane, even as he babbled. Suddenly the man shook his head.

"I'm sure you heard it all. My name is Charlie Flitcraft, anyway. I got married, a couple of kids, bought a house in Queens. Lost money in the stock market, found out my wife . . ." The man stopped talking and gazed out the window.

They rode through the symphony of city noises in silence.

"Do you ever want to chuck it all?" the stranger said suddenly. "Start again? Forget it all?"

"Yeah," Simon said. It escaped from his mouth like a burp from his soul.

There was nothing more to say. They reached Fourteenth Street and the man got out. He paid his fare and gave Simon a twenty-percent tip.

Simon felt uneasy. He couldn't remember the man's face, or exactly what the stranger had said. All he recalled was his own heartfelt "yeah."

Riding home that night, the "yeah" haunted him. He'd said it with no hesitation, his subconscious talking. It had been more than just a dream feeling, a feeling so intense no one but the faceless man could really understand. He knew he couldn't talk about it, even if he had someone he could talk with. But there was no one anyway. He tried in vain to think about something other than the brief ride with the stranger in the dark-colored suit. But he couldn't make his mind forget.

Sean's car was parked in front of the house. His son was leaning over the engine, his upper torso concealed by the open hood. The car, a superbly kept black 1968 Mustang, made guttural noises as Sean fiddled.

Simon parked the cab in the garage and went out to his son. He moved stiffly, his big body an uncomfortable weight, accustomed to the springs of the taxicab's cushioned seat.

"How's it going?" he asked.

"Fine, Dad," Sean said. "Seems like the carburetor was just a little dirty. While I was at it though, I changed the fuel line filter. Seemed to be getting some blockage."

"Better to be safe than sorry," Simon said.

"True, very true," Sean said.

Simon hated the way his son treated every cliché he spoke like a gem. He sensed an insincerity. He longed to take his son aside, man to man, for a heart to heart.

"So, how's everything going? School?"

"Just great. I made the dean's list."

"The team?"

"Brian's out with a pulled hamstring. Looks like I'll be quarterback this season. Not that I'd wish an injury like that on anyone."

"Of course. How about the old love life?" Simon said, giving Sean an awkward wink.

"Well, Mary Ann and I are serious about things. But she wants to finish nursing school. We think it's best we wait until I finish school."

Simon found dark thoughts creeping in. Why couldn't Sean knock the perky little coed up? Or take drugs? Or catch the clap or something, so Simon could throw a fatherly arm around him and offer him advice.

"I got a part-time job too," Sean said. "Working at that electronics store near the school."

"Great. Just great. I don't know how you find the time."

Sean nodded wisely. "Sometimes it's hard. But I seem to be able to make the time. I guess I'm lucky."

"I guess so. Congratulations," Simon said, somewhat sadly. "Did you eat supper?"

"Yes, thank you."

"Well, see you later."

"Nice talking with you, Dad."

"Same here," Simon said.

The inside of the house smelled of that cigar. Who was smoking cigars in his home? Sean wouldn't abuse his body with tobacco, and Melonie abused her body with everything but. Milly had gotten defensive when he asked her, and claimed he was having nasal hallucinations.

For nearly a year, Simon had sensed that Milly had a lover. He didn't dare confront her. But there'd always be that cigar smell, and the note "Out with the girls. Supper in the fridge. Don't wait up."

Who was smoking those cigars? The smell reminded him of his father, a short, potbellied cigar smoker with a bad toupee. Was he flying up from Florida a couple of times a week to have an affair with his son's wife?

There was meatloaf in the refrigerator. Melonie was out—he didn't want to think about where. He heard a roar outside, and knew Sean was off.

Simon moved through the silent house, shutting off the lights that had been left on. He sat on the plastic-covered couch in the living room and listened to the hum of the oil burner in the basement. It sounded like a bum heart, occasionally stuttering. He knew he should call a repairman, but he was waiting for a coronary to force his hand.

As he sat with eyes closed, he could just barely hear his neighbor's television. They were watching Merv Griffin. They always watched Merv Griffin.

He knew what he had to do. He hurried down the steps to the basement.

The floor seemed to drop out from under him as he turned on the light and looked at the bookcase.

It was empty. Naked. Bare wood. There was a note on the third shelf:

> Dear Sy—Got another notice from the bank today. Couldn't take it anymore. Then I got this great idea, sell the books to a collector. Do you believe it, I got $2,300 for all that crap, including the cartons in the garage. We've got more space, some money, and you won't have those silly things to distract you. Hope you understand—Milly.

The note was written in her precise little handwriting, with hearts over the *i*s where dots should be. He reread it three times before he really understood.

He was weak with the numbness that overwhelms in the seconds after a tragedy. She'd threatened to get rid of his books for so long. She'd finally done it. Years of collecting, hundreds of happy memories, familiar characters, erased with one brutal act.

Dead Heat, My Gun Is Quick, Dead Yellow Women, Take It and Like It, The High Window. All gone. All his tough-guy friends, wiped out by a mere woman.

He ran to the bathroom and threw up.

Diamond in the Rough was lying on top of the toilet tank as he stood up and wiped the remains of his last meal from his mouth. Milly had missed the book during her rampage. He grabbed it, squeezed it, and held it to his chest. The lone survivor. Not even she could knock off Red Diamond.

He went out to his ratty chair and sat down. He stared at the book cover. The blonde stared back at him.

He held off opening the book. Literary foreplay. He saw the bookmark embedded in the book's flesh. He would never fold over a corner like some barbarian.

The foreplay didn't last very long. He tenderly opened it, tucking the marker in the rear of the volume. He began to read from his favorite part.

The rod was hot, almost as hot as the blonde that lay sprawled on the floor. Her skirt was hiked up, showing too much thigh. Not for a live broad, but for a dead one. When they're dead, even the best-turned gam is just a piece of meat.

She was wearing a red top that was stained a darker red in a foot square patch on her back. I didn't have to be a Sherlock Holmes to know what that meant.

She had nice hands, long nails, with a polish that matched her blouse. A class act. The fingers were stiff. Rigor was beginning to set in.

I needed a slug of whiskey, but the only thing in my mouth was the stale taste of death. I rolled her over.

It wasn't Fifi and the fear I'd been fighting went down for the count.

It had to be her sister, Lulu La Roche. Of course the killer hadn't known that. Lulu had taken the lead meant for Fifi.

I picked up the piece. Not the blonde. It was a .38. I guessed she was too. But this one was hard. Smith and Wesson. I sniffed the barrel. It had been fired recently. I snapped open the cylinder. Two slugs were gone. One was in the blonde's back. The other one?

It wouldn't have been suicide. No one shoots themselves in the shoulder blades when they want to buy the farm. Someone had done it and split. I guessed I should too.

I'm a shamus. I got a right to go snooping around. But the homicide boys like me to stick to nice clean stuff, like busting in on husbands making whoopie while wifey cooks dinner.

It's a dirty job, but someone's gotta do it. I been in this racket fourteen years. Not much else a busted-down ex-cop can do.

I dropped the rod in the pocket of my trenchcoat. The two-bit coppers in this town would probably just toss it in the bay. And I had a feeling that I'd need it soon.

Simon set the book down on his lap and savored the scene. He could smell the cordite, the blood, the blonde's perfume. He could see Diamond's jaw setting, hear his teeth clenching as he made a silent vow of revenge.

He knew from his earlier reading that Lulu was the younger sister, just visiting Fifi, and in the wrong place at the wrong time. It was Fifi that knew Rocco Rico's secret, the secret that had cost Lulu her life.

Simon even knew who did it, having read the book so many times before. That didn't stop him from enjoying it. The book was a familiar place for him to visit. He knew what to expect of racket boss Rocco Rico. He knew Fifi La Roche had a heart of gold under all that make-up and tough talk. And he knew Diamond would get her before Rocco's thugs did. He reopened the novel.

It had started raining outside and I pulled up the frayed collar on my coat. The cold drizzle ran its icy fingers down my neck. The water washed the sins from the city streets, into the gutters where they belonged.

A busted umbrella lay on the sidewalk, flapping in the wind like a dying bat. The street lights shimmered in puddles on the blacktop. I liked the rain. It helped me think.

Rico would be out tonight with another broad who liked diamonds, furs, and guys with greasy good looks. He wouldn't care about the dead broad. Neither would the cops, since Rico owned them lock, stock and squad car.

The La Roche family had long ago written off their daughters, who dreamed of being stars but never made it to starlet.

Fifi was on the run, waiting for Rico to realize his mistake, and set the dogs loose on her.

The only guy that cared was walking in the rain with drizzle as cold as a dead man's hand on his back and a tight feeling in his gut.

What did she know that got her sister put on ice at the ripe old age of twenty-three? Whatever it was, I knew Red Diamond had to find out. And Rocco Rico and his two bit gunsels, bag man cops and flunky politicians couldn't stop me.

I had the smell of blood and the stink of scandal in my nose, and all the rain on the asphalt couldn't make it go away.

Rocco and I were headed for a showdown and only one of us was going to make it out alive. I hoped it was me, but then I always bet the long shots.

I lit a Camel and sucked in hard. The bitter smoke filled my lungs and came out in a cool, pale blue cloud.

Although he had never smoked, except for one ill-fated episode outside his junior high school, Simon longed for a smoke whenever Diamond lit up.

He felt strange, headachy. He needed someone to talk to. Someone who'd understand the clogged thoughts in his brain. He had to get some air, had to get out.

He set the book down and got up dizzily. He staggered upstairs to the front door. But sticking his head outside didn't help. He could hear Merv Griffin. He had to get away. He walked outside to the garage, ignoring the chill rain.

The cab started smoothly, still warm from the long ride home. The tires screamed as he pulled away.

He drove like a teenager with his first hot rod, eighty-five miles an hour on rain-slicked highway, the wipers struggling to keep marble-sized droplets from blocking his view.

Drivers honked as he whizzed past red brake lights. He hydroplaned along, not feeling the road beneath him. The white lights of oncoming cars reflected off his glistening eyeballs.

He clicked on the radio, and spun the dial until he

heard the Big Band sound coming out of the one working speaker. The Glenn Miller Orchestra was tooting their way through "Rhapsody in Blue." Simon let his head roll with the music.

Then he was in the city. Pedestrians, shocked at seeing an empty cab in the rain, waved frantically. They seemed almost friendly as they waved, but there was desperation in their movements, and obscene gestures as he passed them by.

The city was his. He knew every pothole, every one-way street, every slow traffic light. He knew where the traffic cops cooped and where the tow-truck operators waited for inevitable accidents, like vultures with hunger pangs. He rode crosstown, downtown, uptown, midtown. Cruising just for the joy of it.

He saw the familiar scene through a kaleidoscope, shapes and colors jumbled. Reflections of rectangles on wet pavement. Chrome catching the yellow of sodium street lights. Red light, green light.

The only place he knew that was open was the Balmoral. There were the ubiquitous cabs in front, and their drivers eating inside under the bright fluorescents.

But night-time cabbies were different. They lived behind bulletproof partitions, carried guns, knives, blackjacks. They adopted the demeanor of their riders, the night people of the city.

Simon's cab began to sputter as he headed north on Broadway. It was coughing like a tubercular by Thirty-fourth Street. He was oblivious to the empty fuel gauge until the car gave up and died just south of the Port Authority on Eighth Avenue. Out of circulation in the heart and crotch of New York City. He rolled into a loading zone in front of a bank. He got out without missing a beat and kept walking. He had to keep moving.

LIVE GIRLS, the signs blinked. TOPLESS, LIVE SEX SHOW, NO COVERS, NO MINIMUM, OPEN 24 HOURS, BEAUTIFUL HOSTESSES.

He walked under movie marquees that announced THE NAKED NURSES, BOX LUNCH, BABY'S BEDTIME, GANG BANG ORGY, HARD UP, SEX SLAVES, LEATHER & LACE, TEACHER'S PET.

The seedy barkers, scrawny little men who spoke in a continuous patter, stood sheltered in doorways and urged Simon to come in out of the rain. "Fine women, best in New York. Feel so good, feel so fine, come on in, they blow your mind."

The hookers working the damp streets, desperate, clawed at him and tried to slow his march. "Going out? Want a good time? Got a date? Want to party?" With hot pants and miniskirts barely covering well-traveled loins, they tugged at him.

The faces were all a blur. He moved drunkenly. The air was thin as he took it into his gasping lungs. Where had the oxygen gone?

The women reminded him of stories Pedro told of his adventures on the night shift, of hookers who'd turn tricks in the back of his cab, and tip him ten dollars or a freebie. Of pimps and hookers who fought in the back seat, of a night spent with an aging call girl.

Simon had never been with a prostitute. When women had offered to pay with their bodies, he'd let them ride for free. He dismissed them as too old, too fat, too ugly, or infested with an exotic strain of venereal disease. Why else would they go with him? He'd never been with a woman other than Milly.

She hadn't been a virgin when they married, and she would needle him with hints of her teen-age nights out with the football team. She'd been very popular. Very, very popular, she let him know.

The dizziness was worse. He leaned against a signpost. He had to get back to Long Island. She'd probably be home now, smiling her secret smile. The kids would be home. Did they suspect? What did they think of him?

He blacked out for a millisecond, his grip on the pole

the only thing that kept him from falling into a heap of wet litter.

He began walking again.

He saw her at Forty-ninth Street. Their eyes met. There was no shyness in the blonde as she stepped in front of him.

"Fifi?" he asked.

"If that's what you want," she answered. "Going out?"

Her voice was velvet sandpaper, just the way Red Diamond described it.

She was about twenty-five, with the premature hardness of a girl who'd been around. Her skimpy red dress showed off an ample bosom, and well-shaped, surprisingly muscular legs. Her blond hair was straggly from the rain, but still seemed to glow with its own illumination.

But Fifi was dead, or in hiding, or not real, or . . .

"I ain't got all night, honey," the blonde said, running a finger along his cheek. "You want Fifi to make it all right?"

"What about Rocco and his hoods?"

She hesitated only a second. "Whatever your trip, honey. It'll cost, but it's worth it with Fifi."

"I thought you were dead," Simon said.

"I'll show you I ain't," she said, entwining her arm in his and leading him across the street. "C'mon, we don't have all night."

What was Fifi doing acting like a common whore? It had to be an act, he realized, winking at her. He'd go along with it. There was danger on the street. Rocco's enforcers might be around.

"I'm the best there is, honey. But quality costs. That's thirty-five dollars straight up, fifty bucks for half and half. You want anything special? Around the world?"

"Huh?" he said, not really listening to her. He was figuring how he could get her safely home. Milly would have to understand keeping her under wraps until Red Diamond could pick her up.

The blonde repeated her well-practiced spiel.

"Going around the world would be nice," Simon said. "I went to Canada once."

She laughed. "You're funny. I like that. I'll take you around the world like you never thought."

"I wish I had the time."

"You got all the time in the world. You're with Fifi and it's gonna be all right. Just keep moving."

"I don't know."

"Give it a chance. Just move along," she said, giving him a tug as they turned off Eighth on Fifty-first Street.

She was right. They had to keep moving, get her to safety. Then he could worry about Rocco, and telling Milly about their visitor.

The o on the pink neon LIDO HOTEL sign had burned out, and LID blinked on and off. The stairs were rickety and had served as a urinal to countless derelicts. Neither the blonde nor Simon noticed. She, because it was her fifth trip up them that night. And Simon's mind was on how to get her safely out of the city.

The clerk, a sallow-faced young man reading a copy of *Popular Science,* buzzed them through the locked double doors after "Fifi" signaled him.

"The door to number eight is open," he said, barely bothering to look up. "How long will you be?"

The blonde appraised Simon. "About fifteen minutes." She turned to Simon and said, "Give the man ten dollars."

He took out his wallet and gave the clerk a ten without thinking. She peered into his billfold and saw green. Her grip tightened on his arm.

"I'm gonna show you a real good time," she said, leading Simon down the narrow corridor as the clerk quickly put the money in a locked strongbox. He was back to reading about a car that ran on thickened manure by the time the couple entered room eight.

A bare bulb hung from the ceiling of the drab green

room, illuminating the bed, a wooden chair, a battered night stand and a small sink that were the only furnishings. Fifi shut the door behind them.

The bed was a sway-backed mare that had been ridden too often. The once white sheet was gray and splotched with yellow stains. An Army surplus blanket lay rumpled at the foot of the bed.

The room smelled of liquor, mildew and a goaty human scent. The pungent odors were like smelling salts, snapping Simon out of his fantasy.

"Uh, listen, I'm sorry to have wasted your time," he said. "I've got to get out of here. I really should be . . ."

She was pressing against him, her hands running over his body. Her perfume overwhelmed the other scents. She put his hands on her breasts. She purred as he awkwardly held them.

Her hands were at his crotch, alternately stroking and squeezing. It had been so long. He was dizzy again, weak-kneed and gasping for air.

He felt his fly and his inhibitions going down. Her hands were cold on his erection. It wouldn't hurt anyone, just this once. No one need know.

"Shouldn't we turn out the lights or something?" he asked, his last bit of resistance ebbing.

"Sure honey, anything you want," she said. "Let's just get your pants off." He sat on the wooden chair and unlaced his shoes, putting them neatly side by side next to the bed.

"C'mon honey, I ain't got all night." She watched carefully as he draped his pants over the back of the chair.

"You're looking good," she said, as he heard the switch click and the room went dark. He moaned as she homed in on his hardness and began kneading it like so much dough.

"I bet you're ready to get down and go around the world," she said, raising her voice unnaturally loud for the last few syllables.

Simon didn't notice. He was nearing orgasm, just from her masterful manipulation.

"Uhh, it's so good, just—"

There was a pounding at the door and a deep male voice shouted, "Poh-leese! Poh-leese. Everybody out. The poh-leese are comin'!"

The blonde acted panicky. "My god! Your family! Better hide quick. Get in the closet."

She released Simon and gave him a shove. Limp and terrified, he stumbled to where he guessed the closet was. He slammed his head into the wall.

The dizziness was back and he didn't know what to do. The blonde came to where she'd heard the thump, and gave him another shove.

He groped his way along the wall, found the closet and plunged in. He pulled the door shut behind him.

He heard the door to the hallway slam.

His heart was pounding as he crouched on the floor. He hoped Fifi could handle the cops. What would he say to Milly and the kids if he got caught?

He waited in the blackness for what seemed like hours. The only sounds were his heart and his heavy breathing.

He cracked the door open. The room was dark but he could see everything clearly. Something he couldn't place was missing.

He turned on the light and squinted at the brightness.

His shoes were where he had left them. His boxer shorts lay on the green and white linoleum floor. His pants were gone.

He threw the door to the hallway open. There was no one in the corridor. He ran to the window in his room and jerked open the shade. There were no police cars out on the street.

The blonde was gone. So was his wallet, with ninety-three dollars, charge cards, driver's license and assorted bits of identification.

Simon searched the room in a frenzy, tearing the sheet from the bed, lifting the mattress in the air, throwing the pillows on the floor. Useless. His pants and wallet were gone.

He ran to the small sink and began to heave. The dry retches felt familiar, like he'd purged himself not that much earlier. His body was wracked by the heaves.

He ran around the room in circles until he collapsed on the soiled mattress. He stared at the cracks in the ceiling for awhile, then rolled off the bed and staggered back into the closet, pulling the door shut and curling up into a ball. The linoleum was cold. It felt good.

Simon felt the world spinning as he pressed against the floor. A flickering movie played on the rear of his eyeballs.

Red Diamond. Simon's father. Fifi La Roche. Milly. Rocco Rico. Melonie. Benny. The blond hooker. Pedro. A yogurt yogi. Sean. Nick.

The images speeded up, then slowed and went dark. His bladder filled and he voided it. He cried himself to sleep, awoke, and saw a second showing of the film.

He saw bits of his childhood, growing up clumsy in the Bronx. Not the smartest, not the strongest, not the richest, not the best with girls. Just a face in the crowd. Always someone better.

Simon refought junior high school skirmishes, imagining pushing matches concluded with .38s and .45s. Driving his go-cart at eighty miles an hour on hairpin turns. He recalled an early date, Naomi, a ninth-grade siren in black silk and garters. Teachers who had humiliated him died in sprays of bullets. Hours spent nursing egg creams in waterfront bars. He slept again.

By the third mental movie, Milly, Melonie and Sean were minor characters. The yogurt yogis and cabbies were cameos. He murmured the name Fifi as he slept again.

Light was creeping under the closet door when he was awakened by the voices.

". . . nobody does it better, big stuff," the woman was saying. She sounded young, black and street-smart.

"They all say that, baby. I'll believe that when you earn

33

your money," the man said. He sounded middle-aged, white and tough. "Shit! What happened to this room. It looks like a bomb hit it."

"Don't worry about it," she said. "You won't be caring about no sheets when I get down to business." Simon heard the shade being pulled down.

"I never met a shy whore before," the man said.

"I thought you'd like it better in the dark," the woman said. She sounded annoyed.

"I like my women dark. I don't give a damn about the room. Come here."

There was the sound of movement.

"Oooh, you squeezin' too hard, sugar. Take it easy," the woman said. Simon heard a fly being unzipped. "Mmm. You built for business."

"And ready for you. Go to it."

"Let me put your pants on the chair," the woman said. "Don't want them gettin' messed up."

"I'll do it," the man said.

"Don't trust me?"

"Sure. I trust every twenty-five-dollar whore I meet on Eighth Avenue, especially ones so interested in my haberdashery. Now get to it."

"First I gotta wash you up," she said, practically yelling.

The tap was turned on.

There was a pounding at the outside door.

"Poh-leese! Everybody out. Poh-leese!"

The voice sounded familiar, but Simon couldn't recall where he'd heard it.

"Ow. Leggo of my hair," the woman shouted. "I gotta get out of here."

"You ain't murphying me, bitch," the man growled. "Finish what you started. Get down and get to it."

"You hurtin' me. Leggo. Leggo," she said.

"Ahh," the man screamed. "You bit me."

There was the sound of fist on flesh.

"Jonesy. Jonesy! Help," the woman said.

A door slammed open. "Put your hands in the air, mu-thafucka!" the deep male voice said.

Simon heard the scuffle. There was cursing and grunts from the two men and the woman.

The gunshots were muffled. Five of them. More strug-gling and a few anguished moans. Cursing. Gasps. A long whine, then a sigh, and it was quiet.

Simon's body was stiff from the hours spent curled up on the closet floor. He gingerly pushed the closet door open.

The three bodies lay in a heap on the floor, sprawled together, a mass with six arms and legs of different hues and shapes reaching outward and twisted among each other.

There were three heads on the tangled beast: a black woman, her lipsticked mouth open in a grim rictus of death; a black man, with a close-trimmed goatee that was soaked in blood; and a white man, his face locked in a final sneer, his eyes rolled.

The pimp's white hat, flecked with drops of blood, lay in a corner. Bits of the prostitute's blouse, torn during the fray, were all over the room. The trick's pants were lying on the floor, a cuff just barely touching the pool of blood.

The pimp's gun, a chromed .25 automatic, lay on the floor, lit by a shaft of light from the window. It glowed like a divine tool.

The edges of the scene were fuzzy, like a cheesecake photo shot through gauze. The blur took the hard edge off, made it more unreal. The gore and the blood didn't bother him, he'd seen it before. His breathing was even. He longed for a cigarette.

He picked up the pants with the bloody cuff and slid his legs in. They were a trifle short, but not a bad fit. The polyester felt scratchy against his skin. He reached under the bed, pulled out his shoes and slid them on.

He dropped the pimp's gun in his pocket, thinking, "the

two-bit coppers in this town would probably just toss it in the bay." He had a feeling he'd need it.

He cracked the door open to the empty hallway. No one had heard the shots. And if they had, guests at the Lido would not bother calling the cops. It was a seedy little rat trap on a street of seedy little rat traps, where everyone had a rap sheet, and knew how to mind their own business.

He took one last look around the room. The blur he saw made it look like a picture postcard. Not the kind you'd want to send home to mother, he thought, unless Mom ran a brothel in Tijuana.

He shut the door behind him and moved down the narrow corridor. There was a slight swagger in his walk, a bob in his shoulders.

Too long he'd been confined. Maybe he'd go down to the gym and shoot the breeze about old times. It was too early for that, he decided. It was never too early for a shot of bourbon.

He walked past the front desk. The clerk was nowhere in sight. He opened the heavy metal door and walked downstairs.

Red Diamond hit the streets.

He squinted, blinked and rubbed his eyes as the sun hit him like a slap in the face. The deteriorating bright bulb and neon glitter of the Times Square night was gone. The whores were trying to make one last trick to bring some extra cash to their masters. The pimps, primed with coke, were waiting. The muggers had crawled back under their rocks, and the rest of the human debris returned to the rat-trap hotels, or fallen out in the street.

The whole area was like an aging prostitute. Done up, at night, in the dark, there was a certain allure. During the day, even a blind man couldn't find her appealing.

He reached for the .38 at his waist, to pat his old friend for comfort. All that was there was a roll of fat.

The dizziness swept over him and he nearly fell. He leaned against a parked car and swayed like a sapling in a storm.

A pert-nosed secretary on her way to work gave him a condescending stare. Red Diamond, dismissed as just another Times Square wino. He struggled to compose himself.

What had happened? he wondered, trying to sort out the blurry events of the night before.

He'd been with Fifi, in the library. Thousands of books. They were looking for something. Then one of Rocco's molls, Milly Something-or-other had gotten him in the cab.

He squeezed his head, trying to press the thoughts into order.

The cab. Just like they got Hugo Candless. Nevada gas. Doped up and left for dead. Three stiffs in a pile. But it'd take more than that to knock Red Diamond out for the count. The opening round had gone to Rocco, but the bout was just beginning.

He shoved his hands into his pockets as he threw his shoulders back. His right hand felt the butt of the gun. He took it out and looked at it, puzzled.

A man in a three-piece suit passed, looked at him holding the weapon, and speeded up his walk.

Diamond dropped the gun back in his pocket. It was a .25. A lady's gun. Fifi must've slipped it to him. What a dame.

Diamond walked down the block to the bulletproof glass-partitioned storefront, and ordered a pack of Camels from the gnome safely ensconced inside.

He paid for the cigarettes, and then studied the wallet he'd pulled reflexively out of his pants pocket. It was different, a black cowhide. He'd always carried a brown leather billfold, and the case with the photostat of his license and gun permit.

The name on the driver's license was John Teel. There were some other papers and charge cards with Teel's name on it, and a couple hundred bucks. Diamond didn't remember setting up a cover. What the hell was going on, when he couldn't even trust his own brain?

He'd been Mickey Finned, sapped, punched out and hung over more times than he could remember, but this was the worst. His head throbbed like he'd been Rocky Marciano's punching bag for a week.

He tore open the cigarette pack with the awkwardness of someone who'd never done it before and slipped a cigarette into his mouth. It didn't fit his lips, no matter where he placed it. No coordination, he decided. A good thing none of Rocco's plug uglies were around.

A lady's gun. No grace. All he had was guts. And all he needed was a glass. Full of bourbon.

He struck a match and touched it to the tip of the cigarette as he exhaled. Nothing happened. Then he inhaled.

The hot smoke burned his lungs. He was coughing and choking and gasping for air. There were tears in his eyes by the time he dropped the cigarette and ground it underfoot. Lungs must be shot from that Nevada gas last night, he thought. Have to wait until later. Right now he needed to soothe his throat.

The sign on the Silver Shamrock drew his attention. He guessed it was the Silver Shamrock, since the *I* and *L* were missing from Silver and the *A*, *M* and *R* missing

38

from Shamrock. If there was one thing Diamond could spell, it was the name of every bar in his burg.

A jukebox that wasn't as loud as a jet taking off blasted his eardrums as he pulled the door open. Some dame was singing, if you could call it that. She was panting while some guy beat the hell out of the drums. Harry James it wasn't.

The bar had probably been a pretty decent joint back when Gentleman Jimmy Walker was running the city. Now it was kept dark, so you couldn't see the garbage on the floor, or the names carved into the long oak bar. Not that the patrons would give a damn.

There were a couple of middle-aged, hard-looking, hard-luck guys down at the end of the bar. They nursed beers, not looking up and just barely mumbling to each other. He had seen that kind of mumble before. Ex-cons had it, from years of talking in the yard so no one could see they were talking. They were a feature at every bar he'd ever been to, grifters who spent the day plotting bank heists, and wound up boosting TV sets off the loading dock at Sears.

The rest of the patrons were younger, in their twenties, black. You didn't need to be street smart to guess what they did. Pink suits with diamond cuff links. Wide-brimmed hats, coats with fur collars. They weren't shoe-shine boys making big tips. Pimps. Small fry. Pimples.

There were a couple of women sitting at a table. The temperature outside must've been about fifty, and they were wearing hot pants. They were drinking Cokes. He doubted that they were old enough to drink liquor. Besides, the pimps wanted to take good care of their merchandise.

The guy behind the bar stood in front of Diamond as he sat down on a torn upholstered stool. The bartender was a middle-aged pug with a face as Irish as Danny Boy and a road map of broken blood vessels on his nose. With what he saw everyday, Diamond figured the bartender had a right to sample his wares.

"Gimme a bourbon. Neat. To start," Diamond said.

The bartender poured the drink without saying a word. Diamond slapped a five-dollar bill down on the counter.

"You're new around here?" the bartender said.

Diamond nodded but didn't answer. The bartender lifted a damp rag, and began wiping the long, dark wood counter. He moved away.

It was too early to talk. Diamond had to compose his thoughts. And you never knew if one of Rocco's spies was lurking around. He eased some bourbon down his throat, and listened to the conversations around him.

". . . so I had to lay one upside the bitch's head," a lean young man in a green-checked suit was saying. Jewelry glistened on his fingers as he gestured. "I mean, you let the bitch get away with that, and she'll be walkin' all over you fo' you know it."

"Dig it," another dandy, with a gold earring and maroon outfit, answered. "I had me a flatbacker once. Ten, twelve tricks a night. But she was always gettin' in my face, messing with the other chicks in the stable. I had to cut her loose, tell her . . ."

Diamond returned to his drink. He remembered when he'd worked vice, the little pleasures, like throwing the fanciest pimp in the small holding cell with a couple of puking drunks. But there'd been too many guys on the job who would just take the pimps' money and cut them loose. Street tax, they called it.

The bagmen, the deals on the cuff, the pad. It had gotten so bad, he'd had to . . . ah, but that was water, dirty water, under the bridge.

"Another bourbon," Diamond ordered.

The bartender had taken a dollar out of Diamond's five while he was in his reverie. He brought a fresh bourbon and took another single.

A gaunt six-footer, as garishly clad as his comrades, came in and joined them at the end of the bar. His movements were sharp, jerky, as he rubbed his nose.

"Hey, Blood," Green Suit said. "Where you been?"

"Toot, toot," Blood answered, making a gesture like a trainman pulling down a whistle.

"You got any to share, bro?" Green Suit asked.

Blood shook his head. "But I got me a new snow bitch you gotta see." He took a couple of steps back to the door, opened it, and a woman walked in.

Her blond hair was done up in a bubble cut that added three inches to her five-and-a-half-foot frame. It was a nice frame, properly packaged in a skin-tight blouse and miniskirt. She was about twenty-two, with world-weary eyes that were indifferent as the men appraised her.

Blood beamed as Green Suit and Gold Earring whistled.

Diamond had done a double take, as his eye was drawn back to the fresh meat being brought to market. Could it be? She had an unworldly glow, so out of place in the sleazy midtown bar.

"Fifi?" he mumbled too low for anyone to hear. He knew her past, how, when down on her luck, she'd done things she didn't like to talk about. He stared at her. The face was a little different, but the figure and hair were . . .

"Hey, what you lookin' at?" Blood demanded.

It took Diamond a moment to realize Blood was talking to him. Then he ignored the young pimp.

Blood stepped in closer. The other two pimps smirked. Fifi looked bored.

"I don't want no trouble," the bartender said, knowing Blood's reputation for cocaine belligerence.

"No trouble," Blood said. "I just want the dude to apologize to my lady for staring at her."

The other pimps chuckled. Fifi looked at her nails.

"You hear me, sucker? You say you sorry."

The pimp was used to pushing people around, especially the losers who hung out at the Shamrock. He grew furious as Diamond ignored him.

"Mutha, you hear what I say?" The pimp was within knife range now. There was a dangerous quaver in his voice.

Diamond let his eyes drift up from his drink to meet the pimp's. "I'm the last person in the world you'd want to fuck with." He returned his attention to his drink.

Blood put his hand on Diamond's shoulder. "Tough talkin' ofay, ain't you?"

"Take your hand off of me," Diamond growled.

The pimp pulled his hand back, then snapped it forward in a punch aimed at Diamond's jaw. Diamond was turning, and the blow glanced his cheek. He was off the stool and face to face with Blood as the pimp threw a second punch.

Diamond blocked it with his right, and tossed the half-full glass of bourbon in Blood's face with his left. While the pimp tried to rub the burning fluid out of his eyes, Diamond doubled him over with a solid punch to the gut. Then he bruised his knuckles on the pimp's chin as he sent him to the floor.

"Your name Fifi?" Diamond asked the woman, who had a bemused expression on her face.

"I've used that. And Candy, Trixie, Lola." Her voice didn't sound quite like Fifi's. It was hard, with a hint of a Kentucky twang.

Blood moaned and Green Suit went over and helped him up. Diamond watched him out of the corner of his eye. The bartender had his right hand under the counter.

Diamond sat down and the woman took a stool next to him.

"Do I know you from somewhere?" she asked him, laying a hand on his thigh.

Diamond knew the strip changed people quickly, but

could this be Fifi? There was a cheapness, an emotionless evil about her. Maybe she'd been drugged. She acted like it was just a game.

He caught the movement just in time. Blood was reaching under his jacket. He isn't taking out his wallet so he can pick up my tab, Diamond thought.

I'm moving too slow, he realized. It seemed to take him an hour to reach Blood. By the time he did, the other pimps had hit the floor and the woman was halfway to the door. The cagey ex-cons had disappeared, and the bartender had ducked down behind his counter.

Diamond stumbled as he went to grab the pimp. His 225 pounds hit the pimp's 150, and both men went down. The silvered automatic in the pimp's hand went off, and the mirror behind the bar shattered.

Diamond rolled on top of the pimp. Gravity did the work, as Diamond's bulk knocked the air out of Blood. The pimp was in no shape to scuffle, and Diamond took the gun easily from his hand.

"I eat your kind for breakfast," Diamond said, lifting himself up while keeping the pimp's gun trained on its former owner. "And spit you out before lunch."

I must be losing my touch, Diamond thought, that a skinny punk like Blood could recover from a Red Diamond uppercut so quickly.

The bartender had gotten an ugly sawed-off shotgun out from underneath the bar. He was pointing it vaguely at Diamond.

"Put that thing away," Diamond ordered. "And pour me another drink. I wasted the last one."

The bartender set the drink down in front of Diamond, smiled, and didn't take any of Diamond's money.

Diamond sipped it and watched, in the shards of mirror that remained behind the bar, as Green Suit helped Blood to his feet, and out of the bar. The other pimps followed.

"I guess I cost you some business," Diamond said.

"Every now and then the toilet needs a cleaning," the bartender said. "They weren't buying anyway."

"Any idea where the girl went?" Diamond asked.

"She'll be on the strip tonight," the bartender predicted.

A lean young black man, who had been nursing a beer at a table in the back of the bar, was the only other patron. Dressed in a denim suit, with an easy, predatory grin, he sauntered to where Diamond sat.

"Mind if I sit here?" he asked, not waiting for an answer as he plunked himself down next to Diamond.

"Suit yourself," Diamond said, returning to his bourbon. He took a sip, then told the bartender. "I'll pay for the mirror as soon as I get a few more bucks together."

The bartender nodded cynically.

Diamond was staring off into space. I should be out cruising for fares. Doing what? Cruising, looking for Rocco. Rocco was behind all this, Red Diamond having to worry about the price of a mirror in some dive.

I need some shut-eye, he thought. Cut down on the booze, the broads and the cigarettes. Rocco could afford to party. He had an army of strong-arms to do his dirty work. Red Diamond had no one he could trust, except his two fists.

He felt the stare of the young man next to him.

"You see something you like, or you just window shopping," Diamond said.

"You move real good."

"I'm getting old, kid. You're only as good as your last fight in this life."

The young man nodded. "Where you from?" he asked.

"Around. I been around."

"I thought you was a cop when I first saw you."

"Used to be. A long, long time ago." Diamond studied his murky reflection in his drink.

"Twelve years on the job," he mumbled. "Every dive precinct in the city. As many shoot-outs as reprimands

44

for insubordination. That first time, with Fat Nicky up at Juicy Lucy's whorehouse on the East Side. They took four slugs out of Nicky. I got a commendation. And lost my partner."

Diamond continued to stare into his drink like a gypsy with a crystal ball. But his mumbling became clearer, and more emotional, and his voice grew louder.

"That was on patrol. Turns out Nicky was wanted in three states. Hot-shot bank robber dies in a whorehouse 'cause he wouldn't pay up.

"A couple more things, and they made me a dick. Safe and Loft. A few years there, a few years in Harlem, Chinatown, Lower East Side. I got a habit of telling people what I think. And I classed captains as people. My mistake."

Diamond was oblivious to the rapt attention he was getting from the bartender and the young man.

"So I wind up in vice. Must've been someone's mistake. The best way to get rich, and I wouldn't play ball. They tried all right. My partner takes me aside, explained how it worked. I still wouldn't play.

"Someone starts a rumor I work for the shooflies. Internal Affairs. The squad thinks I'm gonna derail the gravy train. They set me up, so the shit hits the fan and I'm holding the bag. Justice."

Diamond lifted his drink suddenly and belted it back. The bartender set another one down in front of him.

"What have you been doing?" the young man asked.

"A little of this, a little of that. Knocking around. Snooping. A PI. Just another busted flatfoot trying to pay the rent. Then this thing with Rocco came up."

"Who's he?" the bartender asked.

"I can see you ain't been around. Rocco runs the rackets all over this town. Keeps a low profile, but every dirty dollar's got his greasy thumbprint on it. He was behind the frame-up. I been giving him a hard time ever since. Or trying to. He lives in a mansion over in Jersey and I'm

45

drinking cheap booze early in the morning with no place to stay, no job, no nothing."

Diamond didn't notice as the bartender circled his index finger near his temple.

"My name's Sweets, what's yours?" the young man said to Diamond, ignoring the bartender's gesture.

"Red Diamond."

"You need a job, Red?"

Diamond studied Sweets with his bloodshot eyes. The young man was well-built and looked rather clean-shaven to be in a pimp bar.

"What d'you got in mind?"

"I work for someone's got a few businesses. Might be able to use your help."

"I don't run whores or deal drugs. I may be down on my luck, but I got principles."

"Me too," Sweets said. His voice was patronizing and insincere, but Diamond's guard was down. His liquid breakfast was beginning to take effect.

"I gotta get some grub," Diamond said.

Sweets got up as Diamond did. "Mind if I come along?"

"Suit yourself," Diamond said.

Sweets turned to the bartender. "Mr. Brown will take care of the mirror."

The bartender looked quizzical, but nodded acknowledgment.

"The only money I take, I earn," Diamond said. He handed the pimp's gun to Sweets and said, "You can do me a favor and hock this. The money will go for that mirror."

"Whatever you say," Sweets answered, realizing that Diamond lacked the hustler's get-whatever-you-can attitude.

"Who's Brown?" Diamond asked as he and Sweets stepped out into the sunshine.

"My boss. You'll be meeting him later."

Diamond didn't say anything, but he pulled himself up a little taller. He put a bob in his shoulders as he strutted down the street.

Squinting cagily, he glanced up at the clear blue sky. It looked like a nice day.

4

The first pot of java was just brewing in the coffee shop on the corner. The pungent smell, laced with the odor of bacon and eggs cooking on the freshly cleaned grill, gave the place a homey atmosphere.

By the end of the day, it would smell of old grease and strangers' cigarettes, but as he and Sweets settled into a booth, the good scents added to Red's hunger.

There was no conversation until after Diamond had devoured the two eggs, four strips of bacon and two pieces of toast the fat waitress had brought them. She smiled when Diamond asked for seconds and a pitcher of coffee.

"So what kind of businesses this guy Brown got?" Diamond asked as he dug into his second order.

"He got some property around," Sweets said, grinning evasively. "I won't last very long I go putting my boss's business out on the street."

"But I told you everything."

"That's rule number one around here, man. Keep your mouth shut. I don't know what the deal is where you come from. It's okay, cause I know you was jiving."

Diamond didn't know what jiving meant, but since Sweets obviously approved, he decided not to question him. Jiving just came naturally, Diamond figured.

"So what d'you figure Brown wants me for?"

"He don't know about you yet," Sweets said. "I'm gonna take you up to see him later. You interested?"

"I ain't had any better offer yet today," Diamond said, cleaning the plate of the last morsel.

Sweets insisted on picking up the tab. Diamond didn't fight him too hard. The meal might be all he'd get out of Sweets. He liked the kid, but he'd heard too many smooth talkers before. There was something insincere, something he didn't quite trust. But Diamond was busted and the kid was offering him a fresh deck.

"I'll get you a room in the hotel," Sweets said as they exited the coffee shop. "You clean yourself up, get some sleep, and we meet Mr. Brown tonight."

As they neared the Intown Hotel, the idea of sleep grew more and more appealing. Diamond was dragging his feet as he climbed the half-dozen steps into the lobby.

A couple of old men were living out their final days watching a flickering black-and-white television in the lobby. The management had applied generous doses of cheap disinfectant to the lobby floor to try and keep away the smell of death. The three potted plants in the lobby looked as unhealthy as the TV watchers. Everything had seen better days, but at least the rates were by the day, not the hour.

Sweets spoke to the desk clerk while Diamond surveyed the lobby. The clerk, a lean Hispanic with a droopy eye, nodded as Sweets talked.

"I'll be back at six," Sweets said, returning his attention to Diamond and handing him a room key.

The elevator struggled up to Diamond's floor and he struggled to reach his room. The smell of mildew on the threadbare hall carpets kept him awake until he fumbled his key into the lock.

He stepped into the room, kicked the door shut, and had collapsed into a sound sleep on the bed before the echo of the slamming door had died.

48

He was at the airport in Casablanca. A fine mist was in the air as the light from a plane lit up Fifi. "As Time Goes By" was playing instead of the usual Muzak. Then Milly was there, demanding his letters of transit. The letters were bound into a paperback book. She had just grabbed them out of his hand, and the plane was about to take off without him, when the knock at the door woke him up.

He reached under his pillow for the gun, and came up empty. Had they stolen it while he slept?

Then the day's events came back to him, in a blur as fuzzy as his nightmare. He took the .25 out of his pocket and walked to the door.

"Who is it?"

Could Rocco have tracked him down already? Was Red Diamond fated to die in a run-down hotel?

But Rocco's button men wouldn't have knocked, he reasoned as he cracked the door open.

No one was in sight. There was a tray on the floor with a hairbrush, safety razor, mouthwash and a fresh shirt and underwear. He took it in and shut the door.

He stroked his stubbly face as he picked up the room phone and dialed the front desk.

"What time is it?"

"Glad to hear you're up, Mr. Diamond," the clerk said.

"Me too. What time is it?"

"Just about five. Sweets said you should be ready by six."

"Very efficient. You do good work."

"I better. Mr. Brown owns the hotel."

Diamond made a mental note. "Can you get my clothes pressed in an hour?"

"I'll send someone right up."

He took the gun and hid it under the mattress before the bellhop came in. Diamond draped himself in a towel and handed over the clothes he was wearing.

The hop was a white-haired old man with posture so bad Diamond thought at first he was a hunchback. As the hop reached for the clothes, Diamond played with a five-dollar bill.

"You want a woman?" the hop asked in a voice that sounded like newspapers crumbling. "The boss don't like that."

"I want to know about the boss," Diamond said.

The hop reached for the five, and Diamond held it away from him. "What about Brown," Diamond said.

"He owns this place, a couple, three others. They say he's got a half-dozen bars and after-hours joints. Started as a numbers runner way back when. Got a reputation for keeping his word, and did good. A tough piece of work, but he's kept his nose pretty clean. Never touched that drug stuff, and I don't even think he's into gambling any more. Some say he's getting soft."

Diamond let the hop grab the five with his gnarled hand. The hop tucked the money into his shoe, gave Diamond a grin, and walked out with his suit.

Sweets waved furiously as they stood on the curb, trying to flag down a passing taxi.

"Fuckin' cabbies," he said. "Don't want to pick up no nigger no time."

"Don't be so hard on us," Diamond said. "I mean, we got to worry, I mean, us, they got to watch, we, you never know if some, we try . . ."

Sweets was watching him as he fumbled the words.

A battered Buick with a City Car Service decal on one side slowed down.

"Need a ride?" the black man with the scarred face behind the wheel asked.

"I don't need nothing from a damn gypsy," Diamond said.

"My man means yes," Sweets said, pulling the door open and scowling at Diamond.

Diamond grudgingly got in and glared straight ahead during their ride. The driver glared back at him in the rearview mirror. Diamond shifted around, strangely uncomfortable in the back seat.

Sweets said nothing, but a bemused smile played across his face as he watched Diamond fidget.

They got out a few blocks north of Columbus Circle, Sweets paid the fare, and led Diamond to a storefront with *Brown Real Estate* written in small letters on the tinted glass window.

A redheaded secretary with a big smile, and bigger breasts, greeted them.

"He's expecting you. Go right in," she said.

She didn't seem to mind when Diamond winked at her.

Diamond knew he had a way with women, but somehow the flirtation gave him a thrill. Sweets tugged at his arm, and they walked to a door in the back. The secretary hit a buzzer at her desk, and Sweets pushed the door open.

Everything in the room was brown, the wood-paneled walls, the thick carpet, the desk that wasn't as big as a football field, the tables, the upholstered chairs, and the man sitting in the leather chair behind the desk.

His thick neck poked out of a custom-made brown suit that barely covered his broad shoulders. He looked like he'd been suckled on a lemon. His sour expression didn't change as he studied Diamond.

"So this is the guy?" Brown asked in a voice that was like gravel rubbing on sandpaper. "He don't look like much."

"If you're looking for a model, I came to the wrong place," Diamond said. "I've been undercover on a big case. So I don't look like the Prince of Wales."

"Mr. Brown, this is Red Diamond," Sweets said.

Diamond stepped forward and extended his hand. Brown ignored it.

"You ever done any bodyguard work?" Brown asked.

"Yeah."

"General security?"

"Yeah."

"Investigations?"

"Yeah."

"You know your way around?"

"Yeah."

"Okay. I keep a low profile. What do you know about me?" Brown said, leaning back in his chair.

"You own the joint Sweets put me up in. And by the way, you could use some new carpeting. You got a couple of other hotels, some bars and after-hours joints. Used to be in bookmaking, but you're keeping your act pretty clean. Got a reputation for being fair."

Sweets was smiling like a teacher watching his prize pupil win a spelling bee.

"You tell him that?" Brown asked Sweets.

Sweets shook his head.

"What've you done?" Brown said, returning his sour gaze to Diamond.

"A little of this, a little of that. One thing I don't put up with is shit from anybody."

"I'll vouch for—" Sweets began, but a wave from Brown cut him off. Sweets took a candy bar out of his pocket and began gnawing at the chocolate.

The only sound in the room was his nibbling as Brown stared at Diamond. The room must be soundproofed, Diamond realized. The angry street noises of screeching brakes and blaring horns were as far away as if they were in the Catskills.

The staring match continued. Brown looked intense. Diamond looked bored. Sweets ate the bar down to the wrapper.

Brown grinned. "You're hired," he said. "Five hundred

a week, plus expenses. You start tonight. Take it or leave it."

This time when Diamond offered his hand, Brown clasped it and gave him a firm shake.

6

"We gonna visit a couple of places tonight," Sweets said as they stood back out in the street. "You dig?"

"Beats sitting in a hotel room watching the dust settle," Red replied. He puffed on a cigarette and reminisced about times he spent kicking around the great jazz joints of Harlem. He looked northward, and could almost hear the wailing saxes, the women laughing, and the liquor flowing.

He ground out the cigarette as a Black Pride gypsy cab picked them up at the curb. They rode in silence up Amsterdam Avenue. There were no yellow cabs in sight.

"Watch out for that pothole by Eighty-seventh," Diamond cautioned.

"What you say?" the middle-aged Haitian driver said as they barreled hard into a crater as deep as an artillery scar.

"You're gonna mess up your suspension if you don't watch out for that one and the mother over on Broadway and Twenty-third Street."

"How'd you know that?" Sweets asked.

"Because."

"Because what?"

"Just because," Diamond said. He began gazing out the window, taking in the night street scene and hiding the perplexed expression on his own face from Sweets.

53

The number of gentrified white faces on the street diminished as they drove northward. The brownstones appeared more rundown. The foreign imports parked in the street were replaced by flashier gas guzzlers. Overpriced delis gave way to greasy rib joints. As the street numbers entered the triple digits, occasional burned-out cars and boarded-up tenements began blighting the scene.

The thousands of hard-working stiffs, the men and women who kept the city clean and moving, were behind multilocked apartment doors watching video dreams. The hookers, hustlers and heroin addicts had claimed the street for the night.

Diamond reached into his waistband to pat his gun. The missing .38 made him feel vulnerable. He had the .25, but it wasn't the same. What the hell was he doing? The gypsy cab seemed stuffy as he squirmed on the torn upholstered seat. He could hardly breathe. He was about to ask that they pull over when at last they did.

"Hey man, you okay?" Sweets asked as they got out of the cab. "You lookin' a little pale."

Diamond wiped his brow. "Sure I look pale." He forced a weak grin. "That's the price of being a white guy."

Sweets smiled and they entered a noisy bar.

A few red lightbulbs in the ceiling cast a faint light down on a sea of dancing, dark faces. There were about two dozen more people inside than the Fire Department maximum-occupancy sign mandated. They bobbed and shook to the heavy soul beat blaring from a juke box in the back.

Sweets waved to the bartender and shouted something that was inaudible in the din.

Most of the crowd was in their late twenties and early thirties. All were black. The ones that noticed Diamond looked at him with the warmth reserved for rabid dogs and bill collectors.

"How's business?" Sweets shouted to the bartender as he and Diamond moved belly up to the bar.

"Lookin' good," the grizzled bartender with the two

54

gold teeth in front said. "Have it ready in a coupla minutes. Jimmy's countin' it now."

"I'll go help him out," Sweets said. "Pour my friend here whatever he wants," he added, indicating Diamond.

Sweets disappeared into the crowd after a few soul handshakes and slaps on the back with select patrons.

"Bourbon and coke," Diamond said.

The bartender poured the drink and set it down wordlessly in front of him.

As Diamond eased the first sip down his throat, he realized he hadn't eaten since the morning. He reached over past the man next to him, and grabbed a handful of pretzels out of the bowl.

His neighbor, who had been lost in conversation with a pretty young woman with cornrowed hair, saw the white hand snaking by him, and stopped talking. He turned to glare at Diamond.

"They don't serve honkies in here," the man said.

"I didn't order a honky," Diamond said.

The man appeared unamused. He was about Diamond's height, thinner, but his shoulders were broad. With his soft-sculpture nose, and cauliflower ears, Diamond guessed he'd been inside a few boxing rings. He looked like trouble.

Diamond's first thought, barely completed, was to call a cab and get the hell out of there. But I'm Red Diamond, private eye. I've been in tighter scrapes, like that bar in Marseille where the Frenchman sicced three Apaches with sharp knives and killer feet on me. Or the kidnapping caper where I wound up in an Arizona canyon facing six chain-toting Hell's Angels. Or the shootout with Rocco's two-bit hit men.

At the memory of Rocco, he felt a spurt of adrenalin set his pulse into overdrive. He should be out, looking for Fifi and Rocco, not getting into fights in Harlem bars. But he needed money for his search, and he was there, and this man had gotten up and was hovering over him.

". . . you hear me, honky. I don't like your face."

The woman with the cornrow was looking over her boyfriend's shoulder, trying to seem bored. But the glimmer of passion was in her eye, and her tongue flicked briefly across her lips, like a serpent on a hunt.

Diamond had seen that kind before. They sat ringside at the fights, watching the fighters pound each other into Palookaville, not really caring who won. For them, the smell of blood was like Chanel No. 5. Diamond knew her boyfriend couldn't back down, or he wouldn't be getting into her ring that night.

"I don't like my face either," Diamond said. "It ain't much, but it's all I got."

"How about I rearrange it some," the boxer said. He stepped back and dropped his left shoulder a bit as Diamond got up.

No wonder the boxer's face looked like a piece of tenderized meat. If he telegraphed his punches like that in the ring, he'd be little more than a punching bag for any student of the pugilistic arts.

Diamond kept the barstool between himself and the boxer. He was just out of reach. The boxer shifted and stepped in. Diamond twisted his body, putting himself out of reach of a solid punch. The boxer stepped again and there was nowhere for Diamond to move, so he stepped in close. His eyes met the boxer's and he waited for the warning flicker.

The cornrowed girlfriend waited breathlessly. The other customers murmured encouragement as they waited for the ballet to end.

How many saps had played the sandman's tune on this old noggin? Diamond thought. How many dark alleys had he walked down, and crawled out of, after hitting goons in the knuckles with his stomach? It takes a tougher man to take a beating than to dish it out. And pain is just the price of being alive.

There was no fear in Diamond's eyes and the boxer saw it. He knew that once he started, Diamond would play the game to the end without thought of consequence. The boxer started mumbling curses. He had to make his move.

A hand reached over from behind and squeezed the boxer's muscular shoulder.

"Lay off the dude, nigger," Sweets said, his voice low but firm. "He's with Mr. Brown."

The boxer spun, recognized Sweets, and frowned.

"Okay. Then it's okay," the boxer said, turning again to face his disappointed girlfriend.

"I've got to be going," she said. "I've got a man waiting for me." She flounced out.

Sweets sat down on the stool on the other side of Diamond.

"Sorry for the hassle," Sweets said.

"No problem," Diamond answered as he finished his drink.

The deserted boxer was sadly sipping from a stein of beer. He drained it and stared into the empty glass.

"Buy you another?" Diamond asked him.

"Say what?"

Diamond summoned the bartender and pointed to the boxer's empty glass. The stein was refilled.

"Women! You're fucked with them, you're fucked without them." Diamond paused and smiled. "And you never can get fucked enough."

The boxer tried to smile.

"I tell you, I must've been through a couple hundred dolls in my life. A dame like that, she watches you bleed, she takes your money, and runs off with your best friend. I know the type."

"You got it," the boxer said, sliding his stool closer to Diamond as someone plunked a few quarters into the juke box and the disco-soul began blaring. "You handle youself like you been around. You ever box?"

"I fell asleep on the canvas more times than I care to remember."

"You don't got a mark on your face," the boxer said, peering intently at Diamond. "How you do it?"

"Been lucky I guess. But I've pissed blood plenty. Only

57

did it a couple of years. My manager got the money. I got a ringin' in my ears from this Italian guy with an upper-cut that hit me like a Mack truck." Diamond slammed his right fist into his left palm.

The boxer grinned. "I bet I knows the guy. I think I see him fight once in Philly."

"You been to Philly?" Diamond asked.

"Coupla weeks ago."

"What a town. City of brotherly love. Bullshit! I got rousted by the cops when I broke up this big kiddie hooker operation."

The boxer waited for him to go on.

"The chief of police was in on it," Diamond said. "It started out simple enough. Most of my cases do."

Sweets and the bartender were both leaning in, listening.

"This redhead comes into my office. A real first-class doll with a body that just wouldn't quit. The only green she had was in her eyes, but I figured what the hell, it was slow anyway. I'd just have to figure out a new stall for the landlord for a couple of days."

"I hear what you saying," the boxer said.

"So dollface tells me it should be easy enough. Just find her little sister. It seems the kid, she was only twelve, had run off a couple of days earlier. She gave me a picture. The kid was cute, but with that kind of mischievous look that I knew meant trouble."

The patrons at the table nearest Diamond were dis-creetly craning their necks so they could hear him talk.

"Missing persons hadn't done anything. They know most of the time the girl turns up at her boyfriend's house, convinced she's found true love. But I take the kid's picture around to a couple guys that know the street. They seen the kid, and she's with some bad com-pany."

A half-dozen people were clustered around Diamond, but he barely noticed, lost in his reverie.

"Cost me a sawbuck, but I found out where she was in Philly. It's always tough in a strange burg. You never know what's going to turn up when you kick over a rock. I go to the fleabag where she's supposed to be, and I find a dead guy in her room. Neat dresser, he was. Except he had a steak knife where his tie tack shoulda been."

The music got louder.

"Shut that fuckin' racket," someone yelled, and another person pulled the plug out of the juke box. Two dozen ears waited for Diamond to speak.

"Turns out the dead guy was a city councilman. Real conservative type. Church twice a week, whether he needed it or not. Didn't bother to tell Father O'Malley he was dipping his wick in every under-age piece of tail he could get. Kinky stuff too."

Diamond paused occasionally to gesture or emphasize a point. His sincerity was obvious. He lit a cigarette.

"Go on," a man at the back shouted.

"The jailbait I wanted was gone. The trail was cold, so I go to the councilman's office. His secretary looked like a bulldog. But not as cute. Wouldn't let me into his office, said she was going to call the cops. So I paid a late-night visit."

Diamond mimicked picking a lock.

"Seems the guy was being blackmailed. A grand a week, not a bad piece of change. But no clues. So I go out to see Mrs. Councilman at their estate in Bryn Mawr. The place is wallpapered with greenbacks.

"So I'm sitting on the sofa, after Jeeves the butler makes me come in the service entrance, and the grieving widow walks in wearing a lot of perfume, and not much else. She sits close enough to count my eyelashes. Next thing I know, she's playing find the hot dog in my fly."

Diamond gave a lecherous grin. There were whoops and whistles in the crowd packed tight around him.

"Takin' care of business," a man yelled.

Diamond leered, and continued. "I had a job to do and I told her that. She wasn't used to not getting what she wanted. I told her it wasn't nothing personal, and let her keep her hand on my thigh while she told me her life story. Seems she knew her husband and the top cop were in cahoots on the kiddie hooker operation. I got the name of the councilman's aide who actually ran the deal. I told her I'd be back, and headed to the little pimp's place in Balacynwyd. I need another drink."

The bartender hurriedly poured Diamond a generous one. Red nibbled a few pretzels as the tension built.

"So what happened?" a wide-eyed woman in a blue silk top demanded. There were several echoed shouts of "yeah" from the crowd.

"The guy was a real smart aleck. Came to the door of his penthouse apartment wearing one of those shirts with an alligator smiling on it. He had the same kind of look on his face.

"I laid out what I knew for him, guessing some stuff and leaving other things out. Sounded like I had everything but a signed confession from the dead guy. He asked me what I wanted. I told him one twelve-year-old. He thought he had me, just another perv. Took out a photo album, let me have my pick. I picked the little sister, of course.

"He started telling me about problems they had with the kid, how they had to drug her and slap her around. Seems she wasn't quite as willing as some.

"Now I know plenty of guys that make their living off of their ladies. And plenty of ladies that make their living off of guys. But I don't like no one who takes advantage of kids."

The cigarette burned down to the filter, and Diamond slowly, deliberately, ground it into an ashtray. He smiled his best tough-guy grin.

"So maybe I lost my temper a little bit, slapped him around. Hell, I bounced him off the walls like a tennis ball."

"Jack that sucker up," a woman said.

"Right on," agreed a man.

"To make a long story short, I got the kid back. Then I sent all the info to a friend who's a scribe over at the *Bulletin*. The feds came down with a big indictment. The papers boosted their circulation a few thousand. Me, I just do my job."

"Who killed the councilman?" the woman in blue asked.

"I figure it was the twelve-year-old. And I figure it ain't so important the cops got to know about it."

Someone began applauding and soon Diamond had a standing ovation. He smiled and raised his drink in a toast to the crowd. Several men patted him on the back. Two women came up and kissed him. Sweets's grin was straining at his cheeks.

"So what happened with the redhead who first gave you the case?" a man missing his two front teeth asked.

"She was very appreciative," Diamond said, smiling and looking off into pleasant memories.

The crowd began drifting off and someone plugged the juke box back in. The woman in blue lingered.

Her big brown eyes were studying Diamond. Apparently they liked what they saw. Her dark skin had the same shine as the gold bangles on her bare arms. She had sharp little teeth behind thickly glossed lips.

"My name's Carmen," she said. "I think you're bad."

Diamond frowned. "I try not to be."

"Want to get down?" she asked.

Diamond looked at the floor, a worn linoleum with spots of squashed gum and miscellaneous litter. "No thanks."

Carmen nibbled her thumb and leaned in close. "I've never been to Philadelphia."

"You're not missing much."

"Anyone ever tell you you were cute," she said, running a moist finger along Diamond's cheek.

"All the time. Just the other day, this cop stopped me for speeding. Told me I was real cute, doing ninety in a fifty-five-mile-an-hour zone."

"You've got a nice neck," she said.

"It holds my cute head up."

"You're teasing me," she said with a pout.

Sweets interrupted. "We got to go."

"Can I come?" Carmen asked, tangling her arm with Diamond's.

"Anytime you want," Diamond said, slipping free. "But not tonight, dollface. I'll be back."

Diamond noticed the bulge under Sweets's coat as they stepped out into the street. They hailed a cruising gypsy cab and got in.

"You did good," Sweets said, taking the bulge out from under his coat. It was a plain brown bag filled with five-, ten- and twenty-dollar bills. Diamond gave a low whistle of appreciation.

"This is just chump change, my man," Sweets said. "Stick with Mr. Brown and there's a lot more where this came from."

7

After they made stops at a rib joint, a bar and two after-hours clubs, Diamond estimated Sweets was carrying more than twenty thousand dollars cash.

"What happens if someone tries to rob that?" Diamond said, pointing to the bag on Sweets's lap as they settled into a big, brown limousine.

"No one tries to take off Mr. Brown."

"No one tries to take off Brinks, but some guys did," Diamond said. "You can't tell me that the two of us riding around is harder to heist than an armored car or a bank."

Sweets checked that the window to the driver's compartment was closed. Only the back of the driver's head was visible as he guided the big car downtown. The chauffeur wore no cap, and his bullet-shaped head was attached to a neck as thick as an oil drum.

"I change my schedule, make it hard for anyone to guess when I'm coming," Sweets said.

Diamond grunted approval. "That's good. But it's like trusting your nympho girlfriend at a stag party 'cause she says she loves you."

"Say what?"

"That isn't gonna make me sleep a whole lot better," Diamond said.

"How about this?" Sweets said, making a quick movement at his waist. A black Beretta materialized in Sweets's hand. It was pointed casually at Diamond's midriff.

Diamond, equally casually, brushed the muzzle aside. "Not bad. What's that, a nine-millimeter?"

Sweets nodded.

"They're okay. Not a whole helluva lot of stopping power. Which reminds me, I want to get rid of this pansy-ass .25 and get me a man's gun."

"I've got just the man for you. At our last stop." Sweets smiled, and didn't say anything more until they pulled up in front of the after-hours joint on Columbus Avenue.

"Wait here," Sweets said as he got out of the limo, and walked to a man sitting in a white Cadillac.

Diamond slid open the glass partition that separated him from the driver's compartment.

"What's your name?" Diamond asked the brown-suited chauffeur.

"Mitch," he said, making the word a challenge and a threat.

"Mine's Diamond. You always going to be picking us up for the last couple of stops?" Diamond ignored the malice in the driver's tone.

"That's none of your f—"

Sweets rapped on the side of the car, interrupting Mitch in mid-obscenity. "C'mon, Red," Sweets said, as he gave Mitch a reprimanding look.

"Nice talking to ya," Diamond said to Mitch, parting his lips in a grin that was part smile, and part baring his teeth.

Diamond got out and walked with Sweets to the Cadillac. A little man with a big bulge by his left shoulder got out.

"Red's interested in your stuff," Sweets said.

"Call me Vic, how do you do," the man said, shaking Diamond's hand and patting his shoulder. "Come around back."

Vic opened the trunk. There were enough guns inside to outfit a small guerilla army. Mounted on the opened lid were pistols, ranging from a .22 derringer to a .44 Magnum. On the floor of the trunk were display cases holding two sawed-off shotguns, an Uzi, a Thompson and two submachine guns.

Diamond glanced at the cars passing by.

"Don't be nervous, don't be shy, just step right up and make your buy," Vic said.

"What about the cops?"

"Who do you think I get the guns from," Vic said smiling.

Diamond pointed to a snub-nosed .38. "How much?"

"A fine weapon. Only owned by a little old lady in Kew Gardens who took it with her to bingo games. Said it was her good luck charm. Always won, never got robbed."

"Why'd she sell it?"

"She got run over by a truck. Her daughter sold it."

"Doesn't sound so lucky to me. How much?"

"Since you're a friend of Mr. Brown, I can let you take it from me for a mere three hundred bucks. And that includes six rounds of ammo, at no extra charge."

"I thought you wanted something with some stopping power, like a Magnum," Sweets said.

"I like a .38," Diamond said. "It's the gun I've always used. And it beats this peashooter."

Diamond glanced around as he reached into his pocket.

"It's okay," Sweets said. "Don't worry about no brothers passing by. The first law of the street is mind your own business, else someone mind it for you. And the man ain't gonna bust you up here. The place got juice, and the last time there was a bust here, the block got torn up, and the captain got transferred."

Diamond took the .25 out and handed it to Vic. While Vic appraised, Diamond watched Sweets out of the corner of his eye.

He didn't understand the young man. There was something about his speech, his manner, that was vaguely condescending, menacing. Diamond felt like a cow being patted on the back as he was led to slaughter. He shook the feelings off.

"Not a bad little gun," Vic was saying as he slid the clip back into the weapon. I'll take it off your hands. You give me a hundred, and the gun, and the .38 is yours."

Diamond looked at Sweets. Sweets nodded.

"Sold," Diamond said.

When they completed the transaction, Vic climbed into his Cadillac, waved, and drove off.

His license plate read GUNN.

They walked back to Brown's limo, and got in. Mitch started the car up and drove downtown.

"I should've asked him if he had any holsters," Diamond said, the .38 making his jacket bulge like a siliconed stripper's bra.

"You got a carrier's permit?" Sweets asked skeptically.

"No. The cops took it away after the case where I caught the commissioner's son in a Chinese opium den."

"I don't remember hearing anything about that," Sweets said.

"It got hushed up pretty good."

"I see, well, anyway, you carry a gun illegally, you best off without no holster. Less to get rid of if the man comes down on you."

He didn't respond. The whole idea of carrying a gun illegally made him uncomfortable. But Red Diamond without a .38 was like Benny Goodman without his clarinet. It just wasn't natural.

"This is it," Sweets said, breaking into Diamond's thoughts as the limo stopped in front of the Intown Hotel.

"You don't want me to come with you and drop the money off?" Diamond asked.

"Not necessary," Sweets said.

Diamond got out and the big car pulled away from the curb like a fish getting rid of a distasteful worm. At least he didn't have to guess where he stood with Mitch, Diamond thought as he walked to the newsstand across from his hotel.

A skinny Arab kid with hair as black as the desert night nodded to him as he walked up to the counter. Diamond took copies of the *News* and the *Post* from the rack, and requested a pack of gum. The kid slid across his gum, after Diamond pushed a five-dollar bill through the hole in the bulletproof glass.

"You Diamond, right?" the kid asked as Diamond took his change.

"So?"

"You the white guy working for Brown?"

Diamond tucked the newspapers under his arm and lit a cigarette. The Arab shifted gears as Diamond just stared at him.

"You want some weed?" the kid asked.

66

"Weed?"

"Grass."

"Like crabgrass kind of weed?"

"No man, reefer," the kid said. "Jiba Jiba. Ganja. Sinsie. You dig?"

"Reefer. That's muggles, right?"

"Reefer is reefer. No loose joints. The best shit around. Better than Colombian."

"Shit? Are you talking about fertilizer for that grass, or hop?"

"Hop?"

"Maryjane," Diamond said indignantly. "Do I look like a dope fiend to you?"

"You look like a guy who's gonna need it," the kid said.

"What's that supposed to mean?"

"You buying?"

"Information yes, dope no." Diamond slid another five through the partition. The kid pocketed it, and chose his words slowly.

"I know that any white guy gets caught up with the niggers is looking for trouble."

"That ain't even worth five cents."

"Yeah, well how about this: the wise guys ain't happy with Brown. They say he got religion or something. A few of the dealers, not just street guys either, got shot up. And someone snitched some others out to the cops. Someone like Brown."

"Very impressive," Diamond said tauntingly, turning to walk away.

"You wonder why he hired a white guy?" the clerk said.

Diamond turned back. "Why?"

"He's looking for a chump. No one else would go with him."

"Thanks for nothing," Diamond said, as he walked to his hotel.

Diamond ground out his cigarette in an ashtray in the hotel lobby. The television was on, and the desk clerk tore his attention away to give him a big greeting.

Red barely acknowledged it. The newsstand vendor's words had stuck with him like a bad hangover. The elevator took forever to get him to his floor, and he felt like kicking the door in as he jiggled the key in the lock to make it work.

He spotted the dark shape in his closet as he entered the room. He grabbed for the gun in his pocket as he threw himself down on the floor. Just before his pressure on the trigger reached the point of no return, he let up.

He got up and turned on the light. The figure he'd been taking deadly aim on was a brown suit. So the boss was making sure he was in uniform, he thought as he put his gun away with a shaky hand.

What was wrong with him? Red Diamond had been in tough spots before. Maybe Brown's troubles would even flush Rocco out of the underbrush.

He got out of his clothes, tucked the .38 under his pillow, and lay down on the bed. He popped a piece of gum in his mouth, and unfolded the newspapers.

"POLICE BAFFLED BY TRIPLE SLAYING," the *Post* said. Underneath the page-one story was a photo of a body being carried out of a familiar-looking hotel. The two morgue attendants were grinning into the camera.

Diamond felt the trembling begin again.

A pimp, his prostitute, and a man believed to be the woman's customer were found dead in a Times Square hotel yesterday in a case police described as "baffling."

Elmo "Jonesy" Johnson, 32, of no known address, Cora "Candy" Thomas, 23, also of no known address, and John Teel, 41, of Parsippany, N.J., were found shot to death at the Lido Hotel, police said.

"It looks like the three of them killed each other in the struggle, but certain key items are missing," Homicide Detective Pete Anglich said, declining to say what the items were.

An autopsy was scheduled for tomorrow, but Anglich estimated the bodies had been there for at least seven hours.

"It's not the kind of hotel where they want to know what goes on in the rooms," Anglich said.

Two months ago, a fourteen-year-old runaway was thrown from a top floor room. Police believe she withheld money from her pimp, who has been missing since the incident occurred.

Johnson was described by police as "a Times Square regular" with arrests for assault, burglary and pandering. He was released from prison last year, after serving two years of a seven-year sentence for armed robbery.

Thomas had four arrests for prostitution and two for receiving stolen property, police said.

Teel, a garment center salesman, lived in New Jersey with his wife and two children. Neighbors described him as "gruff, and sometimes hard to get along with" but "a pretty nice guy."

"I have no idea what my husband was doing in that room with those horrid people," said his wife, who refused to give her first name and hung up abruptly.

Police have no suspects in the slaying.

Anglich speculated that someone else was in the room, and made off with the missing items.

"We don't know if he, or she, was just an innocent bystander, or part of the murder," Anglich said, adding that the investigation was continuing.

Diamond had trouble reading the last few paragraphs, a bunch of tough-talking statements from politicians who claimed to be concerned about midtown crime, because his hands were shaking so.

He set the paper down, and picked up the *News*. He found the story on page three. Diamond gulped involuntarily, swallowing his gum.

It had virtually the same facts, though the paper had chosen to leave out the name of the murdered trick. The reporter had lengthened his account with details of other recent murders in the area. The article ended by noting that these were the twenty-seventh, twenty-eighth and twenty-ninth murders of the week.

What was it that was so upsetting? Hadn't Red Diamond seen enough stiffs to fill Arlington Cemetery? Big deal! Two dead dirtbags and a John Q. Public who was getting his ashes hauled.

But this was different. "Jonesy!" The sudden explosions. The pile of bodies. The smell of gunpowder and death. He wiped a film of sweat from his forehead.

When you're dead, you're dead. No one cares but the undertaker.

But why had Simon gone there?

The guy's name wasn't Simon. It was John Simon Teel. Just Teel. From Long Island. No, New Jersey. The lawn needed work. The gun needed bullets. All day without a fare. No fair. All's fair.

He shakily threw down the papers, got up, and turned on the television.

Captain Jacobi staggered across the screen, a parcel in his hands, a bunch of bullets in his gut. Gutman. Casper Gutman. The Fat Man.

Diamond lay back down on the bed, his clenched teeth loosening as he recalled one of his toughest cases. The black bird. The Maltese Falcon. He'd let Spade take the credit on that one, but well, Spade was an all right Joe.

Bogart wasn't bad either. A little short to play him, but he had the right moves. Those movie people exaggerated a bit, but they always did that. Diamond lay, hypnotized by the images.

He hadn't gotten a penny out of it. And he still missed Brigid. But she had to take the fall. No twist could make a sap out of Red Diamond. She wasn't like Fifi, but she was a hell of a broad. Not that you could trust her any further than you could throw the Fat Man.

There was a slack-jawed grin on Diamond's face as he watched.

He wondered what happened to that whole crew, after they did their time. He'd heard rumors that Brigid had gone to Vegas, and Cairo had run off with some guy he met in prison. And the Fat Man, he'd gone back to his search, after checking in with Rocco.

Diamond had calmed down by the time the final credits flashed on the screen.

Wonder where the black bird is now? Maybe some pawnshop, right in Times Square, where nobody knows of the treasure under the veneer. Or maybe Gutman has finally gotten it for Rocco, the man who funded his international search.

Who the hell was this guy Brown? Diamond hadn't heard of him before, and all of a sudden he was caught up in the middle of something. He lay back and stared at the ceiling.

Diamond decided to play along with Brown and see where it took him. He needed some cash, and if Brown was involved in shady dealings, Rocco wouldn't be far.

Diamond knew he just wasn't himself. Red Diamond, a three-pack-a-day man, without a butt in his mouth. And nothing, from the Sabrett's hot dogs the Greek sold at his umbrella stand by Central Park, to the veal marsala at that mob joint over by the river, tempted him.

What he wanted was Fifi, and Rocco. Though he had very different greetings in store for each.

With Fifi, it would be nice and slow. Champagne, a big bed, and no wake-up call.

For Rocco, it would be quick. Red Diamond wasn't a sadist. He wanted just enough time to let Rocco know it was Diamond punching his ticket. Then back to Fifi, for more champagne, and . . .

9

Over the next few days, he developed a routine. Up at about noon, then over to the East Side for a quick meal, and the daily search for Rocco could begin. His nights were spent on the prowl for Mr. Brown.

None of the mobster's joints seemed to be where he remembered them. He wondered if Rocco had covered his tracks further in anticipation of some big push. That would explain his renewed determination to get rid of Diamond.

The bartenders, pool club owners and nightclub front men he questioned denied knowing Rocco. Diamond expected that. But when he waved a sawbuck in front of some people, he started getting results.

"I know a guy named Rocco, books a lot of action over in Brooklyn," a shoeshine-stand operator said.

A man Diamond met in a deli told him Rocco owned a bunch of bars, and had moved to Florida.

A woman Diamond found in a grocery store said she knew a Rocco in real estate in New Jersey.

Two kids hanging out by a bus stop earned five bucks each for telling Diamond about the Rocco who had a hot-car ring operating out of a Bronx body shop.

So Rocco had been covering his tracks real good, Diamond thought as he jotted down his notes in a black pad he'd picked up.

But Red Diamond was on his case, and as hard to shake as a lovesick teenager. The cops and the courts did no good with a guy like Rocco. The fix was in from the word go. The only kind of justice Rocco understood came from the mouth of a gun.

Afternoons, he took to collecting gossip, and working out, at Muldoon's Gym, an Irish-sounding joint owned by an Italian where Jewish promoters taught Puerto Ricans and blacks how to fight.

"No offense, guy, but you look like you'd get a coronary if you got in the ring," Vito, the manager, had said when Diamond first showed up and asked for a bout.

Vito was a pugnacious ex-welterweight who lived at and for the gym. The only money he made that didn't get invested in the place went to buying the bottles of gin he'd taken to knocking down with the fervor he once devoted to opponents.

Diamond was indignant. Imagine the nerve, telling former Marine Corps heavyweight Red Diamond he wasn't in shape. But Vito was adamant, and probably right, Diamond realized.

Vito even insisted Diamond sign all sorts of medical waivers before he could attack the speed and sand bags. Vito wanted to see some papers with his name and age on it, and since he had already identified himself as former boxing champ Red Diamond, he couldn't very well use his John Teel ID.

Vito let him slide after some cash changed hands and some smooth talk about forgetting his wallet at the hotel, but that night Diamond asked Sweets to get him some papers.

"What happened to yours?" Sweets asked, with that condescending grin on his face.

"It's confidential," Diamond said.

"No problem. It'll be a couple days."

Three days later, Diamond got his papers. And proved his worth.

Sweets called him at eleven-thirty that morning.

"Mitch called in sick and Mr. Brown needs a driver. I can't make it. Can you do it?"

"I guess. You ever get me that ID, you know, the driver's license?"

"Bet," Sweets said. "Mr. Brown will have it for you. Take a cab to his office. The garage is in his building. Meet him there at two-thirty. He's got to go to Howard Beach."

Before his appointment, he stopped off in a Times Square gift shop that sold "I Love New York" T-shirts, kewpie dolls, obscene ash trays, knives ranging from small to extra large, and holsters.

Despite Sweets's advice, Diamond bought a brown leather holster with a belly clip. Diamond was no cheap gunsel with a bulge in his pocket.

He got to Brown's building by two-fifteen and waited in the garage. Checking that it was deserted, he took the holster out of the paper bag, and tucked it into his waistband.

He took the gun out of his pocket and spun the cylinder, checking the chambers. It sounded like a roulette wheel coming up double zero. He slipped it into his holster, buttoned his jacket over it, and waited for Brown.

Brown tossed Diamond a New York State driver's license paperclipped to a social security card as they walked briskly toward the limo.

There was a moment's awkwardness as Brown waited for Diamond to open the car door for him. Brown cleared his throat, and pointed at the door, until Diamond got the message.

"What's the matter, you a cripple or something?" Red said as he climbed into the front seat.

Brown stood waiting outside.

Diamond started the engine.

Brown got in.

"I don't like that," Brown said, his voice low and mean.

"Listen pal, I'm Red Diamond. I been around the block a few times. I been shot, stabbed, sapped. And I dish it out pretty good too. I'm no flunky. And I'm not going to be broken up if you don't like my manners. I'm the best there is, and you got me for a bargain price."

Brown considered firing him on the spot, but simply muttered, "let's go." Diamond shifted into gear.

It took a few minutes behind the wheel before Diamond felt comfortable. There wasn't much chance to play around in the crosstown traffic. But once they hit the FDR Drive, he was able to press on the gas, and tickle the brake, until he felt he knew the big car's touch.

The steering wheel felt good in his hands. He stroked it, kneaded it, twisted it from side to side, gauging the play. Brown, reviewing some papers in the back, didn't even notice his toying.

Diamond rolled his window down a bit and let the air off the East River stream across his face. He zipped in and out of traffic, keeping the car at a smooth sixty miles an hour.

Most of the guys don't like to go to Brooklyn. They say you never get a fare back, but me, I figure . . .

The thought was lost as a woman in a big Buick jammed on her brakes in front of him. Diamond switched lanes effortlessly, with enough control to have time to glare at her as he zoomed past.

The sunlight glinted off the spidery cables of the Brooklyn Bridge as he rode across. But he was too quick a fly to get caught as he left the Big Apple for the fourth largest city in the U.S.A.

10

Both men were oblivious to the bumps in the roadway, which had more pockmarks than an adolescent's face, as they headed east.

Diamond was enjoying the driving, trying to recall the name of a moody jazz piece that kept running through his head, and speculating why Brown was so cranky.

The boss was reading *The New York Times*.

Diamond had stopped reading the papers after the night of the Maltese Falcon. What the hell did he need the newspapers for anyway? They never got things right.

Cops never told reporters the truth. Pols never told reporters the truth. The wise guys never told reporters the truth. And if any of them did, the reporters would screw it up anyhow. Papers were for wrapping fish and lining birdcages.

Red Diamond wasn't a reader. He was a doer.

He pressed his knees against the wheel and controlled the car with minimal nudges. He felt like he could direct it with just his thoughts. Of course, he had been a pro race driver, until his buddy got toasted like a 170-pound marshmallow during a six-car pile-up.

Diamond took a cigarette out of his pocket, put it into his mouth and lit it. He puffed it without inhaling.

Brown slid the partition open.

"Put that damn thing out. I don't allow smoking in my car."

Diamond slowly removed it from his mouth, and crushed it in the virgin ashtray.

"I got all these bad habits," Diamond said. "Must be I come from an underprivileged childhood."

"Spare me the cheap sarcasm," Brown said. "Just get us to Howard Beach." He shut the partition and picked up a *Wall Street Journal*.

This isn't going to last, Diamond thought. I don't take orders from no one. That's why I had to leave the big agency, go out on my own. It was tough with no organization to back you up, but it was tougher to put up with guff from anyone.

He remembered the case that made him leave the nest. The boss had told him to back off. The retainer had run out and the guy that hired them, a middle-class Joe with a big heart and a bigger mortgage, had run out of dough.

Diamond had a few leads on the guy's wife and kid, who

had disappeared while he was out doing his nine-to-five. The boss said no cash, no work. Diamond wasn't built that way. He found the wife and kid; she'd run off with the Fuller Brush man. But he lost his job.

The car moved easily down the Belt Parkway, a couple tons of Detroit steel guided by Diamond's autopilot.

Brown slid open the panel.

"We're making good time," Brown said without any hint of pleasure in his tone. "Get off on Cross Bay Boulevard. Head south about a mile."

The tires squealed like pigs on the way to slaughter as the limo followed the off ramp to the street.

"We're going to Candida's. 15125 Cross Bay. Park in back." Brown sounded like a guy about to meet his first date.

The lunchtime customers were back at work, the supper crowd hadn't decided yet where to go, as Diamond eased the car into the parking lot.

There were less than a half-dozen cars in the lot behind the one-story, stuccoed, pseudovilla. A black, 1983 Eldorado was parked near the door. Diamond jotted down the license plate number.

"Are you . . ." Brown said, the rest of his sentence lost as a plane on its way to JFK passed by.

"What?" Diamond said, as the black shadow moved over them.

"Are you coming?" Brown growled, as he pulled the brass-plated handle on the heavy wooden door open.

Diamond kept his hand near his holster as he sized up the dozen patrons in the bar. Two groups of working-class Joes in flannel shirts, and a family of five.

It was dark inside, and it took a moment for his eyes to adapt. Details became clearer as he stood and scanned the place. Worn red booths with upholstery patched with tape in a few places. Red- and white-checked tablecloths, with paper placemats that bore maps of Italy. Empty Chianti bottles and faded pictures of Sicily hanging on

77

the walls. Fake Styrofoam ceiling beams. Fake flowers on the tables. But the smells of tomato sauce, peppers and garlic coming out of the kitchen were real.

The customers were looking at Brown like he'd just walked in on a KKK recruitment meeting. The waitress, a stocky brunette in a green and red blouse and a white miniskirt, directed them to a small side room.

The flowers in the little room were real, and the upholstery was unmarred, and looked freshly cleaned.

Diamond locked eyes with the man standing next to the only occupied booth. The man was about six feet tall and built like a refrigerator. He had dark black hair that was greased back from his forehead and a bulge near his left shoulder that Diamond guessed wasn't a copy of the Bible.

Brown strode toward the booth where the sentry stood. Another man was seated there, his back to Diamond. His ears were red and his silver black hair was neatly trimmed.

As Brown sat down at the booth, the man's bodyguard approached Diamond and gestured toward an empty booth. Diamond sat down, facing the bodyguard and the table where Brown was. He was too far to hear the other table's hushed conversation.

Diamond smiled warily at the bodyguard. The man showed as much emotion as a corpse. He had Magnum-size nostrils, with BB eyes.

A younger, skittish waitress, in the same Italian flag uniform, brought both tables bread and butter. She set a basket down between Diamond and the unsmiling sentry, and scurried away.

The man grabbed a chunk of bread and ripped into it. Diamond took his time, gently fingering the knife while he spread butter on the bread. He made a point of sticking his pinky in the air as he nibbled.

The whole meal went like that. The bodyguard tore at his veal piccata, saying nothing, but grunting and smacking his lips like a hog in a trough. When he attacked his spaghetti, the flying tomato sauce made it look like a red snowstorm.

Diamond savored every bite of his excellent veal marsala. He lifted his glass of house wine in his dining companion's direction.

"Salud."

There was no response. Diamond sniffed his wine, rolled a swig around in his mouth, and then swallowed.

"You know, sometimes it's good to act like a fifty-dollar punk in a leisure suit, and sometimes, you should act like a classy guy," Diamond said.

The bodyguard belched.

"Very eloquent," Diamond said. "It reminds me of a remark the Duke of Windsor once made when I was having crumpets with—"

Diamond stopped as he saw Brown get up suddenly from his table. Brown threw his napkin down and stormed past Diamond. Diamond was standing with his hand by his gun.

The waitress was as white as her skirt.

"It's okay, doll," Diamond said, slipping her a ten-dollar bill with his left hand. He began backing out. "The food was delicious. I'll come back sometime without my talkative friend here."

The bodyguard rose from the table.

"Watch it, cuddles," Diamond said. "Lead and linguini make a bad mix."

Diamond kept backing out as the bodyguard walked to his boss. He was leaning over into the booth as they exited.

Brown sat fuming in the car.

"Let's go," Brown ordered, as Diamond started the car and pulled out of the lot. Diamond noticed that two rented cars, each with two men in them, were pulling into the lot as he headed north on Cross Bay Boulevard.

As he drove onto the Belt Parkway, Brown began talking.

"That no good guinea son of a bitch. Who does he think

he's dealing with? Some nigger shoeshine boy just booked his first bet? After the money I made them!

"I don't even know the punk. I'm out of the business, and he wants deeds to my property. Says he'll let me in on a big smack deal. As if I'd touch that shit."

Diamond divided his attention between Brown's tirade, and the rearview mirror.

The two rented cars were coming up fast behind him. Diamond stamped the gas pedal.

Brown stopped murmuring obscenties as the car shot forward. "What're you doing?" he demanded.

"Did you see the black guys in the car with zebra plates?"

"What?"

"That joint we just came from, they take to integration like an Alabama sheriff. And two cars with black guys pulled in just as we were leaving. The cars had zebra plates, rented cars. Following us."

Brown turned around and looked out the back.

"You sure?" he asked.

"I'm going to find out."

The speedometer edged up to 120 and stopped when it ran out of room. There were angry beeps from car horns, barely audible as the limo swooshed by.

One of the drivers following them was outclassed, and soon lost behind a couple of cars. The other driver, in a beige Fairlane, was holding his own.

As they neared the Verrazano Bridge, traffic thinned out. The Fairlane gained a little.

"I don't think I'll be able to shake him," Diamond said. "You got a gun?"

"I haven't carried one in years."

"Okay," Diamond said, letting the car slow down to seventy while taking the .38 out of his holster.

"I'll take it," Brown said, reaching through the partition.

"Red Diamond takes care of his own business. Just stay out of sight."

Diamond set the gun down on the seat next to him, lowered his window, and switched into the middle lane. He was down to sixty miles an hour and the Fairlane was closing fast. The passenger was holding something that looked like a pipe out his window.

Rush-hour traffic was starting to clog up the other side of the parkway, but as they rounded the southwest corner of Brooklyn, the road to Manhattan was relatively clear.

Diamond could see his pursuers' faces in the side mirror. Dark faces with clenched-teeth grins. They looked more scared than happy. The rabbit was supposed to run, not slow down, for the fox.

The pipe in the passenger's hand was a sawed-off shotgun. Diamond wasn't surprised. The stick-up man's answer to an American Express card—Do you know me? I spread enough buckshot in a ten-foot area to turn a man into chopmeat. Fill the bag, sucker!

The Fairlane was a car length behind them, in the left lane.

Looks like they plan to take me out, and hope to get Brown with the second blast, or trust the crash to do their work for them. Sloppy, Diamond thought as he moved the .38 from the seat to his lap.

Diamond lifted the .38 as the Fairlane spurted up next to them. He slammed on the brakes and began squeezing the trigger in the same moment. He got off three shots.

The Fairlane zoomed ahead, with Diamond in pursuit. The shotgun-pointing punk's face, locked in a grimace so exaggerated it was almost comic, was frozen in Diamond's memory. It seemed so much more real than his past adventures. But of course, you're only as good as your last shoot-out.

Diamond felt great. The punk hadn't even gotten off a shot, and the rabbit was in hot pursuit of the fox.

The man behind the wheel of the Fairlane knew how to drive. That was okay. He liked the challenge. And he was gaining slowly.

It was just a gut-level feeling, but Diamond felt he had

been on that road before. And the traffic cops had been waiting. He dropped down to sixty as the Fairlane shot past the ramp where the cops waited.

There was a wail and a flashing red light, and the hounds came out after the fox.

"New York's finest will take care of the rest," Diamond said, allowing himself a smile. "C'mon up."

Brown sat up, adjusted the lapels on his suit, and began talking like they'd just come from a croquet match.

"You know, when Sweets told me about you, I didn't really believe it. So cool under pressure, like there was something missing. But I liked your style, and I figured a white guy can go in places where a brother would stand out."

"Makes sense," Diamond said.

"I'd like to stretch my legs," Brown said. "And I've got a proposal."

Diamond took the next off ramp, and drove to the Sixty-ninth Street pier. He got out with Brown and they walked out to where the wind brought a salty smell to their nostrils, and New York's famous profile could be seen.

"I'm upping your pay to a thousand a week," Brown said. "No more flunky work. From now on, you're my right-hand man. If you want it."

"What's my responsibilities?"

"First thing, find out who set me up. And why."

"Who was the guy you met?"

"All I know is Tony. The message came through Sweets. He's supposed to be a big deal."

"You got anyone in motor vehicle can run a plate?"

"Sure."

Diamond copied the license plate number he'd recorded in the parking lot, and handed it to Brown.

"How'd you know to do this?"

"It was the only car in the lot that looked like it'd belong to a guy who'd set up a sitdown."

"But how'd you know to look?"

"I had one case, involved a dead guy in Central Park no one could ID. I went to the block, wrote down all the license numbers of all the parked cars, ran them, and came up with my guy. Since then, I've always kept track of plates."

Brown bobbed his head approvingly. "You have any theories?"

"I figure one of your own people set you up. Thought you were getting soft. We were supposed to stay long enough for the killers to get there. We left early and they came late. They were sloppy all around, I mean, that was a real cowboy move they were trying to pull."

"You think it was the Italians?"

"They'd usually go for one of their own on a big job. Nice, neat, a good meal, maybe a broad, and a couple of bullets behind your ear. This was amateurs."

They walked on the pier for a few minutes, then got back into the car and headed toward the city.

"You think Mitch set me up?" Brown said abruptly.

"It's a time-honored tradition. Like Albert Anastasia's man just happened to take a powder when Al got into the barber's chair for the last time."

"And Mitch wasn't available today."

"It might be a coincidence," Diamond said halfheartedly.

"I want you to find out."

"I guess I'll go pay him a get-well call."

Brown sat back in the rear seat. "And Sweets didn't want to take the ride either."

"Could be coincidence."

"And I could be the Easter bunny. Damn! Both of those guys have been with me five, six years. I'll give them the benefit of the doubt. Until you tell me elsewise. Then I'll take care of it."

"Just to be on the safe side, you have someplace you can go to until I find out who's behind this?"

"I've got a sister in Jersey I been owing a visit to."

"I think it's time for a family reunion. Now, what's the story behind this meet today?"

"Sweets came to me a week ago, said this guy named Tony was into real estate. Mobbed up, with money to spare. Was going to buy me out, or bomb me out. I get there, this joker wants me to go into drug dealing, and hand over all my real estate. Said he'd heard I had a lot of respect in the black community."

"He sound like he knew about you?"

"Everything."

"Hmmm. He mention a guy named Rocco?"

Brown pondered the question. "No."

"Probably covering his tracks. It sounds like a Rocco scheme, though."

They were nearing the Brooklyn Bridge.

"Why don't you light yourself a smoke?" Brown said.

Diamond smiled, took out a Camel, and lit it. He smoked it without inhaling.

11

After dropping Brown off in Newark, Diamond mulled over what he had been told on the way over.

Mitch was thirty-one, unmarried, a high school drop-out and Vietnam veteran with two dismissed receiving-stolen-property arrests. Nearly made it as a professional football player, he had said, although Brown doubted it. Didn't gamble or take drugs. No steady girlfriend. Lived alone on West Ninety-sixth Street.

Sweets was thirty, divorced, and vague about his background. He'd met Brown one night in an after-hours joint, and talked Brown into hiring him. Street smart, with a good business head, he'd been a real asset to Brown, who treated him like a son. Had a taste for cocaine. Went through girlfriends like a chain smoker through a pack of cigarettes. Had totaled his Porsche a few weeks earlier.

Sweets was the obvious suspect. What did Diamond owe him? He'd gotten him the job, then maybe set him up to be killed.

Whether it was Mitch or Sweets, someone had thought Red Diamond would play the patsy. The graveyards were full of guys who'd thought they could pull a fast one on Red Diamond.

If Sweets was behind the setup, he'd already be underground, or have a cover story planned. Mitch would be easier game, he decided as he cruised Ninety-sixth Street looking for a parking place.

Mitch lived on the third floor of a four-story brownstone walk-up. It had high ceilings, higher rents, and roaches that had come over on the Mayflower. The building had been subdivided into eight apartments.

Diamond hit the buzzers for every apartment but Mitch's, and someone let him in. He walked quietly up the stairs, and then rapped hard on the wooden door to Mitch's apartment.

It opened quickly. Mitch was expecting somebody.

The look on his face was midway between shock and horror as Diamond shoved past him into the room.

Mitch recovered enough to grab for an automatic lying on the end table next to the door. Diamond already had his .38 out, and he slammed it down on Mitch's forearm. The .45 didn't go off when it bounced on the parquet floor.

"That's a hell of a way to greet a co-worker who came to see a sick friend," Diamond said.

"What you want? You surprised me."

"I bet I did. You figured I'd be a guest of the medical

examiner by now. Sit down," Diamond said, gesturing toward a blue velour couch with the .38.

"Your buddy boys screwed up. They tried to play Jesse James with me. You just can't get good help nowadays." Diamond smiled, showing his teeth and a bit of gums. The smile had as much warmth as a hungry bill collector's. Diamond shut the door and moved further into the apartment.

"You can't prove nothing. You ain't got a warrant."

"I'm not a cop, and this is my warrant," Diamond said, wiggling the gun. "Now sit."

Mitch sat down on the sofa and chewed his lip, desperately searching for something to say.

"I didn't, I didn't, I don't know nothing 'bout—"

"Save the witty repartee. Just tell me who put you up to it? I know you couldn't bust open a parking meter without someone to tell you how it's done."

Mitch looked offended, and then glanced over where the .45 lay on the floor. He calculated the distance.

"You couldn't make it to the rod," Diamond said. "I'll step back, give you a better chance. But shooting you when you go for it will be like robbing a cripple."

Diamond took a step back and bared his teeth again.

Mitch leaned back on the sofa and sighed.

"Just lay it out for me, Mitch old pal. What were you going to get for setting up Mr. Brown?"

"Ten grand. You could get a piece of the action too," he said hopefully.

"Not bad. But it'd take more than that for me to play Judas. Now, who put you up to it?"

Mitch chewed his lip some more, and looked expectantly at the door. Diamond felt like he was playing high-stakes poker with a kid.

"All right, who're you expecting?" he asked.

"How you know that?"

"I'm like Santa Claus. I know when you've been bad or good," Diamond said, pulling a straight-backed wooden chair over to where he could watch Mitch and the door.

He sat with the gun in his lap, held loosely, but ready to swing up at the slightest movement. He stared at Mitch, who was unable to meet his gaze.

"I'm not big on smacking guys around," Red said. "Besides, I don't think you're the kind it would do much good. And I'm pretty tired. So we're just going to wait here until your visitor comes. Relax and make yourself comfortable."

Mitch took another longing look at the gun on the floor. Diamond gave him another toothy smile, and they sat.

Keeping Brown's driver, or former driver, always in view, Diamond glanced around the apartment. Men's magazines and soiled clothing lay scattered among the spartan, and sparse, furnishings. The only item that wasn't wooden was the plush sofa where Mitch sat. Posters of bikini-clad starlets and football players were stapled to the badly plastered walls.

"Where'd you get the couch?" Diamond said. "It fits in here like a nun in a porno theater."

Mitch said nothing.

"You should get an interior decorator, and a housekeeper."

Mitch glared.

"How about we cut the small talk, and you tell me who set this deal up? He'll be here soon. Right?"

After getting no answer, Diamond began to hum "On a Slow Boat to China."

The sun was packing it in for the night, and a few final streaks of light were edging through the smears of dirt on the window, when Mitch began to get edgy.

His hopeful looks toward the door grew more frequent, as he shifted on the sofa and worried his lip like a dog with a fresh bone.

"C'mon pal, you look like you're about to explode," Diamond said, getting up. "This is the first time I've ever said this to a guy; let's go into the bedroom."

Mitch got up reluctantly, and they walked down the narrow, clothing-littered hall to the bedroom.

The king-size brass bed was unmade, partially covered by a genuine acrylic leopardskin throw. Centerfolds and posters of women wearing nothing more than their make-up were tacked upon the walls.

"We got to get you a girlfriend," Diamond said as a particularly well-endowed model in a lascivious pose caught his attention.

Mitch chose that moment to play middle linebacker, with Diamond as the quarterback. Red faded back to pass, and then rapped the burly driver's forehead with the .38. Mitch staggered and fell stunned on the bed.

Diamond rooted around in the closet and retrieved some gaudy ties.

"You got terrible taste," he said to Mitch as he bound the man's legs together.

Mitch had a thicker head than Diamond thought and he sat up and grabbed for the gun. The two men wrestled for the weapon. They got tangled in the leopardskin throw. Pillows and blankets flew through the air.

Mitch was younger, stronger, but his feet bound together made him awkward. Diamond clung to the gun like a kid with a new toy. He shoved it against Mitch's neck and pulled the hammer back.

"You got a hell of a seductive approach, but you're not my type," Red said, as he pulled a sheet off his body and started to get up.

Mitch gave a last desperate buck, and Diamond fell over sideways. Mitch was on top of him, one hand at his throat, the other pinning the gun to the bed.

Both men were wriggling, struggling, panting. Diamond broke the grip on his throat and they rolled around the bed some more. They exchanged punches and took turns holding the upper hand.

Mitch tried to spoil the exchange by sinking his teeth into Red's gun hand. Diamond pulled back, and Mitch chomped down on the rolled steel of the .38. He let out a yelp as his two front teeth and a canine shattered like a brittle wineglass.

Diamond jabbed the gun into Mitch's temple, but the driver refused to give up. He grabbed for the weapon, forcing Diamond's finger down on the trigger.

The explosion was muffled by his flesh. Mitch's expression went from a surprised look to a smile, as the pain, and all other feelings, drained from his body.

Diamond pulled himself up and off the bed. He ached in a dozen spots where Mitch had landed solid punches. His neck felt like it'd been tenderized with a two-by-four.

The room reflected little of what had transpired. Not much blood, Mitch lying there with a peaceful expression on his face. The rumpled bed looked more like a sign of a passionate interlude than a life-and-death struggle.

Diamond felt weak, dizzy. It had been him or me, I had to do it, he thought. What about the other three though? What three? The hotel. The closet. Bodies in a heap. Dead. Deadhead. No fare. Got to go home. No books. Who did it? Whodunit.

He went to the bathroom and dryheaved. He threw cold water on his face and tried to rinse the taste of death out of his mouth with Listerine. He weaved down the hall, leaning against the walls for support.

In the living room, he realized he'd left fingerprints all over. He retraced his route, wiping every place he could recall touching with a ball of paper towels he flushed down the toilet when he was done.

He was still having trouble holding himself up when he walked back out to the living room.

Sweets was standing in the middle of the room. He had a candy bar in his mouth, and Mitch's .45 in his hand.

12

"You wanna play shoot-out, or you wanna play smart?" Sweets said, the .45 pointing at Diamond's middle. Diamond figured the odds, and knew he was a fifty-to-one long shot. He let the .38 that was hanging limply at his side hit the floor.

"Maybe you got a brain on top of that motor mouth after all," Sweets said. "Now kick it over here."

Diamond kicked the gun over to Sweets. Sweets put the candy bar in his pocket and bent and retrieved the .38, all the time keeping the .45 on Diamond.

"Mitch dead?"

"He went for me."

"I ain't no court of law. I don't care about no self-defense jive. You know I got to kill you." There was a slight quiver in his voice.

"Mind if I have a last cigarette?"

Sweets shook his head and Diamond slowly took one out and lit it.

"Guess I don't have to worry about it being hazardous to my health, do I?"

"Just get on with it, man," Sweets said, sounding more uncomfortable than Diamond.

"Why'd you bring me into this?"

"I met Tony in the body shop when I brought my car in," Sweets said. "His whole family is mob, but they're soft. So's Brown. We decided it was our time. If Brown went for the deal, that would be it. But he blew his cool."

"And walked out before plan B could go into effect."

"That was a bunch of guys Mitch knew. They were gonna put the snatch on you two when you came out of the guinea restaurant. I got your .25 back from Vic. They were supposed to off him with it, and make it look like you died in the struggle."

"So you set me up like a chump. Figured I was just another knockaround palooka."

"It coulda been anyone, but it was you. I knew Brown was looking for a white guy. And you dropped into my lap."

"What about Brown?"

"What you mean?"

"I mean he's not going to rest once you kill me. He's got to come after you, to keep his respect out on the street, and not have to worry that some pal of yours won't jump out of the shadows and play peekaboo with him some night."

"I'll worry about that later. I've got connections."

Sweets had put the .38 in his pocket, and was gnawing at the candy bar again.

"Why'd you sell out?" Diamond asked. "Who put you up to it?" Diamond took a step toward him.

"Keep back." The hand holding the .45 was shaking. "You're gonna die," Sweets said, as if he was trying to convince himself.

Diamond's cigarette was more than half gone. "Why'd you do it?" he asked. "You got smarts. Brown likes you. You could've taken over slowly."

"I ain't got time. My girlfriend and I do a couple hundred a night in coke. She likes furs. I like cars. We both like the horses. I do all the work, get a thousand dollars a week from him. I got more coming."

The candy bar was gone and Sweets had the .38 back in his left hand. Diamond sensed Sweets was psyching himself up to pull the trigger. The edge in the young man's voice was like a straight razor.

"You never killed anyone, did you?"

Sweets tightened his grip on the guns.

"It's a messy business. Specially with a .45. Blood and bits of bone flying. Lots of times the dead guy starts shitting and pissing. Clearing himself out before the big sleep. It smells terrible. And you hit an artery, the blood spurts ten, maybe fifteen—"

"Stop it!"

"Just want you to know what you're getting into. Lot of guys, they kill their first one, they get nightmares for years. They keep seeing the guts all over the place, the—"

"Shut up!"

"But maybe it won't bother you. Of course, if the cops catch up with you, you're going to be spending a lot of time without wine, women and coke. But maybe that's better than if Brown finds out—"

"Shut up!" Sweets screeched.

Diamond had pulled the bowstring as taut as he dared without snapping it. He took one last puff on his cigarette. The tip glowed like the entrance to hell.

"Look out, behind you!" Diamond yelled.

Sweets nearly fell for the old ploy. He hesitated but a millisecond. Diamond took advantage, and flicked the glowing butt at his face. Sweets flinched just long enough for Diamond to make a headfirst dive at him.

Sweets pulled the trigger on the .45, and a lamp exploded into oblivion. The room was dark. Red butted his head against Sweets's nose, and the young man's lower face was quickly covered with blood. He stretched Sweets's arm with the .45 over his head. The .38 dropped to the floor.

The two men went down, kicking and tugging at each other for the gun. Diamond pressed his full weight down when he got on top, and Sweets gasped for air.

Sweets suddenly realized he had lost control. Like a runner with his second wind, he pushed his body to the limits. Diamond sensed the surge, and it set off the adrenalin in his own body.

He jerked the .45 out of Sweets's hand; Sweets grabbed for the .38. He had it quickly, but Diamond was quicker. He pulled the trigger on the .45 once, and Sweets became a statistic.

It seemed easier. How many had it been? How many notches in his gun?

He wiped the .45 clean of prints and dropped it by Sweets's side. He pried his own gun out of the dead man's fingers, and holstered it.

The report of the big automatic was still in his ears. He thought he could hear sirens outside, above the ringing, and he hurriedly wiped everything he could think of.

He opened the outside door. There was no one in the hall, but he could hear noises downstairs. He ran up one flight.

The door to the roof was unlocked, and he pushed it open with his elbow. He ran to the edge of the deserted roof, and looked down into the street. A police car was pulling up. The cops took their time getting out.

A heavyset woman met them as they neared the stoop. She was gesturing wildly. The cops seemed bored as they followed her in.

Diamond ran to the far side of the roof. There was a twenty-foot gap between buildings. He ran to another side, avoiding the antenna guywires that stretched across the space, deadly garrotes in the dark.

There was a six-foot alleyway separating the building from its neighbor. Diamond backed up and threw himself into the air, landing on the other roof with a comforting thud. He had to traverse three more rooftops before he found an open door into a stairwell. He sauntered down to the street.

A second patrol car had parked in front of Mitch's building and the two officers were occupied keeping the crowd back. Children were making shooting gestures with their fingers, and telling their friends about dead bodies they'd seen.

The cops were more animated now that they knew it was a legitimate call. The homicide dicks would be by. With their "What d'you got, kid?" they'd take the action away from the patrol guys. The cops were hoping the TV crews got there before the dicks grabbed center stage.

Diamond skirted the edge of the crowd unnoticed. The medical examiner's meat wagon had just pulled up, and everyone was watching to see how many body bags the crew was bringing out. A TV news van was pulling up as he walked away. The crowd got excited. Its moment of stardom was near.

Diamond picked the limo up and drove to Brown's garage. He walked by Brown's office on the way out.

"What're you doing here?" Red asked, after Brown buzzed him in.

Brown hung up the phone he'd been speaking into.

"Just putting things in motion. Talking to an old friend who'd be eligible for social security, if he ever bothered to get a number. The only number he's got the police gave him." He pressed a button under his desk and a small section of the wall lifted up. A television set was visible, and a Betamax hummed on as he hit another button.

". . . body found in an Ozone Park lot has been tentatively identified as Tony Lucchini, a forty-two-year-old Queens resident. He had been shot three times at close range, and organized crime is suspected, police told Channel Two. Back to you, Jane," the voice said, as the shot of a rubble-strewn lot disappeared from the screen.

"More death on the Upper West Side," said a smiling brunette. "Fred Cox has the report, live from Ninety-sixth Street."

Cox fended off a pair of teenagers who were trying to shove in front of the camera.

"The atmosphere here is grim, as police discovered a

94

double homicide early this evening, Jane. Two men, both shot to death, were discovered in the apartment of a man identified as Mitch Freeman. Freeman was apparently one of those killed."

The camera cut to a shot of police guarding the doorway.

"Robbery is not the motive, we've been told," Cox said. "There's the detective now."

The cameraman jostled his way to the cop. Even without the cigar clenched in his teeth, the shield pinned to a loud plaid jacket, and the shoulder holster peeking out, the detective would've been as hard to spot as a Great Dane in a pack of Chihuahas.

"Detective Anglich, what can you tell us?" Cox asked, shoving a microphone next to the cigar.

Anglich flicked his ash. "One victim was found in the bedroom. Another in the living room. Both young, male blacks. Shot at close range, and dead when we arrived."

"Had they been shot with the same gun?"

Anglich smiled. "We have to have some secrets, Fred. It's too soon to tell, anyway."

"Any suspects?"

Anglich chewed his cigar. "The investigation is just beginning. We are hopeful."

"Was it drug-related?"

"No comment."

Anglich moved back behind police lines.

"That was Detective Pete Anglich of the Special Midtown Crime Task Force. Back to you, Jane."

The blonde smiled out of the screen again. "We'll be bringing you more details as—"

Brown hit a button, and the screen went dark.

"You don't waste any time, do you?" Brown said approvingly. "You find out why they did it?"

"Not saying I know what you're talking about, I'd guess Sweets just got greedy. And your driver went along for the ride."

95

Brown took out a stack of twenties and put them on his desk. "Thanks," he said, shoving the pile toward Diamond.

"For what?"

"You know."

"No, I don't. Anything that might've happened happened because some guy tried to play Red Diamond for a chump. And Diamond would be a chump if he went around taking blood money."

"If that's how you feel."

"That's it."

"Fine. Listen, that Anglich is a good cop. He's all over town on cases and has more snitches than the Pope has Catholics. It might be good if you make yourself scarce."

"I don't run from no one."

"Well keep a low profile at least, until I find out what's going on."

"I'm gonna go grab a bite, then hit the hay. It's been a long day."

"I still don't know if there was anyone else in on this deal with Sweets. Be careful."

"I always am," Diamond said.

He took a cab down to the Port Authority Bus Terminal. He chose a locker in an uncrowded part of the terminal, and when no one was looking, slipped his gun in. He took the key to the locker, put it in an envelope, and mailed it to himself at the Hilton Hotel. Then he grabbed a cab over to the East Side.

The cabbie recommended a French joint near the United Nations called Mange Chez Joseph. During a couple of his high-class, international jobs, Diamond had learned to pronounce the "c" like an "s" in garçon, and not to go "Ugh, snails" when the client ordered escargot. He felt entitled to some nouvelle cuisine.

A half-dozen different languages were being spoken at the small, candlelit tables as the maitre d' showed him to a table in a rear corner.

Waitresses in slinky gowns moved among patrons wearing dashikis and three-piece suits, turbans and burnooses. The dimly lit restaurant had a natural, international feel. It reminded him of his last big case in Geneva.

"You ready to order?" his waitress asked. A recessed bulb in the ceiling behind her gave her shoulder-length blond tresses a backlit glow.

The details of her face were lost in the dark, but her lush lips had been painted to match the red of her dress, and the voice that came from them sounded familiar.

"I said are you ready?" she repeated. "You make up your mind yet?"

The red gown clinging to her perfect shape gave him a different type of appetite. His hunger, and a little bit of bewilderment, showed on his face.

"What do you recommend?" he asked, staring at her unabashedly.

"Depends what you like," she said, fingering her hair in a way that said more than her words.

He became aware of the faintly playing Muzak, barely audible above the multilingual chatter, and usual restaurant noise. But the bland rendition of "Some Enchanted Evening" filled his ears.

An awareness had been blossoming inside him that this was no stranger he was meeting. It was Fifi. But he had to follow her lead and play it cool.

"Hello. Do you want me to come back in a couple of days when you're ready," the waitress asked.

"Sorry. It's just you remind me of someone I know," he said. "Or knew."

"That's okay. You remind me a lot of my boyfriend," she said. "I mean, my ex-boyfriend. He's a cop."

"I'm a private cop," Diamond said. He knew Fifi had been going out with a cop, but that was a long time ago. He'd sold her out to Rocco. Maybe she was trying to tell him something.

"You still haven't ordered," she said, throwing her hip

forward in a way that made him feel like a farm boy discovering his first red-light district.

"What've you got?" he said.

"Quite a lot to choose from," she said with a confident smile.

"I'll trust your judgment."

She was about to go to the kitchen when he said, "By the way, what's your name?"

"Jane. Jane Doe. What's yours?"

"Red Diamond."

"Nice to meet you, Red," she said before walking away.

What a doll! She would've been a great undercover operator. Heck, she *was* a great undercover operator, he thought, remembering how they'd wiled away the hours during that lonely stake-out in Cleveland. But you'd never guess it by the way she was acting.

The years had been good to her, wherever she'd been. She didn't look a day over thirty, although he knew she was only a couple of years younger than he was. It was amazing what these dames could do with a little make-up.

"Jane Doe?" he said with a smile when she brought him a halibut steak in a light sauce, garlic bread, and julienne-cut string beans.

"That's my real name," she said.

He was proud of her for being so careful.

"I understand," he said with a wink. "How about we get together later, and talk about the people we reminded each other of."

She hesitated, then said yes as if it was something quite daring. "I get off in an hour."

"It'll be a long hour."

The food was delicious and he ate slowly, allowing his eyes to feast on the woman who claimed to be Jane Doe. Well, Fifi never was very imaginative. Except in the bedroom, where she made Houdini look like a dime store magician.

He wasn't the only one watching her. She was easy on

the eyes, and most of the male patrons managed to keep track of her syncopated movements.

He tried to guess who Rocco's henchmen were. The tall black in the dashiki could have any sort of weapon under his flowing garment. The swarthy man in the three-piece suit had a decidedly undiplomatic-looking knife scar on his face. Two men with turbans reminded him of a couple of thugs he'd run into in Calcutta.

He'd had enough killing for one day, and decided whoever it was, he'd just give them the slip. He regretted stashing his gun, but it was too hot to carry. He'd have to get the coppers to give him back his carrier's permit.

After about forty-five minutes, she came back to his table.

"The boss said I can leave a few minutes early."

Good, he thought. That would throw off the timing of anyone who knew her hours. "I know a nice quiet bar," he said, thinking of Garelick's, where they'd first met.

They stepped outside and got caught in a cold rain that cut through the night like a mugger with his first knife. They were soaked in seconds.

"Let's just go up to my place," she said. "I don't usually do this sort of thing, but I'm too wet to go anywhere."

"Don't apologize. Do you want to pick up something?"

"Why, don't you have everything you need on you?" she said, in an exaggerated Mae West impression.

He put his arm around her as she shivered in the back seat of the cab. She smelled good, a hint of perfume mixed with some cooking odors.

"You smell nice," he said.

She snuggled in closer as they rode to her apartment in the East Seventies.

Her apartment was as he expected, warm and sweet and feminine, just like its occupant. Thick carpet, bean-bag chairs, a couple of huge Raggedy Ann dolls. The green of the plants was the only cool color in the yellow, orange and red decor.

She turned the dimmer switch only halfway, and the bright colors created a warm ambience.

"You fix us a couple of drinks while I get out of this," she said, breezing right into the bedroom.

"What would you like?" he asked, although he knew her favorite drink. Or at least what her favorite had been when they'd last met.

"Surprise me," she shouted from the bedroom.

He mixed her a Tom Collins, and himself a straight Scotch. He set his soggy jacket down and carried the drinks into the bedroom.

"Gentlemen knock," she said, making no effort to cover up.

"The door was open. And I'm no gentleman." He appraised her charms, and was pleased to note everything was where it belonged. "Besides, you said I should surprise you."

"Since you've seen the whole shebang, it seems pointless to slip into something seductive."

"You'd be seductive in a burlap sack."

She smiled as he handed her the drink.

"A good guess," she said after taking a sip. "My favorite drink. How'd you know?"

"I'm a detective. Private."

"A private dick, don't they call it?"

"Sometimes."

"What's that line from the movie," she said, brushing a few strands of wet hair from her face. "Oh, yeah, 'I didn't know private detectives really existed, except in books. Or else they were greasy little men snooping around hotel corridors.'" She paused. *The Big Sleep,* with Bogart and Bacall."

She was grinning, obviously pleased with her memory, as she slipped into a nightgown that hid about as much as a yard of cellophane. "Do you like trivia?" she asked.

"That was anything but trivial. I remember it well. The Sternwood case. The general with the wacky daughters. Got a lot of publicity, thanks to that Chandler guy. But it was a tough one. Eddie Mars's boy, Canino gave me a run for my money."

She gave him a quizzical look.

"Not that he's in Rocco's league. Mars was just a front man for Rocco. We know that now, but then it was anybody's guess. Good thing my pal Marlowe helped me out."

Diamond had mixed a stiff Tom Collins, but she downed it in one gulp as she listened to his rambling recital.

"You really a private dick?" she said over her shoulder as she walked to get another drink.

"As real as they get," he said, sitting down on her bed. She returned and sat next to him, her thigh barely touching his. Was she continuing the game because the apartment was bugged? he wondered. "What about you?"

"I'm an actress."

"I was admiring your performance."

She giggled and took another gulp of alcohol.

"I've been in a movie. And a commercial. For the restaurant. I played a waitress. No speaking parts yet, but I've done some modeling too."

The slight bob in her breasts as she talked made him hornier than a herd of rutting goats.

"Tell me about yourself," she said.

"Not much to say. I'm just a knockaround kind of guy, trying to keep my head above water in the big city."

"Who's this guy Rocco?"

"Enough of this game," he said, setting his drink on the floor, and taking the nearly empty glass out of her hand.

Their tongues fenced for a while. He made deep, broad slashes. She favored a darting, rapierlike approach. She lay back and tugged at his pants.

A woman named Milly frowned jealously. Must've been some ex-girlfriend, Diamond figured, as her image was lost behind a cloud as thick as cigar smoke in a small room.

Then he was thrusting into Fifi, and there was no one else in the world.

It was the best it had ever been for him. And the second time, a few minutes later, was even better.

He lit a cigarette afterwards.

She threw a thigh across him. "You're not inhaling."

"I'm trying to cut down."

"It hasn't hurt your wind any."

He blew out a cloud of smoke and kissed her.

"You know, I've never just let a guy pick me up that easy before. But there was something about you, like, do you believe in reincarnation?"

Diamond shrugged.

"I feel like I've known you in a past life."

"You can cut the act, sweetheart. It's me. Red. The guy who saved your life in Bay City."

She gave him a perplexed look. "Was that with Rocco?"

He nodded.

"You want to be Humphrey Bogart. Can I be Bacall?"

"You're everything she was, and more. But there's no time for play-acting. Have you heard anything about Rocco? What crimes he's active in?"

She giggled. "I heard he's in the white slavery business,

you know, kidnapping pretty girls from movie theaters and selling them to Chinamen."

"Hmmm. He was in that racket a while ago, with Cha Hsu Ba over on Mott Street. I wonder when he went back to it."

"And he's got this ring, selling drugs to public school kids. Has guys outside most of the junior highs in the city. They sell candy bars with heroin in it, get the kids hooked, and then make them steal."

"Figures."

Her hands were on him again, but his mind was on Rocco.

"You got any idea where he's hiding out?"

"I'm tired of this game, Red," she said petulantly. "Let's play something else. I've got some whipped cream in the fridge and we can—"

"It's no game, dollface. This one's for keeps."

"Want to play—"

"No games," he said, roughly brushing her hand away from where it was distracting him.

His serious tone cut through the pleasant haze of liquor and lust. He had the obsessed look of Captain Ahab on the bridge as he scanned the ocean for Moby Dick. Red didn't notice the way she stiffened.

"You're serious about this, aren't you?" she said.

"As serious as a slug from a .45."

Her lips fluttered as she tried to think of something to say. She wound up staring mutely at the ceiling.

"Listen sweetheart, once I take care of Rocco everything will be the cat's pajamas. But you've got to tell me more."

"I tell you I don't know anything about him."

"This is not time for fooling around," he said, squeezing her shoulder for emphasis. "If it was anyone other than you, I'd be bouncing them off the walls by now."

She shivered at the violence of his words and tone.

"Don't be scared, angel. I won't let anyone hurt you." His hand traveled up to caress her hair. She pressed him to her with the leg draped over him, hoping to distract him from his obsession.

"There'll be plenty of time for that later," he said, ignoring the well-shaped thigh. "What can you tell me about Rocco?"

"I don't know anything."

"You don't need to cover up. I'll protect you from him. You can come live with me."

"I just met you," she said, raising her voice slightly.

"Don't talk so loud," he whispered. "You never know if he's got the place bugged."

She glanced nervously around the room, momentarily believing him. She struggled to regain control, trying to recall the tips from rape-prevention classes.

"The last time I saw you, I thought you were dead," he said. "I'm a hard-drinking, hard-living guy, but I had a lump in my throat the size of a Studebaker. Even when it turned out to be your sister . . ."

His tender words only alarmed her more.

"She looked so much like you," he continued. "And it was you they were after. We both know that. I can see it so clearly."

Diamond was lost in the painful images. "I thought it was you, spilling your guts all over the floor. Like a bloody, busted doll. I was just a big dummy who got there too late. Even now, when I saw you undressed, I expected to see the scars from those killers' bullets."

"Please, please, this is all a mistake," she said as he ran his hand from her unscarred abdomen down to her buttocks and thighs. "I'm not the person you're thinking of. You really better go."

"Tell me dollface, where's Rocco hiding? We'll never be safe until I send him off to meet the reaper. Where is he?" He squeezed her too hard, and she flinched.

"Ow. You hurt me," she said.

"I didn't mean to."

She marshaled her courage. "I think you better go."

"Not until you tell me more about Rocco."

She hesitated. "Okay. Okay. I heard he had left the city. Yeah, he'd left the city."

"Where'd he go?"

"I don't know."

"Think," he said, unintentionally squeezing her hard as he got caught up in the questioning.

"California. Yeah, Los Angeles. He went to Los Angeles. I heard that, I did."

"It's a big city."

"I'll, I'll get more information tomorrow."

He leaned back. "I'm sorry. I didn't mean to hurt you. I guess I just don't know my own strength."

Her lips were dry as he gave them a peck. "Listen, I've got to be at work early tomorrow. Especially if I'm going to check things out."

"You sure you'll be okay? I can stay here with you."

"Not tonight. There'll be plenty of nights in the future."

"I guess you're right," he said, slowly getting up and getting dressed. "Once we get this taken care of, don't worry, you'll never be out of my sight."

"I can't wait," she said, trying in vain to put some enthusiasm in her tone.

He collected his belongings and got dressed. She put on a terrycloth robe and walked him to the door.

"I'll be back," he said. "You can count on it."

He kissed her and walked out.

She breathed a sigh of relief and slid her three locks into place. As she propped a chair against the door and shut the lights she made a silent vow never to pick up a customer again.

14

What a doll, Diamond thought as he rode back to his hotel. A little bit of a screwball, but hell, that's the price you paid with these dames. She acted like she'd forgotten their times together. On the run, Rocco's goons on their tail. The nights in run-down motels, passing the hours under the covers, with his gun under the pillow as they waited for a knock at the door.

The clerk behind the desk at the hotel, a skinny Puerto Rican kid with too pretty features, was shivering. It wasn't that cold and Diamond walked over to the desk.

"What's going on?" Diamond asked in his best inquisitional tone.

The clerk was as hard to crack as a rotten egg.

"There's a couple of guys waiting for you upstairs," he blurted.

Diamond tensed.

"I think they're cops," the clerk said.

"Why?"

"They showed me their tins."

"Very perceptive."

The clerk nodded. "They looked real, but you never know."

"You let them up in my room?"

"They said they'd get me for all sorts of things," the clerk sputtered. "Please don't tell Mr. Brown. I just got out of the joint. I need the job. It was a bum rap, I—"

"Okay," Diamond said, cutting him off and walking out of the hotel.

He had just cleared the steps when the man stepped in front of him. Diamond reached reflexively toward where his .38 had been.

The man had a Detective Special pointed at Diamond even before he barked "Police. Freeze!"

Diamond froze. He recognized the cop as Anglich.

"Assume the position!"

"Listen, I'm a private—"

"Get against the wall. Now!" Anglich ordered, shoving Diamond with his left hand. The right hand kept the gun aimed at Diamond's midriff.

Diamond placed his hands against the weathered red brick wall of the hotel and spread his legs. Anglich kicked his legs out wider, so Diamond could just barely keep his balance. The cop patted Diamond down and found nothing.

"All right, turn around."

Diamond faced him. Anglich was more than six feet tall, but his droopy posture made him seem shorter. He had the beginnings of a paunch, and a pelican jowl, but the fat was just a glaze over muscle. An unlit cigar was glued to his lips as his hard brown cop eyes sized Red up.

"We'll do this nice and friendly," the cop said. "First I give you some answers, then you give me some answers. My name's Pete Anglich. I work a special homicide detail. Your name's Red Diamond. Claim to be a private eye. I don't like private eyes. I don't like cockroaches either. That doesn't mean I can squash them all though. Just some."

"I guess that means I shouldn't put you as a reference on my resumé," Diamond said.

"You want to be cute, we can go back to the precinct and you can be smart for everyone in the squad."

"I won't crack wise. You got your job to do."

"Good." Anglich returned his gun to his shoulder holster. The tough cop wasn't the kind who needed a gun to take care of himself.

It was nearly three A.M. and no one had seen him frisk Diamond. With the gun tucked away, they just looked like two men talking, though no one would believe Anglich was anything but a homicide dick.

"What were you reaching for when I stopped you?"

"Force of habit."

"That don't answer my question."

"I used to carry a gun. I don't any more. I thought you were going to mug me."

"I look like a mugger to you?"

"You never know. Times are tough, and like I said, it was a reflex."

"So where's your gun now?"

"Damned if I know. Sold it to some guy in Jersey about three months ago."

"But you still got the reflex. Why'd you sell it?"

"You guys are doing such a great job keeping the streets safe, I figured I didn't need it."

The cop rolled his cigar across his lips. "You got a receipt for the gun?"

"Not on me."

"In your hotel room?"

"I'm sure your boys searched that already. Without a warrant, I might add," Diamond said. "No. It was in my wallet. Got stolen."

"You got any ID?"

Diamond reached into his back pocket.

"Take it out slow," Anglich said, putting his hand on the butt of his revolver.

"You frisked me already. Remember?" Diamond said, taking his wallet out slowly and handing it to the cop.

"You can't be too careful." Anglich looked at the driver's license, then flipped through the cash Brown had given Diamond.

"This driver's license looks like it was just printed."

"I told you, my wallet got stolen."

"And you carry all this cash?"

"I just got paid."

"Who do you do your snooping for? Got an agency?"

"Self-employed. I'm a lone operator, just go around like a cockroach picking up the crumbs you guys leave around."

"I hear that you're a strong-arm for Cornelius."

"Who?"

"Cornelius Brown. The guy with everything the color of shit."

"You're misinformed."

"You know the guy?"

"I've heard the name."

"What do you know about two of his guys found dead uptown?"

"That's terrible. I saw it on the TV. Why don't you ask him?"

"I did. He don't know nothing. Told me to talk to his attorney."

"I believe every citizen should cooperate with law enforcement," Red said with a dutiful smile.

"Smart ass. You know you're this close to a trip downtown," Anglich said, holding his thumb and index finger a quarter inch apart. His nails needed trimming.

"The dead guys on Ninety-sixth Street, it was a strange deal," Anglich continued. "One guy dead from a forty-five. The other guy dead from a thirty-eight. There's no thirty-eight, but the guy that bought the farm from the forty-five has a twenty-five in his pocket. And that little cutie had been used before. To kill three people. What d'you think about that?"

"Sounds like a busy gun."

"Over in the Lido Hotel. A pimp, a pross and her john. Two days ago. That refresh your recollection?"

Diamond's stomach flip-flopped. His eye twitched and he brushed it as he struggled to keep control.

"Just what I read in the papers." Diamond's voice sounded weak, far away.

"For a guy with a clear conscience, you look like you just swallowed a ball of shit. What do you know about the three people got killed? My people tell me it was right about when you showed up."

Diamond remembered the advice the old cat burglar had given him on the case of a million dollars in hot rocks.

"A good cop, or a polygraph, can tell you're getting excited, and they figure youse lying," the burglar had said. "The only way to get dem off de case is to make youself excited over sumthing else, like you really mad, or yours hemorrhoids is actin' up."

The burglar's English was lousy, but his advice was good. Diamond forced his fear to change to anger.

"We talked long enough," he snarled at the cop. "Either take me in and book me, or cut me loose. You just about accused me of five murders in five minutes. You want to know where I was when Lincoln got shot? You got enough to make it stick, try it. Otherwise, why don't you go do something useful, like find the guy that took my wallet."

"Don't tell me my job."

"You gonna advise me of my rights?"

"When I want to."

"I'll give you my name, rank and serial number. Before I say anything else, I want an attorney."

Anglich stepped in closer. Diamond could count the hairs in the cop's furrowed brow. He could smell the pungent, unlit cigar. The cop's jaw was thrown out, like he wanted Diamond to take a poke at it.

"I'm going to let you go, roach," Anglich said. "Just to see where you crawl to."

"Is that a dismissal?"

"For now. Don't leave town."

"I'll cancel my trip to the Bahamas."

"You do that," Anglich said, stepping back.

Diamond walked up the steps of the Intown Hotel.

"I thought you were going out," Anglich said, sneering as he folded his arms in front of his chest.

"I changed my mind. You never know what kind of people you might meet on the street."

Diamond ignored the desk clerk and went straight to his room. There were two young cops waiting.

"My name's Dundy, I'm with—"

"With homicide," Diamond interrupted. "I just had a pleasant chat with Anglich. He got me for a dozen killings, but I got off on a technicality."

"We just wanted to—"

"I know what you want," Diamond said, taking off his jacket. Either show me a warrant, arrest me, or get out of my room."

"We thought you might be able to help us with our investigation."

"I'll give you a call," Diamond said, continuing to peel off his clothing. "Don't hold your breath. I'm tired now and I'm going to sleep."

Diamond was wearing only his briefs.

"You hang around much longer, I'm gonna scream rape. If you have any questions, talk to my attorney."

The two cops exchanged questioning looks, and left.

What a day, Diamond thought as the bed sagged under his weight.

A shoot-out, a couple of killings, and finding Fifi after so many years. Not bad, not bad at all.

And it wasn't often you got to bully a couple of homicide dicks and get away with it. Of course, Red had been around the block a few times. Those wet-behind-the-ears rookies didn't stand a chance. They were still playing with cap pistols when he was going toe to toe with the toughest thugs on earth.

He went to sleep with a smile on his face.

15

"You awake?"

"I am now," Diamond said, groggily recognizing Brown's raspy voice on the phone.

"We should get together and talk. I don't like to talk on the phone. It's so formal." He said each word like he was underlining it.

"I understand. What time's good?"

"I got an appointment in fifteen minutes. How about three? At the zoo. You remember that little statue I got in my office?"

Diamond rubbed his eyes and tried to recall. Of course. There was a foot-high statuette of a brown bear in the corner of Brown's office.

"Got it. That animal's cage at three."

Both men clicked off the line at the same time.

Diamond dressed and walked over toward the East Side. He circled the block twice, and periodically stopped to check his reflection in store windows. It was an old technique, but had come in handy when he'd cracked the hit-man operation being run by a bunch of vets in Miami. He was confident he wasn't being followed.

Diamond stopped off at the Hilton. The desk clerk said there was no mail for Red Diamond.

Mange Chez Joseph was crowded with the lunchtime trade. Businessmen talking about football, profit margins and women. Lawyers talking about golf, judicial decisions and women. Diplomats talking about soccer, international relations and women. Some media types talking about tennis, exclusive stories and women. A few tables were occupied by females, who talked about office politics, entertainment gossip and men.

Fifi was waiting on a table with four gray-suited attorneys at it. She nearly dropped the heavy tray she was carrying when she spotted Diamond. She made her delivery, cutting short the flirtatious banter from an attorney with blow-dried silver hair.

She hesitantly approached Diamond, who was standing in a quiet spot near the telephone booths.

"Hi angel, you look like hell."

Fifi had rings under her eyes and the puffy, drugged look of the sleepless.

"I'm fine, just fine," she said with the enthusiasm of a groom at a shotgun wedding.

"Those guys weren't bothering you, were they?" he asked, pointing to where the lawyers sat. "I could straighten them out pretty quick."

"No, Red. No! Please don't. They're regulars."

"I don't like guys looking at you like they did. They ought to show some respect to my gal."

He reached to embrace her and she stepped back, holding the tray in front of her like a shield.

"Not here, Red. Not now."

"Okay, Fifi. Are you sure you're okay? Nothing happened with Rocco or anything?"

"My name's not Fifi. It's Jane," she said, her voice a mixture of nervousness and exasperation.

Diamond gave her a big wink. "You are a good actress. Sure, Jane, I understand. Listen, things are heating up for me. The cops think I killed these five people. We might have to skip town."

"We?"

"Sure. I'm not gonna let you out of my sight, after what happened in Frisco that last time."

"I've never been to San Francisco."

Diamond winked again. "Yeah, that's right. Well

113

maybe now would be the time to go. Or Los Angeles, or Chicago. Or London or Paris. We got a whole world to explore, just the two of us. After I take care of Rocco."

"Five people you killed?" she asked, just realizing what Diamond had said.

"It's a bum rap. Besides, they deserved to go. Not that I did it or anything. At least for three of them."

Horrified, she covered her mouth with her hand.

"It's a tough world out there. That's why you need me. We'll blow this burg, take care of Rocco, and then have all the time in the world to get to know each other again." He gave her a lecherous, loving smile.

In the dim light of the restaurant, and high on his own obsession, Diamond couldn't see that his beloved had turned as white as bone china.

"What time do you get off?"

"Tonight. Nine," she answered, as if in a stupor.

"Maybe I should hang around until then."

"No. No. No. I'm okay."

"I know you're one tough tomato. And I got some chores to do. I'll be back here then. We'll go to your place, pack it up, and begin the hunt."

"But I don't want to go—"

"No ifs, ands or buts. We've got to move quick, before Rocco has his goons crawl over us like ants at a picnic. I'll be back at nine sharp."

He gave the benumbed woman a peck on the cheek and left.

Diamond cabbed down to Macy's, where he bought himself a suitcase, a new suit and a trenchcoat. He dropped the gear off at his hotel, then walked up to the zoo. He made sure he wasn't tailed.

Brown was looking into the bear enclosure like a kid on his first class trip.

"Beautiful, ain't they?" he said, pointing to two bears who were sitting on the rocks.

The floor of the cage was littered with Crackerjack

boxes and Coke cans, the bears' coats were far from glossy, and they looked a little flabby. But when they moved, thousands of years of predatory breeding showed. In simply climbing over a rock, they showed a strength and grace that transported them from their bleak surroundings.

"Yeah, they are," Diamond said. "I ever tell you about the case up in the Yukon, where Rocco's guys threw me in a bear pit?"

"Another time," Brown said, tearing his gaze from the animals. "The boy at the hotel said the cops rousted you last night?"

Diamond nodded.

"He said the cops forced their way into your room. I ought to sue the bastards. They find anything?"

"Only my dirty shorts."

"Good. He said there was no one there today. Yet."

"I haven't been tailed all day. I made sure of it. These kids they're making detectives couldn't find their pecker in the morning without a snitch."

"Yeah, but Anglich is from the old school. He worries me. I'd like you to take a vacation."

"Anglich is a good cop," Diamond said, leaning on the metal railing. "He won't give up. Will that license you got me hold up?"

"Pretty much. Not if he really looks into it." Brown handed Diamond a thick envelope. "There's two thousand dollars in there. I'd like you to take a rest. Just go relax. Sit in the sun and drink for a week or so."

Diamond had misgivings about taking the money, but he knew it would help Fifi and him in the search for Rocco.

"Thanks," he said, pocketing the envelope.

Diamond left Brown ogling the dark brown beasts.

There was no one staked outside the hotel. Diamond wondered what Anglich was up to. Had the investigation spun off in another direction? Had some new murder diverted the cop's attention? Or was Anglich just giving Diamond some rope, in the hope that . . .

"I didn't tell Brown you let the cops up in the room without throwing your miserable body in the way," Diamond told the pretty boy night clerk who was just coming on. "But if it ever happens again, I'll make sure you're out on your butt. And then I will personally stuff you in one of those boxes," Diamond said, indicating the mail slots behind the desk.

"Yes sir."

"Good. Now, is there a back way out of this place?"

"Yes. If you take the elevator down to the basement, you can go out the service entrance on Forty-fifth Street."

Red nodded and took the elevator up to his room. He packed his bag, went over the room once to make sure he'd left nothing behind, then rode down to the basement. He found the rear entrance, past large carts full of soiled linen and overflowing metal garbage cans. He pushed the creaky door open and walked briskly down Forty-fifth.

He entered the Port Authority on the Ninth Avenue side, and checked his suitcase into a vacant locker. He had a few hours before he was due to pick up Fifi, and decided to kill the time making the rounds in Times Square. He wouldn't be seeing it for a while.

As he strolled the strip, he drew nods and greetings from a couple dozen of the characters who called the area home. No longer the territory of Runyon's guys and dolls, the hardened hustlers seemed more from the world of Kafka, or Darwin.

But survival of the fittest among the human debris meant that a strung-out junkie with a Saturday Night Special was greater than Albert Schweitzer, if the humanitarian was foolish enough to walk through the area unprotected. There was no human dignity, no sign of civilization, that couldn't be violated for the right amount. The wind sweeping down the avenues didn't blow the sins away, it just sent a chill deep into Diamond's marrow.

The efficient grapevine had spread word that he was Brown's trusted aide. And a suspect in five murders. It meant a lot more on the street than a seat on the stock exchange.

Diamond knew that half of his so-called pals would be detailing his whereabouts to Anglich as insurance against their own foibles.

So he chatted with a runny-nosed barker outside a massage parlor, and told him he was going out to Montauk for some deep-sea fishing.

At the coffee shop where he grabbed a hot dog and some greasy french fries, he mentioned a dying aunt in Ohio to the sympathetic waitress.

To the bouncer at the Dude's Social Club, he hinted of a sitdown with a Mafia don in Sicily.

Others heard of big investigations in Milwaukee, Houston and Atlanta. A few discovered he was going for a rest in Florida and the Caribbean.

Not bad for a couple hours' work, he thought as he sauntered down the street. That should keep Anglich busy for a while.

He was feeling good about himself as he passed the massage parlor at the corner of Forty-fourth and Eighth. Any real street person would've ignored the tumult inside and moved on. But Diamond let his curiousity lead his feet to the doorway. ·

The pimp, Blood, was holding a frail girl by her long blond hair, and slapping her face.

"What do you mean, you won't do that. Bitch!" His dark hand was slapping a bright red on the girl's pale skin.

"I can't. I just can't. Please," the girl whined.

"We don't want no trouble here," a fat woman with too much make-up, who was seated behind the desk in the foyer, said. "If she can't do it, one of the other girls can."

A portly man with a waxed mustache, who looked like

the banker character on a Monopoly card, took advantage of the scene to slip out the door, giving Red a nervous grin as he edged past.

"There you go, bitch," the pimp said, jerking the girl's hair. "You lost the trick."

"And we lost the business," the fat woman said. "She gotta go. Too much trouble."

Her words intensified the pimp's anger and he back-handed the girl. His blow caught one of her teeth, cutting her lip and his hand. He grabbed her neck and squeezed.

"Wait till I get you back to the hotel. I'm gonna whip your butt like it's never been whipped."

The girl was turning blue when Diamond stepped over and laid a heavy hand on the pimp's shoulder.

"You got a physical problem, don't you?" Diamond said.

As the pimp spun, Diamond caught him solidly on the tip of his jaw. A second punch, to the stomach, folded the pimp over. Diamond lifted his knee up hard, doing an unpleasant thing to the pimp's face.

"I'm gonna call the cops," the fat woman threatened. Three young hookers were blasé as they watched from a couch in the rear. The sounds of sex that had been coming from the plywood cubicles stopped.

"How old are you?" Diamond said to the girl, who was just getting the color back in her face.

"Fifteen."

He believed her. The girl's still adolescent body looked more pathetic than alluring in the hot pants and low-cut top she was wearing.

Diamond gave the fat woman a toothy, mirthless smile. "You may pay enough to run a whorehouse, but even crooked cops get hot on a contributing-to-the-delinquency-of-a-minor beef. Do you want me to dial them for you?"

"I don't want no trouble. I run a respectable outfit. He

told me she was eighteen," the madam said, pointing to where Blood lay unconscious on the floor.

"Don't believe all that you hear. How's about I take this garbage out for you and leave it at the curb."

"Fine. I don't want no trouble."

Diamond grabbed Blood by the fake fur collar and dragged him out. He picked the thin pimp up and dropped him into the steel mesh garbage can. He crumpled the pimp's Mississippi-gambler hat into a ball, and stuffed as much as he could into his mouth.

"Where's your garbage?" he asked the madam when he reentered her parlor.

She pulled a big wastepaper basket, with soiled tissues, used condoms and a couple of candy wrappers in it, out from under the desk. Diamond walked back into the street, dumped the basket over Blood's head, and then returned to the parlor.

"C'mon, I'll drop you off at the Children's Shelter," Diamond said, gently putting his arm around the girl.

"That's where I came from. He'll find me there," the girl said as they began walking south.

"Can't they protect you? How'd he get his hands on you?"

"The pimps wait outside. The counselors try and chase them. Ever since a counselor got shot last week, the pimps have been coming around more than ever."

The girl had begun crying, then abruptly stopped. The tears had made her awkwardly applied make-up look even more garish.

"You're really neat," the girl said. "Like a knight in shining armor. My name's Gwen. What's yours?"

"Red Diamond. I'm no knight, just the kind of guy that doesn't like to see kids get slapped around."

The girl seemed to have regained her composure. It must be nice to be young, to heal quickly, Diamond thought. He glanced at a clock in the window of a pawnshop they were passing. He had less than an hour until he was to meet Fifi.

"That was so neat. Boom. Boom," she said, mimicking Diamond's punches with her tiny fists. She giggled and looked at him with goo-goo eyes.

An embarassed Diamond said, "Listen, Melonie, we've got to get you straightened out."

"I said my name was Gwen."

"You look like a Melonie to me."

"You can call me whatever you like. I'll be Melonie if you want me to."

"I don't want anything. Where are you from?"

"Los Angeles."

"What the hell are you doing here? You don't need to travel three thousand miles to swim in a sewer. You can find enough trouble on Sunset Boulevard."

"I just wanted to see New York."

"Next time, take a guided tour. You seen enough?"

"I guess."

"Great. I'm sure the shelter can put you in touch with your mom and dad."

"Just Dad. Mom ran off with her guru. Can't I come stay with you?"

Diamond shook his head in disbelief, and she took that as a no.

"Are you married?"

"No. But I got a girlfriend, who I'm going to as soon as we get you straightened out."

They were in front of the shelter, an old building that some amateur artist had decorated with a big mural of smiling children.

A half-dozen pimps were leaning on cars parked near the building, vultures in garish, multicolored plumage. They eyed Gwen and made low whistles as she approached with Diamond.

"You go inside," Diamond told her. "I've got some business to take care of out here."

The girl looked back at him worriedly as she was buzzed in through the double security door. Diamond walked over to the biggest, loudest-talking pimp.

He was dressed in gold lamé, with a small gold earring in his left ear. He was over six foot, but no more than 160 pounds. He was so wrapped up in spouting his wisdom to his buddies, he ignored Diamond's approach.

"Hey, scumbag, did you whistle?" Diamond asked.

The pimp spun around. His five peers were silent.

"Say what?"

"I said scumbag. Though that may be an insult to the birth control people."

"What you want?" the pimp said, fingering his earring, trying to figure out what Diamond was up to.

"I want to kick your miserable ass down the street. But I'd hate to get my shoes dirty like that."

"You want to step outside?" the pimp said, straightening out of his casual slouch.

"We *are* outside, asshole."

Diamond was about two feet from the man, his hands loose at his sides, his eyes narrowed, keeping track of the pimp's hands, and the movements of his associates. "You know who I am?"

"You the dude that works for Mr. Brown," one of the other pimps said.

"The guy that killed five people," another whispered.

Diamond smiled modestly. "I haven't offed anyone in a few hours now. That makes me edgy."

The gold pimp was tugging at his ear like he was going to pull it off. "What you want?"

"I want this street clear. Now. And forever. I see any of you around, I'm gonna start breaking heads. Got me?"

"This is a free country, I know my rights," the gold pimp said. The quiver in his voice belied the confidence of his words.

Diamond grabbed a fistful of the gold fabric. "You have the right to remain silent. You also have the right to bleed profusely when I smash your pretty face into a wall. You want to hear about your other rights?"

Three of the pimps had slunk away while Diamond berated their colleague.

"Gotta go," said one of the remaining ones, as he and his friend took off. Diamond was alone with the golden pimp.

"I'm making this my block, I see you around here, you're gonna become part of the sidewalk," Diamond said, shoving the pimp away from him. "Now get back under your rock. The next time I see you's gonna be the last time you see anyone."

The pimp scuttled away. When he was a safe distance, he yelled out "Motherfucker" and spit on the ground. Diamond took two steps toward him, and the pimp started sprinting north up Eighth Avenue.

There were a dozen faces pressed against the glass, watching the show from inside the shelter. When Diamond was buzzed in, he was greeted by a round of applause and cheers from the counselors and their wards.

The clean-cut male and female counselors looked like they'd just come from an audition with the Mormon Tabernacle Choir. The kids looked hardened, suspicious and yet strangely hopeful. The slight traces of youth that hadn't been beaten out of their features made them that much more pathetic.

Diamond gave a polite nod to everyone he passed, and walked into the cubicle where Gwen sat.

It was similar to the cubicles in the massage parlor, but a not quite professional carpenter had cut out large window holes. And instead of a mattress on the floor, there was a desk that hadn't been new when the shelter bought it.

One of the clean-cut minions was leaning over the desk, whispering in the ear of the stern-faced man who sat behind it. The counselor finished and hurried out, giving Diamond a big praise-the-Lord smile as he passed.

Gwen was looking off into space, feeling safe as a child in responsible adults' hands.

The head of the shelter, a gaunt priest with deep-set brown eyes, looked like he was living in hell while praying for heaven. He had the closest thing he could manage for a smile on his face.

"My name is Father Docherty," the priest said. "Gwen told me what you did. And I heard what happened outside. I can't condone violence, but I thank you."

"It was nothing, Father. I just want to make sure she's in good hands. I've got to go now."

"Wait. I spoke briefly with her father. He asked that you bring his daughter home. He wants to thank you personally."

"I've got business to attend to. I can't go flying out to California just for a pat on the head."

"Her father said he'd take care of everything. He's arranging a flight out of Kennedy tonight."

Diamond frowned. "I've got business."

"More important than this young girl's salvation?"

"That's your department. Mine is not quite so nice. I'm sure one of your helpers would like a trip."

The priest rose from behind his desk and extended his arms. "This is your chance to do a little bit of good in this world. There is evil all around. I have no doubt you've seen it, maybe even contributed to it. With this act, you can make a small part of the world a little better."

He spoke with an intensity that would've been impressive from the alter of Saint Patrick's Cathedral. In the small room, it was overwhelming. Docherty allowed a long pause, as his words echoed silently off the walls.

"Many people have come to me as penitents," Docherty continued. "And a good priest gets so he can read souls like a doctor reads X rays. I see that you are troubled, there is something more beneath the surface than your tough-guy shell. It is something you must work out for yourself, and I cannot fault you for that. But I ask you, will you say no to this child?"

Docherty was pointing at Gwen, who sat slack-jawed, waiting for a heavenly thunderbolt to punctuate the priest's words.

"You got a way with words, Father. I'll do it."

The almost-smile returned to the priest's face.

"A good clergyman only helps others recognize the decency in themselves," Docherty said.

Gwen's eyes were pouring forth enough tears to make Noah nervous.

"Wipe your eyes, Melonie, and let's go," Diamond said.

"I thought you said your name was Gwen," Docherty said, a trifle annoyed.

"Melonie's the nickname he gave me," Gwen said, as if she was talking about an expensive gift.

"Hmmm," the priest said. "Whatever. You better pack."

"I don't have anything," she said. "Blood took my clothes when he gave me this," she said, indicating her hot pants.

Docherty reached into a cardboard box behind him, and fished out a worn overcoat.

"It's not much, but it's better than walking around looking like a harlot," the priest said.

Diamond got up and took his wallet out of his pants.

"That'll do until she gets something better," he said, fishing three hundred dollars out of his wallet.

Gwen slipped into the coat and Diamond dropped the money on the priest's desk.

"If I had known this was such an expensive place to shop, I don't know if I would've come," Diamond said, comfortable with the wise-guy grin back on his face.

"You would have," the priest said, tucking the money into a strongbox he produced from a desk drawer.

"I guess I would have," Diamond said, putting a protective arm around Gwen as they stepped toward the door.

"Go with God, my son," Docherty said, a tear forming in his eye.

16

Red looked at his watch as the taxi picked them up. It was 8:45. The pudgy, thick-lipped cabbie leered at him through the bulletproof partition.

"You and the little lady want to take a ride around the park?" he asked, his voice an oily whine. He shamelessly ogled Gwen's scantily clad adolescent body.

"Just get me to Mange Chez Joseph. Second and Forty-first. Go crosstown on Twenty-eighth, it's the quickest way."

The curt way he barked out the order cut off the cabbie's comments, but didn't stop his smirk when he saw Gwen put her head on Diamond's shoulder.

"Why don't you use that mirror for watching cars instead of passengers," Diamond growled.

The cabbie returned his gaze to the road, mumbling under his breath about sensitive child molesters.

"Sit up straight, why don't you," Diamond said to Gwen. "And button up that coat."

Gwen lifted her head and gave him a goo-goo look. She made a passing effort at closing her coat, then set her head back on his shoulder. She sighed.

"You're not as mean as you talk."

"I'm meaner," he said, pulling a cigarette from his pocket and lighting it. He inhaled a bit, coughed, and put it out. He checked his watch a couple times before they got to the restaurant.

"Is this person you're going to so important?" Gwen asked.

"She's the best," Diamond said, not noticing the teen-ager's jealous pout.

And when the maitre d' stopped them at the door to Mange Chez Joseph, Gwen spitefully let her coat fall open.

He gave Diamond a contemptuous look, usually reserved for small tippers and those who ordered well-done steak tartare.

"If your daughter was properly attired, it might be different," the maitre d' said in unctuous, pseudo-French tones.

"I'm not his daughter," Gwen piped up.

"Oh." The maitre d' lifted his nose higher.

"I'm not here to eat your slop," Diamond snarled. "I got a buddy in the health department says this kind of joint has low lights so the roaches don't have to wear sunglasses."

The maitre d' was shocked. Gwen giggled.

"Where's Fifi?"

"Who?"

"Fifi, oh yeah, I mean Jane. Good-looking blonde, was waiting tables here before."

"Jane Doe, you mean. She left. You should too."

"When I'm good and ready. Where'd she go? How long ago?" Diamond demanded.

"Perhaps you'd like a police escort from the premises?"

"You're the second guy wanted to sic the cops on me tonight. The first one should be outta Bellevue in a month."

The maitre d' sized Diamond up, catching the maniacal gleam in his narrowed eyes.

The maitre d' dropped the fake French accent when he decided to cooperate. "She left several hours ago. Said she was leaving the city for good, something about an acting job. Going to do a commercial in California."

Diamond felt like he'd been punched in the gut.

He left, with Gwen trailing a few paces behind him.

"Who's Jane, who's Fifi?" Gwen blurted out. She hadn't wanted to ask, but her jealousy got the better of her. "Is she your girlfriend?"

Diamond just walked out to the curb and sat on top of a covered garbage can. He tried to pull his shoulders over his head.

Why didn't Fifi wait? he wondered. They could've escaped together. Instead of Fifi, he had a kid who should've been worrying about the prom, but looked like a case of the clap about to happen. Fifi was gone, and he had to play transcontinental nursemaid to Melonie. Or Gwen. Why were these dames always changing their names?

"Scuse me," the apron-clad Puerto Rican kid said, setting a box that smelled of dead fish down near Red's feet. "I got to stack this neat or they won't take it."

Diamond put his feet on top of the box.

He was oblivious to Gwen's concerned look. He never should've left Fifi. Could they have kidnapped her? Or maybe the crazy dame just ran off. She was his main twist, but she sure was screwy.

He was sure her apartment was cleaned out. She'd had a few hours' lead time. He was about to go back in and ask the maitre d' exactly when she'd left, when the Puerto Rican busboy returned, and set down a box filled with empty wine bottles.

"You know Fifi?" Diamond asked.

"Quién?"

"I mean Jane. Waitress. Knockout blonde."

The busboy gave a low whistle. "She some hot number."

"You know where she went?"

The busboy got a cagey look that Diamond had seen on the faces of dozens of corrupt cops, greedy hotel clerks and hungry stool pigeons. He reached for his wallet.

"I don't know, man," the busboy said.

Diamond took out a five.

"She used to live on Seventy-third Street."

"I'm not buying history."

"I heard her tell the boss she was going to Los Angeles. California."

Diamond handed the kid the five, and took another one out. "When'd she leave?"

"Early this afternoon. Maybe three-thirty."

Diamond paused, and the busboy waited expectantly.

"She tell the boss she going to be an actress," the busboy said. "But she tell me the real reason."

Diamond gave him the five.

"She say some guy was after her. *Muy loco.* She say she was scared. He killed a whole bunch of people."

The busboy tucked the money into a pocket in his apron and hurried back into the restaurant.

That explained it, Diamond thought. *Rocco!* He'd scared her. He must've sent someone snooping around, and she just ran, without thinking, not realizing Red Diamond was the only one who could save her.

He got up off the garbage pile.

She was heading to Los Angeles. Probably just a flight or two ahead of him. What a lucky break. For both of them. He'd drop off the kid, then track Fifi down. Together they'd get Rocco, and he'd write a happy ending.

"C'mon kid, we got a flight to catch."

They walked to the Hilton, Diamond enjoying the brisk night air on his face. It took him a while before he noticed the girl had trouble keeping up with his long-legged strides.

The night clerk at the Hilton, a florid-faced man with a dark brown toupee, gave him the same supercilious look the maitre d' had.

"You can't bring that up to the room," he said, pointing at Gwen.

"Unless you want to eat that finger, you'd better put it back up your nose where it belongs," Diamond said. "You got any mail for Red Diamond?"

"Are you a guest here?"

"The orgy down the hall from me was too much. I'm staying at the Plaza now. The service is much better."

The clerk harumphed, and very slowly checked the mail box. He handed Diamond the package addressed to him as if it contained a dead rat.

Diamond threw a dollar on the counter. "Here, go buy yourself a new wig. And next time, don't sweep any dirt under your rug."

Gwen was giggling again as they walked out. She entwined her arm with his.

"You sure know how to handle yourself. I bet no one pushes you around."

"Not anymore. You get to be my age, Melonie, you realize the people that like to push are the ones who need pushing."

"How old are you?"

"Too old. Old enough to be your father. Now button up your coat and stop making cow eyes at me. You'll get me locked up as a damn pervert."

They took a cab to the Port Authority Terminal. In a cramped, overpriced store that specialized in raincoats for patrons of porno theaters, Diamond got the girl a new outfit. She put it on like he was giving her a designer gown from Paris.

At a photo shop, he bought a lead-lined packet used to protect film from X rays.

He retrieved his revolver from the locker and slipped it into the photo pouch when there was no one around.

"What's that? A gun?" Gwen asked wide-eyed.

"Forget you ever saw it," Diamond said, as he slipped the pouch into the suitcase he removed from another locker.

"What are you doing?"

"Wrapping it so it don't get stale."

"C'mon. Seriously."

"Wrapping it so it doesn't show as a gun shape if they put it through a metal detector."

"You're so smart. I bet you're the sharpest guy I ever met."

"You must be hanging out with dummies."

Gwen got insulted, and stayed silent for all of five minutes. But as they rode in a limo to the airport, she chattered about how great he was.

"You're so neat. Is every private detective like you?"

"Not everyone. Some. And I'm not so neat. I'm just a guy who roots through other people's dirty laundry, finds the thing that needs to be washed most, and holds it up to the light."

"But you're so smart. And so tough."

"If I was so smart, I'd be rich. And tough guys are a dime a dozen."

"My daddy's rich, and he's not so smart."

"Don't talk that way about your father."

"It's true. All he cares about is business. I told him I was running away, and he didn't stop me."

"He probably didn't believe you. So you proved you could do it. Satisfied?"

"I guess." She leaned her head on his shoulder.

"Tell me about your father."

"Daddy used to be in the army. I don't remember much about that. But he talks about it sometimes. He used to call me Major Gwen. And I'd have to salute him."

It wasn't a pleasant memory, and the girl looked on the verge of tears.

"What's he do now?" Diamond asked.

"He's head of some big company. Always flying off to meetings. Especially recently. The way he's been talking, I guess business has been bad. It's cash flow this, and overrun that."

"So he's got a lot on his mind. And maybe he didn't give you as much attention as you wanted. But I bet he stills cares about you."

"I guess."

They got to the airport with a half-hour to spare. Gwen

used the time to go to the ladies' room and wash the remaining make-up off her face.

She grew more and more jittery, and childlike, as they waited for the announcement to board. When their flight was finally called, she bounded up the ramp like a kid on her first trip to Coney Island.

Her rekindled freshness made Diamond think of his own lost childhood. From the orphanage, to life on the streets, running messages for the speak-easy owners, joy-riding through the Bronx streets, becoming quick to run, and quicker with his fists.

Until the time he'd punched out the cop who was shaking down his buddy's father. The judge had given him a choice. He picked boot camp over jail. Then he wound up a cop, and . . . ah, it was just a bunch of faded snapshots now.

As the No Smoking—Fasten Seat Belts sign flashed on, Diamond leaned back in his seat. Both he and Gwen were lost in their memories.

Sam Spade, Phil Marlowe, Shell Scott, Lew Archer. He'd have to look them up if he got a chance. Go out for a few drinks. Maybe they'd help him get the lay of the land. Swap a few war stories. See what they'd heard about Rocco. What a great bunch of guys. The last American heroes.

Maybe he better not contact them, he decided. Never know how gossipy they were. They sure got a lot of ink from their exploits. Good guys, but glory hounds. Sometimes they even took credit for his cases.

Red would have to handle it himself. You never know, Rocco might've even gotten to them. He was bad news, that guy.

The plane roared across the continent.

17

The sun was just getting up back east as Diamond and the girl stepped out of the airline terminal.

Los Angeles! It had been quite a while. For a reason he couldn't understand, the first thing that struck him was the cabs. Green and White, Red Top, all different names, and no yellow cabs. It just didn't seem natural.

Then he saw the palm trees, looking like fat pineapples sprouting from the ground. Yeah, it was L.A. all right. The cars may have gotten smaller, and come from Tokyo instead of Detroit, but some things never change. He remembered the infamous "Red Tulip" case, the girl found in the parking lot, her body . . .

"C'mon, the limo is here," the girl said tugging at his arm.

A sullen-faced pretty boy was holding open the door of a black limousine that waited at the curb. He gave the girl a perfunctory greeting, and all but ignored Diamond.

The girl questioned the driver, who gave monosyllabic answers to her inquiries, as they rode north on the San Diego freeway. Diamond kept his eyes closed, but his ears open, as the other two talked.

She had chattered through much of their flight, possessed with the energy only speed freaks and the very young have. But he had picked up enough bits of information to make the drowsiness he felt worthwhile.

When Gwen began reciting her adventures in New York to the chauffeur, Diamond dozed, and mulled over what he knew. He trusted the teenager's perceptions.

Most kids knew a hell of a lot more than adults gave them credit for. The kid playing punchball in the street was usually better informed than the cop on the beat.

Edward Manfred was a longtime military man who had headed Army Intelligence for a while. Retired, he had moved into private enterprise, and was currently the chief executive officer and chairman of the board of Hitech Industries, a conglomerate that did a bunch of things that the girl wasn't really sure about. She did know he was having some sort of business problems.

Manfred was sixty-four, had been married four times, divorced three times and widowed once. He had two daughters, and was disappointed because he never sired a male heir. He was a cold fish, but Gwen thought he liked her best.

Diamond dozed until they pulled up at a pair of wrought iron gates with lion heads welded to the black metal frame. The chauffeur, whom Gwen called Todd, pressed a button in the car, and the gates swung slowly open. They rode down a driveway that wasn't as long or as wide as a freeway until they came to the house.

It reminded Diamond of plantations he'd seen when he'd been tracking a Southern belle who'd disappeared.

There were a half-dozen small statues, artfully lit by small spotlights, displayed around the massive lawn in front of the two-story white building. It was like Tara, without the slaves.

"Do you want me to take your bag?" Todd asked.

"Frankly, my dear, I don't give a damn," Diamond said.

"What?" Todd said, giving him a quizzical look.

"Sure, go ahead, if it makes you happy."

Gwen was already bounding up the steps to the high front door. She leaned against one of the columns on the veranda, waiting for Diamond and Todd to follow.

Todd walked ahead of him, and opened the door for the three of them. Two black-uniformed women were waiting inside.

One was a dumpy, rather plain, middle-aged woman with her hair pulled back in a tight bun. She was crying, and threw her arms around Gwen as soon as the girl was through the door. Gwen returned the embrace, and also broke down in tears.

The other woman was a well-tanned brunette, who looked haughtily amused at the emotional scene. Her uniform was cut lower in the chest, and higher at the thigh than the other woman's. She sized Diamond up with confident eyes, and let the tip of her tongue brush her lipsticked lips like a lizard tasting the air. Diamond winked at her, and her face returned to a bland aloofness.

"Why, oh why?" the governess kept repeating between sobs. Gwen couldn't answer. The governess led her away, and Todd disappeared with Diamond's suitcase.

"What's your name, gorgeous?" Diamond said.

"Rosalie. You're Diamond, right?"

He nodded.

"I'm the maid. If you need anything, just whistle."

She walked away slowly, the uniform clinging revealingly to her hips. Red gave a low wolf whistle. She looked back with an acknowledging smile, and was gone.

He stepped out of the foyer, into a larger room, cluttered with antique furniture and bric and brac. The only sound was the ticking of a big, ornate grandfather clock. The sun outside was beginning to gather strength, and it shot a beam of strong light onto one of the Persian rugs laid out on the polished parquet floor.

He had picked up a little knowledge about antiques during the Back Bay caper involving a Boston banker who'd embezzled a million, and was examining a Louis Quatorze chair, when Todd reappeared soundlessly.

"Mr. Manfred will see you now," Todd said.

"What's your title?" Diamond asked as he set off after the young man.

"I'm the general's aide. That can mean driving, acting as butler, valet, bodyguard, or baby sitter." He said the last word with disgust. Todd seemed looser now that Gwen was not around. He moved casually, confidently, with the natural grace of an athlete, through a half-dozen rooms.

"You work out?" Diamond asked, as he followed.

"Some," Todd said, obviously flattered. "It's quite a workout just walking from one end of the house to the other."

"It is a large home."

"Quite a spread all right. I've seen smaller football stadiums. And they don't have as many doors."

Todd gripped the brass handle on a heavy oak door, and they stepped into a room that was done up in Oriental art. There were Chinese rugs on the floor, Indian statues of Kali and Shiva on pedestals, and ornate shoji screens and triptychs. There were a half-dozen bare spots on the wall, where something had obviously been hanging.

"What happened there?" Diamond asked, pointing to one of the bare spots.

Todd pulled open another heavy door at the other side of the room. "The general will see you now," he said, waving Diamond in.

A man with a shock of snow white hair, capping a face as weathered as a mountain peak, was sitting behind a huge nineteenth-century mahogany desk. He didn't look up from the papers he was perusing.

Well-oiled guns gleamed from the dark wood-paneled walls of the master's den. Custom-made rifles, shotguns with hand-tooled barrels and stocks, matched dueling pistols, revolvers and automatics of every caliber, from derringers to .44 Magnums. Enough weapons to satisfy a South American general.

The man rose slowly from behind the desk, his perfect posture making his six-foot-six-inch height all the more impressive. His movements were slow, not from the weariness of old age, but with a regal dignity. His strong chin was thrust forward, as if he were posing to be sculpted. His grip was firm but cold as he shook Diamond's hand.

"Thank you, sir, for returning my daughter safely."

"The kid would've liked it if you had been there to greet us."

Manfred gave him a frosty look. "My daughter knows my feelings. I will speak with her shortly."

"She's just a kid."

"She's a Manfred," the retired general said tersely. "Would you care for a cup of coffee?"

"Yeah. I take my java black."

Manfred motioned with a finger, and Todd left the doorway where he had been standing.

"Your name is Red Diamond. It seems vaguely familiar. Have we met?"

"No. But you might've read about some of my work. I've gotten a little ink over the years."

"I trust that doesn't mean you are indiscreet?"

"Don't worry about it. These guys like Chandler and Hammett and the others pick up my stuff, and the stuff other good dicks do. But they always mess up the facts, and never get the real names."

"Chandler? Hammett?" Manfred said as he returned to the thronelike leather chair behind his desk. "Are you making mock? Are you really a private investigator?"

"I ain't made mock in years," Diamond said. "And I'm a shamus. Done work in all forty-eight states. And a bunch of places overseas."

"You mean fifty states?"

"I never was too good at math. Or geography."

"What are your credentials?"

Diamond held up his fists, then tapped the side of his head with a forefinger. "I don't have no degree from a matchbook school for sleuths, if that's what you mean. I been in the business twenty years. I've been shot, stabbed, knocked on the head, worked over and drugged. But I've never taken a bribe, blown a case, or a client's confidence."

"Do you have references?"

"Like I said, I'm discreet. My clients don't go for their business being put out on the street. Besides, I've got a job to do."

"I could pay quite well."

"I'm sure you could. What do you want me to do? Find whoever took those Oriental paintings?"

"How did you know that?"

There was a knock at the door, and Rosalie walked in, carrying a silver tray. On the tray was a small pot of coffee, and some tiny pastries.

Rosalie poured Diamond a cup of coffee, and then bent over a little further than necessary, giving him his coffee and a view of her ample charms. Her cups ranneth over.

"Would you care for a little tart?" she asked.

"I like them the usual size."

She left the tray and exited, closing the door behind her.

Diamond had watched Manfred as she executed her bump and grind. The general was more interested in getting back to their conversation than in enjoying the view.

"Does she do windows?" Diamond asked.

Manfred pondered the question for a moment.

"Yes, she does. She's not used to company. I suppose that's why she's putting on the show. I'll speak with her about it."

"It doesn't bother me. I just wondered what her responsibilities were."

"If you mean do I sleep with her, that's none of your business. And the answer is no. I don't think I like your manner. Or your dirty mind."

"Occupational hazard. You go through enough garbage, and you get so you can't get the smell out of your nostrils. I don't get to sit in many flower gardens, Mr. Manfred. So after a while, I start to make assumptions. I'm not apologizing for it. It's the kind of thing that makes some guys go to the bottle, and some guys corrupt. Me, I'm just tired."

Diamond sipped his coffee. It was good and strong.

"How did you know my artwork was stolen?"

Diamond inhaled a pastry, then slowly nibbled a second. He took another long sip, letting Manfred wait.

"The blank spots on the wall. You haven't redecorated, so I guessed it happened pretty recently. The stuff had that long rectangular shape, so I figured it was Japanese or Chinese art. And it was in with all that other Oriental stuff. You want to tell me about it?"

"Three nights ago, someone came in. I was on a business trip in Phoenix. Despite an extensive alarm system, they made off with what I estimate is six million dollars in paintings."

"Nothing else was taken?" Diamond said, looking at the obviously expensive weaponry gracing the den wall.

Manfred shook his head. "Strictly Japanese wood block works. Seven of them."

"Insured?"

"No."

"Why not?"

"That's none of your business."

"You notify the police?"

"No."

"Why not?"

"That's also none of your business."

Diamond drained the coffee cup. "Mr. Manfred, it seems like your business is none of my business. I've got to be going. Thanks for the hospitality." He got up.

"Sit down."

"You're not in the army anymore, General. And I'm not one of the hired help. I've got a woman I'm tracking, and I don't have any more time to play twenty questions with you. I can recommend a couple of good investigators I know out here, or you can go to the cops. Art thieves ain't my ball of wax anyway."

Manfred got up. At first Diamond thought the old man was going to go for him, but then his stern features softened.

138

"I'm sorry, Mr. Diamond." The words were not easy for him to say. "After forty-five years of barking orders, it gets to be a bad habit."

"I've got a few of them myself."

"You said you were tracking a woman. Perhaps you'd be more interested in helping me find my daughter."

"The older one?"

"Yes, has Gwen told you about her?"

"No," Diamond lied. Gwen had said Alison was twenty-nine, with the brains of a gerbil, and the morals of a Tijuana hooker. According to the girl, Manfred had spent enough on abortions for Alison to feed half the nation's poor. Diamond doubted it was a completely unbiased portrait.

"I have never had much luck with women, as my alimony payments will attest. I suppose it was some sort of whim of the almighty to have two of my former spouses bear me two more females. And more troubles.

"Gwen is really a good girl. Quite a little tomboy, and now at the stage where she's not sure she wants to be one of the boys. Alison is different. She's always been rather striking and from an early . . ."

His words were lost on Diamond as he handed the investigator a framed picture of Alison that sat on his desk. Diamond had been set to recommend Marlowe, or Archer or Scott, or anyone of a dozen dicks boiled hard in the Southern California sun.

But the words froze in his mouth as he studied the five-by-seven-inch framed color photo.

It was Fifi. Sure, the nose was smaller, more pert. But Diamond knew the kind of work those Tinseltown plastic surgeons could do. The hair style was different, shorter, but still a dazzling harvest of blond fibers.

Fifi had hinted she came from a wealthy family. And as Diamond studied the deep blue eyes that gazed out, somewhat defiantly, from the photo, he was convinced.

". . . always a problem. Horrid taste in men," Manfred

was saying. "Almost deliberately bad. Do you understand?"

Diamond nodded, gently squeezing the frame. "How long ago did she disappear?"

"About a week ago. She went off. The maid said a dark-skinned man in a red sports car picked her up when I was out. I had a private detective make inquiries, with no results."

"I'll need the shamus's name and address, and you'll have to call him to authorize his talking to me."

"Then you'll take the job?"

Diamond nodded.

"I'm very glad. What is your retainer?"

"Whatever's fair. I'm not that interested in getting rich. Just finding her."

"I value that kind of dedication. Would five thousand dollars be a fitting reward for bringing my first daughter back?"

"I don't want a reward. Use it as a retainer, and toward expense, for getting Fifi back."

"Fifi?"

"Alison."

"I see. Now, you said you were tired. Can I have a bedroom fixed for you?"

"It'd be a pleasure."

Manfred tapped a button on his desk, and Todd knocked a few moments later.

As the manservant led him to a second-floor bedroom, Diamond tried to sort out what he'd learned. Manfred was afraid Fifi had boosted the pictures. That was why there were no cops in on the action. Diamond didn't mind, it just made the field clearer for him.

He was trying to figure out how and why Fifi had skipped out, flown to New York, gotten a job as a waitress, and then flown back. He decided he was too tired to try and deduce what the crazy dame was up to.

The sandman's knockout punch hit him fast and hard.

18

Red awoke to the warm California sunlight forcing its way through a gap in the dark velvet curtains. He stretched slowly and got up, scanning the room he'd ignored in his exhaustion.

There was a small writing desk, a couple of chairs and a dresser, all with ornate scrollwork and a rich wooden patina similar to that of the headboard on his bed.

His clothing was hung in the closet, or neatly folded and put away in the dresser. His gun was in the top dresser drawer. The fired shells had been emptied, and it had been reloaded and freshly oiled.

There was a knock at the door, and before he could answer, Rosalie was in the room. He noticed for the first time he was naked, but made no effort to cover up.

"Todd undressed you," she said. "I figured I'd help you get dressed. I heard you moving around."

He just smiled. "I was going to take a shower."

"Maybe you'd like me to rub your back?"

"I wouldn't want to get spoiled."

She came to him slowly and then pressed against him hard, parting her lips and pressing them against his. He let her tongue explore his mouth. When she stepped back, he was hard. She looked down, and smiled.

"Or is there something else I can help you with?" she asked.

"I understand you were the last one to see Fifi?"

"Who?"

"Manfred's daughter, Alison."

"What's the matter, you don't like brunettes?"

She was pressing against him again, her clothing a stimulating roughness against his bare flesh.

"I need a man," she said. "Don't you like me?"

"Like a bee loves honey. But what I want now is some information. Who did she leave with?"

Rosalie stepped back, annoyed. "A short guy in a green car. I didn't see the license or anything."

"Hmmm. How long have you been with Manfred?"

"About three months. He had the same staff for fifteen years, then he began going through help like there was no tomorrow. If you're worried about him getting jealous, don't be. I give him a blow job once a month or so, and he's happy."

"Very nice. Had Fifi, Alison, talked about anything before she left?"

"We didn't talk much. We didn't have much in common."

Aside from hot pants, Diamond thought. "What about the stolen paintings?"

"You're interested in everything but me? Are you more Todd's type?"

"What's that supposed to mean?"

"Figure it out. And I got an alibi for when the paintings disappeared. I was out with a bunch of friends." The sultry tone was gone from her voice. Her words were harsh, hostile.

Diamond grabbed her and kissed her hard, grinding his body into hers. "I'm going to take my shower now. I'd like a rain check."

She gave him a confused look as he walked toward the bathroom. He shut the bathroom door, and cleansed away the cloying smell of her perfume under a hot spray. Then he let cold water blast his body.

After singing himself a few choruses of "In the Mood," he stepped out and toweled himself off. Just like a teenager again, taking cold showers to get women off his mind.

Rosalie had gotten to him. She had more moves than the Harlem Globetrotters. And it wasn't like Red Diamond was a celibate. But it was too early in the game to get tangled up with her. There was something about Rosalie that set the hairs on the back of his neck standing like the crowd when the "Star-Spangled Banner" is played.

A cold-cut buffet that could've fed a pack of wolves was waiting for him when he got downstairs. The governess apparently doubled as the cook, at least since the high staff turnover began, and she rewarded Diamond for bringing back her charge by trying to stuff him like a turkey.

He was just downing his second sandwich when Todd poked his head into the dining room.

"Sleep well?" Todd asked.

"Like a babe in its mother's arms. The boss around?"

"He's at his office. Downtown. Are you going to begin looking for whoever stole the artwork right away?"

Diamond smiled. "Why?"

"Just curious."

"Does Manfred pay you to be curious?"

Todd smiled back. "So you're the cagey type."

"Loose lips sink ships."

"Mr. Manfred instructed me to tell you the detective firm he used earlier was Wellington Hargrave Investigators. They're in Century City," Todd said coolly. "The blue Ford outside is at your disposal. And if you tell me the name of your firm, I will have a check prepared for you."

"I prefer cash."

"I'll arrange it," Todd said.

He had just left when Gwen entered. She was wearing a conservative white top, and a plaid skirt of modest length. She had a fresh-scrubbed look and rosy cheeks.

"You look like something out of a Norman Rockwell painting," Diamond said.

"Who's he?"

"A guy that does a lot of magazine covers. How you doing, kid?"

"Fine, Mr. Diamond, how are you?"

"Great. And call me Red."

"Okay, Red," she said with a nervous giggle. "My nanny said I don't have to see my tutor today, and I thought maybe I could show you around."

"I'll have to take a rain check." Diamond felt a passing awkwardness, as he remembered he'd just used the same phrase to stall Rosalie's advances.

"Don't you know it never rains in California?"

"It will when I'm here," he predicted.

19

A bronze plaque riveted to a red brick building announced the firm of Wellington Hargrave Investigators, Ltd.—International Headquarters. The small, forty-year-old building was ancient by Los Angeles standards. It stood within view of the Century City towers, the high-priced ghetto for the most expensive attorneys.

The receptionist had a high-fashion face, framed by immaculately coiffed black hair. She saw Diamond, cracked her gum, and looked bored.

"I know I'm not Clark Gable, sweetheart, but how about you stop chewing your cud long enough to tell the boss Red Diamond is here to see him."

"Do you have an appointment?"

"No."

"Mr. Phipps is quite busy. If you state your business, perhaps I can set something up at a future date."

But after Diamond mentioned Manfred's name, the receptionist instantly stopped her masticating, whispered into an intercom, and he was shown to Bradley Phipps's corner office.

The large room was decorated with the kind of modern furniture that looks great in the showroom but is uncomfortable to use. The walls were filled with diplomas, letters of thanks from celebrity clients, and the Daumier prints that lawyers love as much as a fat retainer.

Phipps, his lean body covered by a custom-made, three-piece suit, rose from behind the smoked-glass slab on chromed posts that served as his desk. There was a slight sneer on his bespectacled face as he extended a perfectly manicured, perfectly tanned hand.

Diamond squeezed the hand a little harder than necessary. Phipps gave an exaggerated wince. Their distaste for each other was mutual.

"You a lawyer?" Diamond asked.

"I am a member of the bar. I find the attorney-client privilege invaluable when running the agency. Do you have any degree?"

"I'm a member of Garelick's Bar, got a degree in hard knocks. Class of forty-two. I dropped out of high school."

"I see."

"Yeah, life's tough. I was thinking of going back for ballet sciences, but my bunions put an end to that."

The only sound in the office was the Muzak which dribbled down from a speaker recessed in the ceiling. Diamond sat down in a chrome and leather chair in front of the desk. He had to lean forward to avoid being swallowed into it. He lit a cigarette after noticing there were no ashtrays in the office.

"So what do you know?" Diamond asked.

Phipps lifted a file folder from his desk. "Alison Manfred, D.O.B. 1/2/53, female, white, height—"

"Skip the description. I can see her in my dreams. And I don't need to hear that crap about her screwing around and getting abortions. What about the disappearance?"

"Went off with a man described by maid Rosalie Rodriguez as tall white male, about forty, in a yellow convertible. About seventeen hundred hours last Saturday. No signs of violence, no missing persons report filed."

"What do you know about Rosalie?"

"Been with Manfred for three months, thirty-two, female, Hispanic, divorced. We didn't think it necessary to get any additional information."

"Are you currently investigating anything else for Manfred?" Diamond asked, dropping an ash onto the shag carpet.

"No. Why?"

"Just curious. What did you do to find Manfred's daughter?"

"We checked the computer banks, for credit card purchases and such, and found no trace. Operatives visited six of her most recent ex-boyfriends, to no avail. All of their stories checked out."

"Did Fifi ever work?"

"Fifi?"

"Alison."

"She tried getting employment as an actress, but was not very successful. An operative visited her former agent, but he refused to cooperate. He's a shady Hollywood Boulevard operator by the name of Sid Levy."

"Did your investigator smack him around a bit?"

"Mr. Diamond, we are in the twentieth century. None of my operatives resort to such Neanderthal tactics. The age of kicking in motel doors is gone, in case you haven't heard. People have rights. We didn't get some of the most prestigious clients in the world by doing that sort of thing."

"Well la de dah. Did you find her?"

"Obviously not. Or I wouldn't be meeting with you."

"Maybe if you kicked in a couple of doors, you could've returned her by now, and collected your overpriced fee."

"Any further questions?"

"No. I'd like a copy of the file."

"That's our work product."

"How's about I call Manfred and tell him you won't cooperate because you're afraid I'll succeed where you and your college boys failed?"

Phipps glared at Diamond. "I'm sure he'd dismiss it. However, since you obviously need help in your blundering about, I will furnish you with a photocopy of the list of persons we contacted, and their addresses. Will that be all?"

"It's been a pleasure," Diamond said, rising out of the chair. "And the next time you start talking Neanderthal, just remember the taps you've put on phones, kids you've snatched and garbage you've been through. It's a dirty job, even if you've got a fancy office and a bunch of degrees."

20

Sid Levy's office was on the sixth floor of a building just south of Hollywood and Vine. There was no receptionist, and Diamond walked into the cluttered cubbyhole where Levy did business.

The agent was on the phone, and waved him to a seat. Instead, Diamond walked to the window and looked out through the grime.

A couple of cops were getting out of a black-and-white, and rousting a bum who was wallowing in his own effluvium in the street. The cops ignored a loony holding up an illegible sign and screaming at the top of his lungs. Tourists and Boulevard regulars showed moderate interest in the scene. The fabled intersection had declined as far as Damon Runyon's Forty-second Street.

". . . no problem, sure. Perfect. Yeah, I know, you need her yesterday. Yeah, like a rabbit. For that kind of money, you're lucky you don't get a fat lady on Social Security, no . . ."

Levy was talking a mile a minute, in a raspy, tough-guy voice. He was a late-middle-aged man with a pot belly and a bald head. His feet were up on his battered wooden desk. The cigar in his mouth dribbled ashes on his generous gut.

"Okay, okay. A deal's a deal. Right, we got to take a meeting real soon. Love you too." He slammed the phone down and muttered an obscenity.

"The guy wants a good-looking redhead for his fucking car commercial who'll give him and his partner a blow job off camera. All for a hundred bucks." He took his feet off the desk and focused his attention on Diamond.

"And what can I do you for?" Levy asked.

"My name's Red Diamond," he said, leaning over the desk.

"Great name, but it's been used. I can set you up for some portfolio shots with a close personal friend who happens to be Clint Eastwood's favorite photographer. You got a great cop look, and I know a show that's casting."

Diamond tugged the cigar out of the agent's mouth, and ground it out on some papers on his desk.

"I got a great cop look cause that's what I am," Diamond said, pulling back his jacket so his gun showed. "And it sounds like you're just another sleazy little Hollywood pimple."

"You got no right coming in here," Levy said. His voice had gone up an octave. "I paid off the Hollywood vice boys just last week."

"I'm looking for a girl that's missing," Diamond said. "I find her, I don't care if you sell your mother for quarters."

"I was just kidding about that blow job. You didn't show me no ID. Or read me my rights."

Diamond picked up the phone and dialed a number.

"Hi, Chief, this is Diamond. We were right, it is a front. Pandering. And resisting arrest. Yeah, I had to slap him around a bit. Do you want to send a wagon over? Think it would be good to let the TV boys know about it? Okay. No, the marks won't show. I'll call back when I need a car. Okay." He hung up the phone on the National Weather Service recording.

"I got a wife, kids, you don't want to do this to me, I haven't been busted in—"

Diamond grabbed the agent's collar.

"Tell me about the girl. Name's Alison Manfred, blond, late twenties, nice face and figure. Might have used the name Fifi."

"I could fill the Hollywood Bowl with girls fitting that description. What's so special about this one? Some schmuck was in a few days ago asking about her."

"She's the one that's gonna get your little business shut down."

"Okay, okay, I'll check my files."

Diamond released Levy and he walked to a gray filing cabinet. Rooting through the drawers, he pulled out a bunch of old newspapers, a half bottle of soda, a dirty plate and a pair of frilly pink panties.

"I wondered where these were," Levy said, tossing the panties in a wastepaper basket. He set the plate and bottle down on his desk. A roach was swimming in the flat soda inside the bottle.

"Nope, no one by that name. I got a couple of Fifis, but they're all dark haired. That Frenchie look," Levy said. He held up an eight-by-ten glossy of a homely middle-aged woman with enormous breasts.

"I remember this one. The face, eh, but such a body. I got her a job doing—"

"Maybe it'd help you down memory lane if we went downtown."

Levy threw up his hands. "Search me. Search the office. Look through the files. If you see this woman, may God strike me dead."

"It won't be God that does it," Diamond said. He took out a Polaroid of Alison he'd made from Manfred's framed photo. "You got five seconds."

"That schmuck private detective with some company with a fake British name showed me the same thing. Said I could make some money. What sort of money is there?"

Diamond grabbed the agent by the scruff of the neck. "Not enough to pay your medical bills." He drew back his fist.

"All right, all right already."

Diamond shoved Levy back to the file cabinet. He began digging again, and turned up a couple of hangers, a man's shoe and a 1967 San Francisco phone directory. He pulled an eight-by-ten out from between the pages.

"Ali Malone, she called herself."

Diamond took the photo. It was Fifi all right, wearing false eyelashes and nothing else. Her tongue was flicked to the corner of her mouth. Diamond felt disgusted. He tucked the picture into his pocket.

"Any chance of my getting a reward? I found the picture right after that other guy was here. I never forget a face, or a pair of tits. You can tell a lot about a broad by her tits, like if they—"

"Why didn't you call him back?"

"I wanted to make them sweat a bit."

"Smart guy. Now I get it for nothing. Her address, when this was taken, how'd she come here, everything."

"Any chance of getting—"

Diamond took a menacing step toward him.

Levy started talking fast again, but this time his voice was a high-pitched whine. "I should've known he'd get me trouble. Jimmy Randall. He's brought them in before, but this was a real looker. Last Monday they was here. A real looker, though I don't think she could act worth a shit."

"Do you have a photo of Randall?"

"All I got from him is this," Levy said, handing Diamond a business card that read "James Randall—Talent Consultant—Parties Our Specialty."

"What's he look like?"

"About your height, thinner, with blond hair. Maybe thirty-five. Looks like a typical California beachboy gone to pot. And coke. And pills."

Three roaches were exploring the plate on Levy's desk as Diamond left.

He drove to the address on the business card, a yellow, two-story stucco building on Santa Monica Boulevard that had seen better days. Randall's name was not posted on any mailbox. Diamond leaned on the bell at the manager's apartment.

"Yeah?" said the blowsy, fiftyish blonde who answered the door. Her two hundred-plus pounds were inadequately draped in a bright, floral muumuu.

"I'm looking for James Randall."

"So am I. The bastard skipped out owing two months' rent. You a cop?"

"Private, why d'you ask?"

"You look like heat. I got no idea what he did in there. I don't go sticking my nose in my tenants' business."

"But I'm sure a smart lady like you doesn't miss much."

"Maybe," she said, pushing open the screen door and giving Diamond the once over. "I guess you don't look like a pervert. C'mon in."

Diamond nearly tripped over one of the four overweight cats that was prowling the apartment. Not used to visitors, they eyed him suspiciously. The place smelled of kitty litter and old food.

He accepted her offer of a cup of coffee as they sat down at the folding card table in the kitchen.

"Why do you want this guy?"

"Him and his girlfriend owe my client money."

"Which one?"

"What do you mean?"

"Which girlfriend? He changed them like I change my underwear."

She looked embarrassed, then coy. Diamond reassured her with a smile. He took the Polaroid out of his pocket.

She studied it for a minute, then patted it against her forehead. "This is the latest. Classy-looking, but more frazzled than in this picture. I wondered what she saw in him. Then again, I guess people make dumb choices when they're young and in love."

She continued to tap the Polaroid print against her head, lost in a bygone bittersweet memory.

"Ain't that the truth. By the way, this coffee is great," Diamond lied, trying to bring her gently out of her reverie.

"I make it myself," she said, handing the print back to him. "I don't go for that instant junk."

"Me too. You have any idea where they went?"

"No forwarding address. I'd like to find him—he wrecked the place and skipped out without paying the last two months' rent. The landlord made me foot the bill for the damages. The creep."

"Aren't they all. When did Randall leave?"

"About three months ago. Middle of the night."

Diamond was disappointed. From her vehemence, he was hoping they'd just skipped out.

"What can you tell me about what went on there?"

She hesitated. A cat purred and rubbed one of her varicose legs.

"Confidentially, of course."

Their eyes locked for a minute, and then the floodgates opened.

"Well, he didn't have any regular work. Was collecting welfare, I know, because he signed a check over to me once. He had these girlfriends who, well, they looked like hookers. They'd go out about five at night, and come back maybe five in the morning. Noisy too. A couple times they tried bringing guys back here. I put my foot down. I run a respectable place."

"I'm sure."

"There was a lot of traffic to that place anyway. At all hours. Guys in fancy cars would come, stay no more than fifteen, twenty minutes. Real flashy types."

"Do you remember any of the cars, their license-plate numbers?"

"What do you think I am, a snoop? Besides, you can't really see the license numbers from here. But they was some cars. Rolls Royces. Mercedes. Corvettes and those fancy cars with names like a mountain lion."

"Jaguar."

"Right."

"I was wondering, Miss . . . ?"

"Kowalski. Anna Kowalski."

"Miss Kowalski, I was wondering if—"

"Call me Anna."

"Thanks, Anna, anyway, I was wondering if I might see the inside of the apartment?"

"It's been rented."

"Darn."

"Wouldn't have done you much good. We got these three Mexican guys, come in and prep the apartments. Go through them like gangbusters. Don't leave a drop of dust behind."

Diamond frowned.

"Wait a minute. Snort."

"What?"

"S-N-O-R-T. That was on one of the license plates. You know, custom plates. On a Mercedes. Snort."

Diamond stood up. "Thanks for your time, and the coffee. I appreciate it." He took a couple of steps toward the door.

"Sorry I couldn't help more," she said, clearly sorry the talk was over. "All they left me was a stack of bills."

Diamond spun around. "Can I see them?"

"If I still got them," she said, walking to a drop-front desk in the cluttered living room. Two cats followed her, while the others watched Diamond. A soap opera, the volume turned down low, played on the black-and-white television set on a coffee table.

Kowalski pulled a half-dozen envelopes, held together with a rubber band, from out of the pile. Two were from collection agencies, one was from the gas company, another from the phone company, and two were personal letters.

"Would you mind if I opened these?" Diamond asked.

"I got one strong rule. I don't commit no federal crimes. It got my late husband fifteen months in prison, messing around with our taxes. I don't cheat on taxes, and I don't open my tenants' mail."

Diamond tugged at an ear, and squeezed the envelopes. "You know, it would make sense for me to take these with me. I'm going to find Jimmy, and I'll be sure to give them to him. And I'll make sure he pays you the money he owes."

"You will? You know, the owner makes me suffer for every dead beat. But I told you that."

"I'll make sure Jimmy pays you. You have my word, Anna."

"I guess it would make sense for you to take them. They're not doing any good just sitting on my desk."

"You're a doll."

She coyly covered her mouth with her hand.

"I'll be in touch."

"Do that," she said, as he walked out into the fresh air.

He went to a nearby Denny's, and ordered a light meal to cleanse his palate of the bitter coffee.

While he waited for his order, he tore open the envelopes. The two collection agencies had sent routine letters warning of dire consequences if Randall didn't pay up immediately. He owed a doctor $287 and a furniture company $306.

One personal letter was from a woman who put big circles above the *i*s. Her grammar and penmanship were terrible. She lived in Chicago, and was complaining about not getting any child support from Randall for their four-year-old daughter.

Just your basic dead beat, dirtbag, Diamond thought as he deciphered the depressing letter. She sounded desperate and stupid. He hoped for her sake she was at least good-looking.

The other letter was from a guy who had just gotten out of Lompoc federal prison after doing two years on a drug bust. He blamed Randall, and wanted money.

Tough dice, buddy, Diamond thought. That explained the heavy traffic to Randall's apartment. The young man was apparently merchandising drugs as well as sex.

A broad grin spread across his face as he opened the phone bill. There were more than a dozen toll calls in the Los Angeles area, and five long-distance calls.

Diamond tucked the envelopes in his pocket, wolfed down the food the waitress brought, and left her a generous tip. He got a couple dollars change from the cashier.

He drove to a pay phone, and began calling the different numbers.

21

The first nine calls produced nothing worthwhile. Diamond got pay phones that were picked up by passersby after he let them ring interminably, disconnected phone numbers, a restaurant under new management, and a bowling alley where the man answering the phone hung up on him when he asked for Randall.

He jotted down the address of the restaurant and the bowling alley in his small black notebook.

"Hello?" a man answered suspiciously on Diamond's tenth phone call.

"This is Red. I'm a friend of Jimmy's."

"I told him not to give my private-line number to anyone," the man said, annoyed.

"It's important. He's jammed up. I'm in the same business as he is. He told me to give you a call."

"I see."

There was a long pause. Diamond waited, listening to the traffic noises on Santa Monica Boulevard. A gay man in a leather outfit strolled by, winked at Diamond, and kept on walking.

"What do you have?" the man on the other end of the phone line finally said.

"I don't like to talk on the phone."

"Shirts or pants?"

Diamond hesitated. "Both."

"I only go for shirts. And I'll need a half-shirt as a sample before I'll do business."

"I'd like to come out with the goods. Where are you located?"

"Didn't Jimmy tell you?"

"He couldn't talk."

"Okay. You know where the Bel Air Estates are?"

"I can find it."

He gave Diamond an address. "That's page thirty-two, D-five, in Thomas Brothers."

"What?"

"Thomas Brothers. The map book. You new to Los Angeles?"

"Just got here a few days ago."

"How do you know Jimmy?"

"From Chicago."

"All right. See you in a couple hours."

Diamond killed some time buying a Thomas Bros. map book, and visiting the restaurant that Randall had called.

The map book was helpful; the trip to the restaurant wasn't.

Half a shirt, he wondered, as he drove to his appointment. He remembered from his file on the case of the Sicilian knockout that dope dealers used all sorts of codes. Boy and girl, shirts and pants. Coke and heroin.

He sure as hell wasn't heading into the garment center.

His destination was a Spanish-style adobe house that the king of Spain would've felt comfortable in. The name on the mailbox at the foot of the long driveway was Anders. The house was just barely visible from the road, the orangeish walls hidden by a squad of Italian cypress that stood like good little soldiers on sentry duty.

Diamond bounced the heavy brass knocker off the oaken door a couple of times and got no answer. He walked along the perimeter of the blooming flower bed.

He froze as a mastiff trotted over, sniffed him, and then walked away to water a tree. There was a blonde sitting in the Jacuzzi that fizzed like a carbonated drink. She was wearing as much as the mastiff. She was sipping a Bloody Mary and looking vapidly at Diamond. She didn't look old enough to drink.

"Why don't you take your clothes off and join me," she said, her words slightly slurred.

"Not today. How old are you, anyway?"

"Sevent—"

"That's none of your business," a man's voice said from behind Diamond.

He was not much over five feet, and a healthy potbelly poked out of the green silk kimono he wore. He had thinning hair, a Groucho Marx mustache, and an Old West–style six-shooter in either hand. Both guns were pointing at Diamond.

"State your business, and make it snappy. I've got an itchy trigger finger."

"And a minor sitting buck naked in you tub drinking. Put the guns away, Tex."

The girl in the Jacuzzi giggled.

"Get in the house, Gretchen," Anders said.

"But you said we could play horsey-horsey before the guy came here with the coke," she complained.

Anders glared at her. Diamond looked smug.

"Get inside," Anders growled at the girl.

"You're no fun," she said, rising out of the water like an adolescent mermaid. Her lean, muscular body left a trail of water as she walked drunkenly into the house. She made no effort to cover her nudity.

"You're trespassing, buddy. Better make it good," Anders said.

"I'm Jimmy's friend. And I figure trespassing isn't as bad as contributing to the delinquency of a minor, statutory rape, and a few other charges any creative D.A. could dream up."

"You're a half-hour early."

"That's no crime, at least where I come from."

Anders scratched under his arm with one of the guns. He looked like the kind who didn't know how to use the guns in his hand, and Diamond gambled. He reached in and took out a cigarette.

"Put the guns down," Diamond said. "You impressed the girl a whole lot already. Let's get down to business, and you can get back to horsey-horsey."

"You a comedian?"

"Just put down the rods and applaud."

"I'm not applauding until I get back the money Jimmy owes me. Did you bring the fifteen thousand dollars?"

"You didn't say anything about that on the phone."

"I didn't figure you'd come if I did. Where is he? And where's my money?"

"Lee?" the girl called from the sliding-door entrance to the house. She had put on her clothing.

Anders turned, and Diamond drew his .38.

"Looks like we got a Mexican standoff," Diamond said.

"Damn kids," Anders muttered. "Get back in the house, Gretchen."

"I've got to go back to class," she said, turning and

leaving the two men with guns pointed at each other.

"She's a student of mine at UCLA. It's not what it looks like. I was just giving her some private—"

"Lessons. I can guess in what. You ever shoot anyone?"

Anders didn't answer.

"It makes a terrible mess. And it's hard getting over, all the blood and guts all over. I ought to know. I've shot about thirty-seven guys in my time. Only nine of them lived long enough to know it."

The guns wavered in Anders's hands.

"The girl is gone. We can shoot it out, or talk it out. It's your move."

Anders hestitated, then let his hands drop to his side. Diamond kept his weapon trained on the man.

"I thought you were going to put your gun down too," Anders said.

"You were mistaken. Now set yours down on the floor in front of you, real slowly. Then tell me about Jimmy. And please don't do anything stupid."

Anders reluctantly set the guns down. "How come you're asking about Jimmy if you're a friend of his?"

"I lied. I'm a private dick, trying to track him down. You're going to help."

Anders grinned. "Really? That's wonderful. I'll help you any way I can. I thought you were in with him." He sounded positively jovial.

"Where is he?"

"If I knew that—"

"So what do you know about him?"

"Jimmy Randall is known as Jimmy the Greek. He deals coke, grass, Quaaludes, heroin. Anything he can get his hands on. Looks like a typical beachboy, until you see his eyes. They got that kind of rat cunning, you know the type?"

Diamond thought of all the rats' eyes he'd looked into, and nodded.

"Mainly deals coke. Usually pretty good stuff. Maybe fifty, sometimes seventy-five percent pure. Never

159

stepped on. Uses it to get into places where they wouldn't let him clean the cesspool, if he didn't have it. Big Hollywood types, names. Rock stars. Not bad for an ex-porno star."

"He's into that?"

"Not anymore, though he still travels with some of that crowd. Always has a different girl. Most of them look pretty trampy, but his new one is quite a piece."

"This her?" Diamond said, showing him the Polaroid.

"Yes. He was telling me Tuesday he had a big deal, and the girl was part of it. I asked if he had her hooking, just curious, you understand, and he said 'Not this one.' It must be something big, because he had all his girls available for a price."

"Nice guy."

"There's plenty of them around. He's smarter than most. Used to say 'A key is the key.' "

"Meaning?"

"A key, a kilogram of coke, and you can get just about anywhere in this town. With a good-looking girlfriend that gives good head, you're set. Plenty of guys like that, but like I said, he's smarter than most. Maybe too smart for his own good."

"Like how?"

"Well, the reason I figure he didn't get back to me with the money is he shortchanged the wrong guy."

"You know who?"

"Vinnie Vargas. M-A-F-I-A."

"One of Rocco's boys," Diamond said.

"Who?"

"Never mind. Tell me about Vargas."

Anders looked around, as if there was a mob hit man hiding behind a cypress. After assuring himself they were safe, he said, "Vargas came here about ten years ago from back east. Went to this guy named Cohen who had a small production company, and demanded in as a partner. Cohen told him to suck an egg."

Anders paused dramatically.

"Cohen was found a couple of days later, in a car trunk. Choked to death on a hard-boiled egg. Vargas bought the company from the widow for a song. Some other businesses he got interested in had late night fires. He's now the biggest porno distributor out here. That's how Jimmy met him."

"And he beat him on a drug deal?"

"That's what I heard. This is all confidential, right?"

"Right. How do I find this Vargas?"

"I'm going to his house tonight."

"What?"

"He's a good guy to know. Can be very helpful."

"I'll bet."

"You can come as my bodyguard. But promise me you won't do anything rash. I don't want him as an enemy."

"What time is the party?"

"Eight."

"I'll pick you up at seven-thirty."

Anders was pleasantly excited. "You know, if this bodyguarding thing works out, we could strike a deal. I'm looking for a few good men, to put together my own security team."

"For what?"

"I'm a libertarian survivalist," Anders said. Seeing Diamond's perplexed look, he continued, "Big government has got to go. They've legislated themselves into our sex life, our private life. When the end comes, whether from an earthquake, a war, or a revolution, this country will need strong leadership. Big government will collapse, and the people will take over."

Anders had worked himself into a soapbox fervor. "The strong, the prepared, will run the country. Do you know I have enough food stored up to last me a year?"

"One question?"

"What?"

"Do you have any hard-boiled eggs?"

22

He found the central library (Thomas Bros., page 44, C-3) easily. But he got lost twice under the mosquelike, domed structure. After fifteen minutes in the maze, a librarian, an elderly black woman in harlequin glasses, took pity and acted as his guide.

He learned where the 10-K financial disclosure forms were kept, where the microfilm and microfiche was housed, and how to use the machines to read the material.

After an hour of reading, his eyeballs began to throb from the fine white print on the blue cards. He drove back to Manfred's home.

Todd let him in, telling him, "Mr. Manfred is waiting for you in the study."

"I'm gonna take a shower and freshen up. Tell him I'll report to headquarters in about a half-hour."

Diamond had barely undressed in his room when he heard someone trying the knob. He stepped behind the door. As it was pushed open, he jumped out, grabbing the intruder from behind. His hands pressed on soft, feminine flesh.

Rosalie gave a frightened yelp, which he muffled with his hand over her mouth.

"You scared me," she said.

"You could get yourself killed coming in here like that. I've got dangerous reflexes."

She stepped back and watched the blood throb to his

groin. "I see," she said with a lecherous smile. "You take a lot of showers. Got a dirty mind?"

"It's hot. And I don't like the smell of the people I spend my days with."

"What did you find out today?" she purred, coming in like a pirate about to board ship.

"A little of this, a little of that. I haven't put anything together yet. Why d'you ask?"

"Just curious," she said before pressing her lips against his. He didn't fight, but he didn't encourage her.

"My tub's going to overflow if you keep that up," he said, pulling away.

"I'd just love to hear what you do. It's so exciting."

"There's plenty I'd like to tell you. Even more I'd like to show you. But business before pleasure."

She grasped his most outstanding feature.

"You trying to pump me for information?" he asked.

"Maybe. You drive me wild."

"I've been through some tough interrogations. It takes a while to make me spill."

"Did you have a hard day?"

"Not as hard as the night's going to be." He took her hand away from him, spun her around, and gave her a pat on the rump. "Run along now."

"Are you coming back?"

He didn't answer. He walked into the bathroom, shut the door, and took a long, cold shower.

Todd was waiting in the hallway when he stepped out.

"Did you have a fruitful day?" Todd asked.

"Yeah. Real peachy."

As they walked down the long corridor, a smiling Todd sought to make pleasant conversation.

"You have such a fascinating job."

"It beats parking cars," Diamond said, trying to compose his thoughts for his meeting with Manfred.

"You get to meet all sorts of people, each like a piece

in a jigsaw puzzle. And only you can put together the whole picture. Speaking of pictures, how is it going in terms of getting the paintings back?"

He tried to slip it casually into the conversation, but it stood out as much as a nun in a porno theater.

"It's coming along," Diamond answered in the same casual tone. "It shouldn't be more than a week before I've got the caper cracked."

"Any suspects in mind yet?"

Diamond gave him a wink. "You'll be the first to know."

Todd stumbled on the edge of an Oriental rug. Diamond caught him with an outstretched arm. "Better watch it kid, or you'll be taking a fall."

Todd clutched Diamond's arm. "If, if someone were to get in a jam, could, could you help them out of it?"

"No guarantees. But I don't go out of my way to hurt no one, unless they deserve it. I've helped guys out of a bind before."

Todd watched his back as Diamond entered Manfred's den. The retired general was standing near his gun collection, working the action on a sniper-scope-equipped AR-15. He lovingly returned it to its niche on the wall.

"I'm not used to being kept waiting by employees."

Diamond sat down without answering, pulled a huge crystal ashtray sitting on Manfred's desk toward him, and lit a cigarette.

"I trust you have a good reason for this impertinence."

"I'm not an employee. I'm an independant contractor hiring out my services. I haven't been sitting on my duff all day waiting for orders."

"I'm not used to people talking to me like that."

"You better get used to it if you want my services. Red Diamond doesn't take guff from no one."

"I don't like your manners, Mr. Diamond."

"It's been such a busy day, I must've skipped my Emily

Post reading. I don't give a damn what you think about my manners."

"I don't allow such—"

Diamond got up. "I don't feel like sitting here all night and hearing about what you don't like. Do you want to hear what I found out? I've got a party to go to."

"You're going to a party on my time?"

"That retainer you gave me don't give you the right to run my life. You can have everything back. You let me sleep in a bed in your house. It beats the Holiday Inn. If you want, I'll give you a sawbuck when I check out. And I'll leave a tip for the chambermaid."

The two men had a staring match. An antique clock ticked away the time. Manfred's eyes flickered, then jumped to the clock. "I don't have time for this," he said.

"If you want me to play in this ball game, I have to play by my own rules. If you want another servant, with a piece instead of a serving tray, get yourself another wimp like Phipps."

"You've met Phipps?"

"It's been a busy day."

"What did you find out?"

Diamond flipped open his notebook. "My first break came with the agent. I got strong with him, and he fell for the old phone-call-to-headquarters routine. I had made good use of that before, in a case that went down in history books as *Die, Dying, Dead.* There was this guy—"

"Skip the war stories, and tell me what's happening with my case."

Diamond grumbled, then went through a quick synopsis of all he had done. Manfred still looked disinterested.

"What about my paintings?"

"I figured you'd be more interested in your daughter."

"You figured wrong."

"Don't you care?"

"I care. I don't want her going off and disgracing the Manfred name. But she is free, white and more than twenty-one. If she chooses to fly from the nest, that's her business."

"How can she leave such a warm and sentimental guy?"

"Spare me your dry wit, Mr. Diamond. I believe children should know the value of discipline. If they have not learned it by the time they are Alison's age, then so be it. Is there any indication she's involved in the paintings being stolen?"

"Too early to tell, but I doubt it. She's not that kind of dame."

"You seem to have more confidence in her than I do. Anyway, what's your next step?"

"I'm going to hear from you on a bunch of things. Like about the hired help here. And the background on the paintings. And do you know a guy named Jimmy Randall?"

"Randall? Blond hair, tall and thin?"

"Sounds about right."

"What do you know about him?" Manfred asked.

"I'm doing the questioning."

Manfred harrumphed, and there was a long pause. "He worked here, for about a week or so, last month. I didn't like his attitude, and terminated him."

"What did he do?"

"General responsibilities. Driving, some security. He was totally unfit as a butler. Under the influence of drugs, I suspect. And paying too much attention to Alison. Why do you ask?"

"I think she ran off, or was taken away, by him."

"But he doesn't fit the description Rosalie gave."

"She's given a bunch of descriptions. How'd you hire her?"

"I had the same staff for more than a dozen years. Then the butler went through a second childhood, fell in love with the maid and ran off to the Caribbean. The chauffeur had retired to Palm Springs a short time before."

"When did this happen?"

"About six months ago. Only the governess remains. Rosalie was sent here by the American Referral Service. They also sent Todd. And they had sent Jimmy Randall. All came with glowing recommendations."

"Even Randall?"

"Yes."

"I see. Tell me about the art."

"They are original works. Wood blocks by Japanese masters. Hokusai, Yoshitoshi, Shunei, Hiroshige, Kuniyoshi. Are you familiar with their work?"

"I've heard of Hokusai, and Hiroshige."

"Well, I have photographs. Though they don't do the work justice. The exquisite detail in the lines, the flow and texture, the artistry. Anyway, I can give you a list."

"Why weren't they insured?"

Another harrumph, and pause.

"Let me guess, they were hot," Diamond said.

"I do not traffic in stolen goods," Manfred said. "It's a matter of provenience. Do you know what that means?"

"Yeah, they were hot. When did you get them?"

"Almost forty years ago. I was serving in Japan, and they came into my possession."

"Well, you don't have to worry about the statute of limitations. Did you ask Phipps to check it out?"

"No."

"Why?"

"I had thought the matter would be cleared up by itself. It hasn't."

"So you know who took the paintings? Or you got a ransom note for them."

"I've told you all I care to," Manfred said, sliding a thick stack of hundred-dollar bills toward Diamond.

"Who had the paintings?"

"I don't know."

The phone on Manfred's desk buzzed and he picked it up. "I said no calls. Oh, yes, okay."

He covered the mouthpiece and returned his attention to Diamond, who was pocketing the money. "I'll talk with you tomorrow. This is an important call."

Diamond got up. "The more I know, the better it is for everybody. Otherwise, I'm going to kick over some rocks you might not like kicked over."

Manfred was speaking quietly into the phone as Diamond walked out.

The road rose and the mountains parted and the lights of Los Angeles twinkled down below. Anders prattled on about the libertarian movement, the imminent end of civilization and how Diamond could guarantee himself safety and survival by becoming the first recruit in Anders's private army. The little professor was wearing a pungent cologne that filled the car. Diamond was very glad when they pulled up outside of Vargas's home.

It was a giant wooden hexagon, perched on stilts and set down on the mountainside just off Mulholland Drive. They could hear the music and chatter from the party as they parked in the driveway, behind a Mercedes with the license plate STUD, which was next to a Jaguar with the license plate RICH, which was behind a Rolls with the license plate FAMOUS.

"Wait a second," Diamond told Anders as they stood on the threshold of Vargas's house.

Diamond walked up and down the street, looking at license plates. He found the Mercedes, a red SEL, with the plate reading SNORT.

A Filipino houseboy with an expressionless face and a red jacket opened the door for them.

The rooms radiated like spokes off the center of a wheel. One spoke was missing, and the living room stretched to the outer wall. Through a huge window Los Angeles, a giant glittery body with freeway veins, could be seen.

About fifty people were standing and sitting around the sunken living room. The women were competing to see who could show the most cleavage and thigh, with their outfits either see-through, low-cut, miniskirt or side-slit. There were more women than men, with most of the females in their mid-twenties.

The men averaged at least twenty years older, and most weren't so eager to show their flesh. A few were the lean, tanned types, with gold chains on hairy, bare chests. The rest had prosperous potbellies and jowls of success.

"Lee, glad you could make it," said one of the hairy-chest types. He had less gold around his neck than the vault room at Fort Knox.

"I'd never miss one of your parties," Anders said. "Vinnie, this is Red. Red, Vinnie."

Diamond and Vargas shook hands. Diamond felt Vargas recognize the gun bulge at his waist. When their eyes met, there was the flicker of tension between two beasts.

"Any friend of Lee is a friend of mine. What line of work are you in, Red?"

"I'm a private eye."

"I did a film about that once. *The Private Dicks.* Maybe you saw it?"

"I don't get out to the movies much."

"I'll have to give you a few passes to one of my theaters. Take a friend. You'll enjoy."

"I thought you were only into production and distribution. I didn't know you owned theaters too."

Vargas froze, and Anders disappeared.

"Just what do you know about me?" Vargas said, throwing a heavy arm across Diamond's shoulder in a

169

gesture as friendly as a tiger's growl. "All I know about you is you brought a gun into my house. I don't like that."

"Don't worry. I won't take it out unless I need to."

"You don't look like the kind who comes to this sort of party."

"What sort of party is it?" Diamond asked, slipping out from under Vargas's arm.

A small man in a white suit pushed up to Vargas. "Vincent, Vincent. You've done it again. The party is super. Just super."

While Vargas was accepting the man's effusive praise, Diamond eased back into the crowd. He knew Vargas would find him later.

A fat man with a brandy snifter in one hand and a cigar in the other was crushing a couch under his mammoth bulk. He was holding court, gesturing expansively, and regaling an audience of about a dozen with anecdotes.

". . . on location in the desert with Lola. She'd screwed every guy on the set at least once. If she had the dicks sticking out of her she's had in her, she'd look like a pink porcupine."

He paused to allow his audience to laugh.

"So we're halfway through the shooting, and everyone comes down with the clap. The whole damn crew. Including the butch script girl. We had to trek into Mojave for shots. The doctor made a fortune. That's why I say, expect the unexpected."

Diamond got a Jack Daniel's at the bar, and drifted over to the huge window. He sipped the drink and looked out.

"Beautiful, isn't it?"

The woman had sidled up next to him. She was about forty, well made up, well dressed, and well plastered. She swayed as she fought to keep her balance in her own personal earthquake.

"What's your name?" she asked.

"Red Diamond."

"That's a nice hard name. Are you a hard guy?"

"Hard enough."

She was leaning against him. She took the half-empty glass from his hand, and finished it.

"I like the taste of semen," she said.

"I prefer a burger and fries."

"Do you think I'm forward."

"A bit."

"Does that turn you on?"

"Not particularly."

"What does?"

"Snow White and the Seven Dwarves, a bull whip, two goats and the Mormon Tabernacle Choir."

"Are you making fun of me?" she said, drawing herself up and preparing to make a scene.

Anders came over and put his arm around her. "Lola dear, I see you've met my friend Red."

"He's quite rude."

"Take her away and give her a spanking, will you, Lee? I want to keep my virginity."

Anders gave Diamond a reproachful look as he tugged the drunkenly sputtering woman away.

A well-dressed young man, one of the few people wearing suits, was talking animatedly to a cluster of four men as Diamond edged over.

". . . invest in the distribution scheme. It sounded like a Ponzi setup, and I told him that. If he would guarantee the principal against residuals, I told him he could count me in."

The conversation began to die, and the four men wandered off. The man in the suit stood still, a bemused expression on his face, a glass of white wine in his hand.

"Are you in banking?" Diamond asked.

"No. I'm Sammy Hoyt. Big Sammy Hoyt."

He noticed Diamond appraising his five-foot-eight-inch frame, and smiled.

"I guess you're not a fan of Vargas films. I've got twelve inches of acting ability that's in great demand."

"I see. Or rather I don't see."

171

Both men laughed.

"Look at this crowd. Sidney Sullivan, three hundred pounds of director, sitting there like he's a bloated Hitchcock. But there's no boys here tonight, so he'll go home disappointed. Or cruise S and M Boulevard."

Hoyt's glassy eyes roved across the crowd. He was under the influence of some drug, but still within his limits.

"Lola, over there by the punch bowl, used to be his wife. A marriage made in heaven. She'd be screwing the father while Sullivan was seducing the son."

"I met her."

"She must've zoomed in on you. Most of the people here she's fucked already. She's always looking for a fresh—"

"Face."

"Yeah, face. This place is enough to keep the vice squad busy for a year. I see a half-dozen S-and-M freaks, a couple of coprophiles, a bunch of actresses who've never acted except to fake an orgasm, a founding member of FFA, pedophiles, animal lovers and more bisexuals than you can shake a stick at. The coupling possibilities are unlimited."

"You sound bitter."

"Hell, freaks pay my salary. Keep me in coke and Quaaludes. And one of these days, I won't be able to get it up, and some new schmuck with a big dork will take over the limelight."

Hoyt finished his drink.

"But what's your story?" he asked. "With all this snatch floating around, you're talking to me. Are you queer? You know, I only do that stuff for the movies. It's not my scene."

"Me neither. I'm looking for information."

Hoyt refocused his eyes. He wasn't as high as he was pretending to be. "What kind of info?"

"About Jimmy Randall."

"Why?"

"I have to find him."

"You and half the people in this room."

A petite brunette, who seemed vaguely familiar to Diamond, came over and rubbed Hoyt's crotch like a superstitious bettor with a rabbit's foot.

"Big Sammy want to party with Little Ginny," she said, a squeaky-sexy voice coming from her thick lips.

"Not tonight, Ginny. I've got a headache."

Diamond placed her voice; she'd played the ingenue in a dozen films. But her face, after being nipped, tucked and tightened by a half-dozen expensive plastic surgeons, was a death's-head mask of its former self.

Ginny frowned and flounced away.

"The only good thing I can say about Jimmy is he ripped off Vargas on a coke deal. It's not unusual for Jimmy, but it was for Vargas. I heard he hit the ceiling."

"Do you know where Jimmy is now?"

"He dropped out of sight. Some people think he's dead, but I know he's too smart to—"

Hoyt froze as he saw Vargas barrelling toward him, being trailed by a six-footer who couldn't be anything other than hired muscle. The six-footer moved in an awkward amble, his shoulders bobbing, his arms swinging forward and back.

"Ginny said you have a headache?" Vargas said.

"That's what I told her," Hoyt replied.

"Tony here is very good at treating headaches," Vargas said, nodding toward the six-footer. Tony smiled a disjointed grin; his jaw didn't seem to fit together properly.

"Vinnie, I really don't want to—"

Tony wrapped Hoyt in a long arm and squeezed unaffectionately.

"The man said he don't feel like it," Diamond said. His voice was a low growl, coming up from next to his gun.

"Never mind, I'll do it," Hoyt said with a shrug.

He waved to Ginny and walked to the bedroom with the

173

enthusiasm of a death row convict walking his last mile.

"That was a bit heavy-handed, wasn't it?" Diamond said to Vargas.

"What I do with my employees is my business. Let me introduce you to Tony. I got a feeling you'll be meeting each other again."

Tony stuck out a hairy-knuckled hand which Diamond accepted. Both men squeezed as hard as they could, trying to keep dead-pan expressions. Tony was crushing his hand, until Diamond stomped on his instep. Tony yelped.

"Sorry. So clumsy," Diamond said.

Tony drew back his fist. Diamond unbuttoned his jacket and let his throbbing hand drop near his gun.

"Enough," Vargas barked. "For now."

The man in the white suit waited until Vargas and Tony had walked away before approaching Diamond.

"You're very brave. Or very stupid. My name's Mike Hart." He offered his hand. Fortunately, he had a weak handshake.

"Who is that guy Tony?"

"Used to be a stuntman. Supposed to have broken every bone in his body. When it's wet out, he aches all over. Gets real mean. Fortunately, it don't rain much here. Got so many metal pins in him, they don't let him through the detectors at the airport. But he's probably broken bones on as many other people as himself."

"Nice guy."

"I don't think he likes you much."

There was a commotion at the door, and four men and two young women came in. Three of the men wore black silk jackets with "Duk Fukers" embroidered on the back. One had a crew cut, another a Mohawk haircut, and another an Afro that was streaked with purple. The fourth man had thinning black hair, a pale yellow leisure suit, and nearly as many gold chains as Vargas.

The two young women were pudgy brunettes whose clothes were in disarray. The excessive make-up they wore was smeared.

Mohawk haircut reached into the blouse of one of the brunettes and pulled her by her breast toward a bedroom. The rest of the group, except for the man in the leisure suit, followed the couple toward the bedroom, pausing momentarily to grab a bottle of Scotch from the bar.

Yellow suit glad-handed his way through the crowd to Hart.

"Mikey, Mikey, how you doing?"

"Just fine, Billy. Still getting fifteen percent of your clients' herpes?"

The men were embracing like old friends, but their words dripped more venom than a leaky rattlesnake.

"Cute. I didn't know you stole old jokes as well as clients," Billy said.

"You don't have to worry. I have some standards. Where'd you pick up the two young ladies? I haven't seen them on the Sunset Strip."

"That's because you're so busy cruising Santa Monica Boulevard. These two were hitchhiking. Turns out they're big fans of the group."

"Such good taste," Hart said sarcastically.

"We must take a meeting some time. I'd be happy to give you tips on getting name talent."

"That desperate I'm not."

"So you admit you're desperate?"

"Fuck you."

"You're not my type," Billy said, as he began drifting away. "Nice talking to you."

Hart mumbled some obscenities, then turned back to Diamond. "Just your basic no-talent rat made it big. Billy Walters. I remember when he was hustling drunks on the boulevard. Started dealing coke, then got into 'talent management.' People like him give the business a bad name."

"You know a guy like that named Jimmy Randall?"

"The Geek. I've met him a couple times. Haven't seen him around in a bit. No great loss."

Hart was watching jealously as Walters mingled into

175

the center of the crowd, and took a thick envelope out of his jacket.

A blonde in a miniskirt and high boots took a hundred-dollar bill out of her purse, rolled it tight, and stuck one end in her nostril, the other end in the envelope. She pressed the other nostril shut with a finger and inhaled deeply. She leaned back, sniffled and gave a happy whoop. Other members of the cluster repeated the ritual.

A gaunt redhead, whose pale body was visible through her white see-through dress, came to Hart and Diamond after filling both nostrils.

"You're not going to join us?" she asked Hart.

"I'd rather die," Hart said. "Wanda, this is Red."

Her hands seemed to have a life of their own, floating like nervous butterflies from her hair, to Hart's wrist, to Diamond's shoulder, and then to her face.

"How about you, Red?" she said, tugging at her split ends.

"I like my coke in a can."

"That's kicky," she said, patting his cheek. "Is this your first Vargas party? I haven't seen you around. It's quite a freak show. But it's the only way to do business in this town. Right, Mike?" She tapped Hart's cheek.

"More gets done at parties and lunches than in the studios," Hart said. "On the business end at least."

"Then these clowns try and make a movie with a nose full of coke and a belly full of booze," Diamond said. "No wonder they flush ten million dollars down the tubes."

Wanda pulled her hands back. "With an attitude like that, you won't get very far."

"I don't want to."

"He's got a point," Hart said. "Look at a creep like Walters. Uses gold records as frisbees. What has he got going for him except a Colombian connection?"

"What more do you need?" Wanda said, before walking quickly away.

"What does she do?" Diamond asked.

"Used to be a secretary at a record company. Gave the best blow jobs in the business, I heard. Now she's a singer. People say it's a waste of a great mouth."

"Everyone knows everybody else's business here."

"Red, this town thrives on sex and drugs. You may not know where someone lives, or where they bank, or what their middle name is, but you know their favorite position and their pet drug."

"Do you know a girl named Fifi La Roche? Might also be calling herself Ali Malone, or Alison Manfred, or Jane Doe?"

"There are so many, different shapes and sizes, and all the same. A little talent, a lot of ambition, and a sex life that would make the happy hooker blush."

"Fifi's not like that."

"If she travels with this crowd, she's like that. There are different levels in the entertainment business. We're about three or four from the top. The people here have had a little success: a couple of talking parts in movies; a low-budget feature they've made shown in drive-ins; a record that nearly made the top ten. These are people who can smell success, but haven't tasted it."

"What about Fifi? About five feet six inches, blond, well-built. Blue eyes." He showed Hart the Polaroid photo.

"Cute, but typical. They all come here. Every prom queen who doesn't land a rich boyfriend in the jerkwater town she comes from. Every cocktail waitress who has ever been told she ought to be in pictures. Every jilted girlfriend who thinks she's going to show the world. They come here, get fucked, and either hang around and get fucked some more, or go back to their town with their battered tail between their legs."

"I know, life is tough."

"Sure it's tough. But out here they got the carrot as well as the stick. It makes it worse. They hold the carrot out just a little too far for you to grab."

Hart waved to a lanky young man with curly brown hair and tight designer jeans.

"But life goes on. Mustn't give up hope. Like that fellow," Hart said, his mood lightening as he pointed at the young man. "I just got him a TV spot. And he's got the most delightfully tight tush."

The lights went out suddenly and a seven-foot video screen on one wall glowed on. The image was of a big bed, with Big Sam and Ginny in the middle. Sam was indeed big. And bored. Ginny was writhing and moaning. The amplified sounds of sex came out of concealed speakers in the living room.

"What a show," Hart said. "The last time, he had two girls in there who didn't know about the camera. It was super. Just super."

"I'll bet."

"You don't like women?" Hart said hopefully.

"I like them. I also like my privacy."

"You shouldn't be so old-fashioned."

"I'm just an old-fashioned kind of guy. A broad, a bottle, a fireplace in a log cabin somewhere."

"So primitive. Not even any amyl nitrate?"

"You said you knew about Randall?" Diamond said abruptly.

"The Geek. There's a fellow who knows how to play the game. And cheat at it too."

"You have many dealings with him?"

"I do legit stuff. I don't handle his kind of action. I mean, it's one thing if a cute guy or girl wants to ingratiate themselves with a producer or director. But his talent only had one kind of ability."

"Any idea where he is now?"

"He's been keeping out of sight. Otherwise, he would've been here tonight," Hart said. "Anyway, did you know Sam was the one who was closest to him."

"You said was?"

"I suspect Jimmy may turn up in pieces in the desert. He made a lot of enemies. Excuse me, I have to go circulate," the agent said when he saw the curly-haired young man standing alone.

"One last question. Who has the Mercedes with the license plate SNORT?"

"Big Sam," Hart said, and then he was gone.

After a few more minutes, the video show was over. Judging by the sweaty faces and hard breathing in the audience, it had been a success.

Hoyt came out of the bedroom with the same bored expression on his face. He ignored the ripple of applause, walked over to the bar, belted back a straight Scotch, and walked over to Anders. After a few words, he made his way to where Diamond stood. Vargas and Tony were watching them from the far side of the room.

"Thanks," Hoyt said.

"For what?"

"For trying to step in with Vargas."

Diamond dismissed his thanks with a shrug.

"Listen, Jimmy has burned me too. Borrowed a thousand dollars and split. I know this girl, though, who's still real tight with him. Might just know where he is. She's flaky, but I think she'll tell me. I don't want no one to know, else it will get back to Vargas. He's the only one I hate more than Jimmy right now."

"Great. When should I get in touch with you?"

"Tomorrow afternoon, Scorpio Studios."

They separated and Diamond wended his way to Anders.

"Let's split," Diamond said.

"The party is just beginning. And this little dear wants to learn about phallic symbolism in the classics," the professor said, stroking the bare arm of a statuesque brunette. "I'll stay and educate her."

Diamond stepped out into the cool night air without saying goodbye to anyone. It was quiet. No music, no chatter, no heavy breathing. Too quiet. The hair on the back of his neck rose like a snake charmer's cobra as he moved toward his car.

He spun as Tony's blackjack was nearing the peak of its arc. The blow missed Diamond's head, but caught his right ear, and the bells began to ring.

Diamond swung and hit a tightly muscled stomach that seemed indifferent to the blow. Tony blocked the next and hit Diamond with a breath-draining blow to the middle. Diamond folded, and the blackjack caught him on the top of the head.

He was lying on the ground, clutching his stomach, and Tony pretended he was a soccer ball. He booted a few goals.

"You're not welcome here, shamus," Tony said. "Mr. Vargas don't like no one snooping around. He told me to go easy on you. Next time . . ."

Diamond heard the man's footsteps fading. He lay on the ground, curled in a fetal position, and tried to pull himself together. The front door opened, there was a blast of happy noise, and Tony reentered the party.

Diamond lost track of how long he lay there, but when he heard the front door open, and a group of noisy revelers approaching, he forced himself to his feet and staggered to his car.

He drove back to Manfred's mansion listening to the blues and feeling old.

Diamond was curled up in a fetal position, surrounded by nude bodies dotted with bullet holes. He thought they were dead, then they began to writhe in a grotesque orgy of zombielike sex. He tried climbing over the pile of bodies to reach Fifi. Then a woman in a maid's uniform rose up out of the pile, pointing a gun at him. She cocked the hammer, and there was a click.

The click was real, and he awoke with a start. He reached under his pillow, slid the .38 out, and pointed it at the door.

The figure silhouetted in the hall light was undeniably female. Without saying anything he let her tiptoe over to his pants. She began to rifle his pockets.

"Looking for anything?" he said, and Rosalie jumped. She pretended she was neatly folding the pants, then came to him. She was clad in a light blue robe that gapped open in front.

"You startled me," she complained.

"This isn't the first time a woman's tried to get into my pants when I wasn't in them."

She was close enough now to see the gun in his hand. He heard her sudden intake of air, then replaced the gun under the pillow.

"I was waiting for you to come to me," she said. "It's cold out here. Mind if I come under the covers."

"Not tonight. I'm tired and sore and not in the mood."

"What happened? Where were you all day?"

He was tired and lonely enough that he nearly told her. But the image of her searching his pants froze his tongue.

"Tell me about your day?"

"Uhhh."

She shook him. "C'mon, you can trust me."

"Uhhh."

The next thing he knew, the early morning light was seeping in, and there was a gentle knock at the door. The clock on the nightstand said eight A.M.

"Come in," he said groggily.

Gwen tiptoed in, her shortie nightgown displaying the muscles in her thin legs as she padded to him. She threw herself down on the bed in a move designed to be seductive, but which came out cutely awkward.

"I haven't seen you around, Red."

"I've been here, trying to sleep, when I'm not working for your father."

She sniffed the air, and picked up Rosalie's perfume. She gave Diamond a suspicious look.

"Has Rosalie been here?" she asked jealously.

"She's the maid. I guess it would be her job to be here. Are you checking up on the help?"

"I'm here about them. My governess won't tell me why, but she warned me to watch out. I thought you'd want to know. You should be careful too."

"What else did she tell you?"

"That's it. I tried questioning her. I imagined I was you and did it just like you would. But I don't think she knows anything specifically."

The idea of the scrawny teenager as a private eye brought a smile to his face. She smiled back, and played with the hem of her nightgown.

"Red, do you think I'm sexy?"

"Not yet, kid, but a couple years from now, you'll be a menace."

"What do I need to learn?"

"You need to learn how to wait. Your hormones got to catch up with you. Just enjoy yourself the way you are now."

She leaned over and tried to kiss him on the lips. He pushed her back, giving her a gentle peck on the cheek.

"Everything comes to those who wait," he said. "When I was a kid, I worried about having to shave. I wanted face hair so bad, I would've killed for it. Now, feel this."

He took her hand and rubbed it on his stubbly face.

"A couple years from now, I wouldn't be able to control myself. And it's bad business taking the client's daughter to bed."

Like a puppy desperate for love, she switched her attention-getting tactics. All business, she sat up seriously and said, "I want to be a private detective. I bought a bunch of books on investigative techniques. Do you know how many points of similarity it takes to match up a fingerprint?"

Diamond patted her cheek. "No, but I know a good sleuth needs his beauty sleep. I'd love to talk, kid, but I'm bushed."

"Can I stay here and go to sleep with you?"

"Now, how would that look?"

"Well, okay. I'll go. But you promise you'll teach me how to be tough? How to be a private eye just like you?"

"Sure. Just let me go to sleep." His head was on the pillow by the time she reached the door.

Diamond looked at the clock when there was another knock at the door. It was almost ten A.M.

"C'mon in."

It was Todd. "Mr. Diamond, I have to talk to you."

"You and everybody else. Welcome to Grand Central Station."

Todd gave him a quizzical look. "It's very important."

Diamond stretched. His body ached from the beating he had taken, and for the sleep it still needed. "It always is. I need a hot bath and a couple cups of coffee. I'll talk to you in an hour or so."

"But we mustn't be seen."

"Where do you want to meet?"

Todd walked over to the window and pulled the curtain open. He pointed to a grove of palm trees at the far end of Manfred's estate.

"Over there. Please come."

It was a few minutes after ten-thirty when Diamond entered Manfred's den.

"You look tired," Manfred said. The retired general was looking pretty haggard himself. The skin on his face seemed to be sagging away from his skull. "Learn anything last night?"

"Got a few leads on your daughter's friend, Randall.

The answer to where those paintings are is in this house."

"Why do you say that?"

"It was obviously an inside job. I looked over your security system the other day. It's quite effective."

"Can't a professional get around that?"

"Sure. But any good pro still has an inside man, or woman. To help get the lay of the land, make sure the goodies aren't moved at the last minute."

"I see."

"Did Randall work here long enough to learn about the system?"

"Its existence, yes. The details, no."

"It's so neat, I'd normally think you were the prime suspect. An insurance deal. I read a couple articles about Hitech in the *Wall Street Journal*. And the 10-Ks don't look so good. I'd say a chunk of cash would help keep that Japanese conglomerate from swallowing you like Jonah and the whale."

Manfred tried to appear arrogant and angry, but Diamond had seen the flicker of fear. There was a nervous twitch at the corner of the retired general's thin lips.

Diamond reached over and took a list of paintings off Manfred's desk.

"This the art in question?"

Manfred grabbed for the list, but Diamond pocketed it.

"One other thing. I'm moving out. I don't want everyone here knowing my comings and goings."

"Where will you be?" Manfred said weakly.

"I'll call."

"From now on, I want to know exactly what you're up to." There was an old man's quiver in his voice.

"I'll let you know when there are any major developments."

"You're quite an irascible fellow," Manfred said, trying to sound friendly.

"If that means a pain in the ass, you're right. I do things

my own way. Let the chips fall where they may. The cops don't like me. The crooks don't like me. Sometimes my clients don't like me. But I get results."

Diamond met the governess in the hall. He questioned her about the warning she had given Gwen, but she had nothing to add. It was based on woman's intuition. Diamond asked her to keep her ears open, and she said she would.

He went up to his room and packed his bags. No one interrupted him. He took his luggage out to the car and put it in the trunk.

Diamond walked around the house. The grounds were nice. He had seen smaller parks. Azaleas, camellias and roses exploded with color. Through a clump of bottlebrush and jacaranda trees, Diamond saw, in the distance, a pair of gardeners working.

As he neared the rendezvous point, the soil grew sandier, and was landscaped with plants from the desert Los Angeles would be if they hadn't connived to steal enough water to feed the thirsty millions.

Everything was jagged, spiny, sharp. Pincushion and barrel cacti, aloes and agaves, towered over by Desert Fan, Royal and Washington palms. Todd was waiting behind a thick Yucca tree, invisible to anyone watching from the house.

"I'm glad you came," Todd said.

"I hope you're going to make the trip worthwhile."

"I'm in a jam. I got involved in a crime, and I think I'm going to be set up as the fall guy."

"Go to the cops. First guy in gets the best deal."

"You don't understand. It involves the stolen art."

"What happened?" Diamond said, lighting a cigarette.

"I, I, I—"

"Spit it out. It can't be anything I haven't heard."

"I came here in 1970. Hitched, from the Midwest."

"I don't need your life story."

"Please listen. My father was a minister. I had to leave. I got caught in a barn with another boy. We, we were doing it. Everyone in town knew. I went from being the most popular guy in town, captain of the baseball team, to being Todd the fairy."

"So you came out here to get away. What does that have to do with stolen art?"

"I was broke. I wound up hustling guys on the boulevard." He looked down and nervously kicked the ground with the toe of his shoe.

"But I got out of it. I got listed with a referral service and started getting good jobs. I was out of that scene. Do you understand?"

"Yeah. Go on."

"One day, this Randall showed up. Knew all about my background. He told me he'd squeal unless I went along on this deal, to steal the paintings.

"You don't understand. He'd never understand. I'd be ruined. I'd have to go back to hustling. I couldn't do that. I'd kill myself first."

"How'd it get set up?"

"I got the plans for the alarm system. A few days later, this Japanese guy called. We met at a sushi place in Little Tokyo. He told me what I had to do, then we went to a hotel, and he made me, he made me—"

"What did he look like?"

"About thirty-five. Maybe five feet eight inches. Well built. Short black hair. And he had these tattoos all over his body. Dragons and samurais and fans. And he was missing a piece of his pinkie."

"What?"

"The tip of his pinkie, I forget if it was his left or right. I asked him, and he got real mean, he, he—"

"Okay. Have you seen Randall since?"

Todd shook his head. "I spoke to him once, and he threatened me. He also made it seem like he had something on Mr. Mánfred."

"Like what?"

"I don't know."

"Did the name Rocco Rico ever come up in the talk?"

Diamond heard the crack but it was too late to do anything. Todd's head exploded like a watermelon dropped from a second-story window. Diamond hit the ground and had his .38 out. He wiped a piece of Todd's face from his own.

The gardeners were looking around, unsure of what had happened. They were the only figures in sight. Diamond felt for a pulse on Todd's wrist. It was a futile gesture, and he knew it.

The governess and Gwen were studying in the library. Rosalie was polishing silverware in the kitchen. Manfred was in the master bathroom. Apparently no one in the house had heard the shot. It was a quiet domestic scene, except for the dead man by the grove.

Diamond took Manfred into the den. The sniper-scope-equipped AR-15 was missing. Manfred sagged into his chair as Diamond recounted Todd's last words.

"We've got to call the cops pretty quick," Diamond said. "You better level with me, and do it fast."

Manfred covered his face with his hands. He gave a convulsive shudder.

"I've been a fool. It wasn't supposed to come to this. No one was supposed to get hurt."

"This is no time for twenty-twenty hindsight. Spill it!"

"Hitech is in trouble. The technology changes so fast, it's just impossible to keep up."

"You going to read me the Dow Jones average?"

"Please, please, let me compose my thoughts."

"There's no time."

"About a month ago, I knew I couldn't hold it together. This Japanese holding company, Tanaka Industries, was going to take us over. I approached the president of the company with a deal. He could have the paintings, if they backed off. He seemed interested."

Manfred was pulling at the skin of his face. His tall body was bent nearly double.

"I was supposed to get time to insure the paintings. We'd wait a couple months, then arrange a burglary. But the paintings disappeared. Negotiations broke off. I lost the paintings, and I'm going to lose the company."

"You said before you didn't know where the paintings were?"

"I spoke to Tanaka after the robbery. He claimed he never got the paintings. I think Randall may have double-crossed us both. I don't know who has them. I don't think he'd be able to fence them to just anyone."

"Rocco could handle it. He's got the connections."

"Who's he?"

"My problem. We'll give the cops a limited version. Stonewall them, for now," Diamond said, pointing to the phone on Manfred's desk.

The retired general slowly dialed the police.

Murder was too big a crime for the San Marino Police and the Sheriff's Homicide Bureau handled the investigation of the ultimate crime during its rare appearance in the community.

When Lieutenant Rick Browning, the head of the bureau, arrived, the technicians and deputy medical examiner going about their grim work quieted down. Browning's arrival officially signified this wasn't just another routine murder.

Browning had been playing golf, on his day off, when the call came in. He had gray hair, gray eyes and rosy red cheeks. He was wearing a golfer's cap, yellow slacks and a frown. He had been winning when he was interrupted.

Diamond was standing with him near the spot where the lab boys had tried to draw a chalkline on the blood-soaked earth. The yellow Crime Scene—Do Not Enter ribbon fluttered in a weak Santa Ana wind. The air was hot, but moving. It didn't cool the homicide lieutenant who was less than pleased with the answers Diamond was giving.

"So let me hear that again. You were standing out here, just talking about life?"

"That's right," Diamond said.

"That's bullshit."

"Like Mr. Manfred told you, if you don't believe it, take me in, and he'll have his attorney get me out before you can say habeas corpus."

"You got a permit for that gun?" Browning said, pointing to the .38 at Diamond's waist.

"I told you no. But we're on Manfred's property, and I'm authorized by him to carry it."

"I could confiscate it as evidence."

"But the coroner already told you, in front of witnesses, that Todd was shot with a rifle, from a distance."

"You make it hard for me, I make it hard for you."

"Lieutenant, I don't want to make it tough on anybody. I got my job to do, just like you."

"But you won't tell me what your job is?"

"I told you I'm an investigator."

"Apparently unlicensed. And investigating what?"

"I have to talk to my client."

"Manfred?"

"I never said that. Unless my client releases me to talk, I can't say a damn thing."

"This is murder."

"I don't like it anymore than you do. It doesn't do much for my reputation to be talking to a guy, and he winds up spilling his brains on me. But I got an oath."

Browning let loose a few oaths of his own.

"Don't leave town," he ordered, after he and Diamond had gone around a few more times.

"I wouldn't think of it. I'm starting to like it here."

Manfred was in his study, face buried in his hands. There were a half-dozen empty spots on the wall where police ballistics experts had taken guns they wanted to examine. Manfred had trouble talking coherently. Diamond poured him a Scotch, and left.

Rosalie had asked for and gotten the rest of the day off. The governess was taking care of Gwen. And Diamond had work to do.

He went back to the library, and read everything he could about Tanaka's corporation. Details were sketchy about the foreign company, and its head, Kenino Tanaka. The company was one of Japan's largest, with investments in microchip computer technology, sophisticated photographic equipment and precision machinery.

Tanaka was a mystery man, never giving interviews, with ties to powerful conservative politicians in his native country. He was sixty-two, married to an American woman, with no children.

Diamond cross-checked the gossip columns and feature magazines. There were hints and innuendos, but nothing conclusive. Reading between the lines, Diamond gleaned it was not a happy marriage, and Tanaka had some connections with Japanese organized crime, the Yakuza.

A somewhat tawdry detective magazine had a big article about the Yakuza, tattooed men who lopped off a pinky when they screwed up.

Rocco's name didn't turn up anywhere, but the whole operation had his greasy paw prints all over it. The mobster was trying to get legit, using more front men, and investing in good businesses. But that didn't prevent him from using his favorite tactics: blackmail, extortion and murder.

Diamond rented a motel on Ventura Boulevard, in

Sherman Oaks, that had direct phone lines. Then he went to a pay phone with a fistful of change and began making calls.

Tanaka's secretary said the boss couldn't see him for at least a month. His calendar was as packed as the microchips he made. Manfred's name carried no weight with the icy-voiced secretary, and Diamond didn't leave his own.

Hoyt was more helpful.

Hoyt's voice sounded strange, and Diamond asked what was wrong.

"I'm talking through a fat lip," Hoyt said. "Tony wanted to know what we had talked about, and I wasn't too cooperative. Him and Vargas were pissed. So Tony worked me over a bit. But he screwed up." Hoyt chuckled. "He wasn't supposed to leave any marks. But I resisted. So they have to postpone shooting the latest epic while I heal."

"You okay?"

"Better than Anders. He was in a bedroom with three little chickies when they barged in and beat the crap out of him. He didn't have anything to tell them. But they didn't believe that."

"Tough break."

"Yeah. I bet he's going to be celibate for quite a while. But listen, I got an address for you. Out in Venice, on Wavecrest Avenue." Hoyt read him an address. "That's where our friend was, at least up to three days ago."

"Great. You get anything else, call me at this number," Diamond said, giving him the motel phone number.

"Take care of yourself, Red. Vargas don't like being beaten by anyone."

"He better learn to like it, now that Red Diamond is on his case."

26

Diamond parked a block from the address Hoyt had given him. Skateboarders and roller-skaters, wearing headphones to blot out the world, zoomed past as he walked down the palm tree-lined street. The sound of carpenters erecting more condos overpowered the noise of the surf.

He knocked on the door of a one-story bungalow with peeling yellow paint. A young woman, her long blond hair pulled over to a braid on one side of her head, opened the door. A loosely fitting dress covered what looked like a promising body. She didn't appreciate Diamond's noticing that.

"What do you want?" she demanded in a voice as New Jerseyish as the Garden State Parkway.

"Is Jimmy around?"

"He rents the place out in back. Only he split a couple days ago." She started to close the door.

"I need to talk to him. Know where he went?"

"You a cop?" She pronounced the last word like it was a vile obscenity.

"No. A friend of his."

"He's a creep. I didn't think he had any friends. Are you a Gemini?" she asked abruptly.

"Damned if I know."

She looked at him amazed. "What day were you born?"

"September sixteenth. Why?"

"That means you're a Virgo, the virgin."

"Honey, you're thinking of the wrong guy."

"That's good. I'm a Capricorn. Jimmy was a Gemini, you know, two-faced. I can feel you got good vibes."

Diamond glanced down to see if his fly was open. It wasn't.

"I could do a full horoscope work-up on you. Only twenty bucks. Tell your past, present and future," she said.

"Not today. Can I take a look at where Jimmy lived?"

"It's a mess. I haven't cleaned it out yet. But I need the landlord's permission to show it."

Diamond took out a twenty-dollar bill and held it aloft. "How about an advance payment on the horoscope?"

She grabbed the money, went inside, and came back with a key. They walked around back and she let them in.

The place smelled of decaying food and mildew. There were half-packed cardboard boxes lying on the floor. A furry brown thing, either a giant mouse or a small rat, jumped out of a carton and disappeared behind the refrigerator.

"Looks like he left in a hurry," Diamond said.

"Yeah. He owes a couple hundred bucks."

"Can I look around?"

"Suit yourself," she said, leaning against the door frame. "You'd have to clean the place up yourself. I don't do that sort of work."

Diamond prowled the three-room apartment. A couple of posters of rock stars were still tacked to the peeling wallpaper. There was a soiled sheet on the mattress lying on the floor. A window in the bedroom was patched with cardboard and newspapers. Diamond had seen more luxurious flophouses.

The woman was tapping her fingers impatiently.

"What's your name?" he asked.

"Elaine."

"Elaine, I'd just like to sit here a while," he said, plopping down on a cushion that made an impolite noise. "You know, feel the vibes. If it's okay?"

"I guess. You into TM or something?"

"Something like that."

"It stinks in here. I'll be in my apartment."

He waited until he heard her apartment door slam before getting up and rooting through Randall's boxes. They held the usual, albeit worn, assortment of housewares, dishes and personal bric-a-brac. The only items out of the ordinary were some spent .45 automatic shells, and a large hash pipe.

The last box to be examined was filled with papers and books. The scholarly tomes included *Grow Your Own Grass at Home* and *Synthetic Chemical Stimulants.* There were a couple of thrillers about Nazi plots to take over the world thirty years after the fall of the Third Reich.

Diamond was just about to give up when he noticed a business card stuck in one of the thrillers as a bookmark. It was Manfred's card, with his business address and phone on the front, and his home address and phone on the back.

Diamond went through the books again. In one entitled *The Use of Opiates throughout History,* he found Kenino Tanaka's card, with a phone number and Santa Monica address on the back.

He pocketed both cards, put the books back in the boxes, and left.

The fresh air coming off the ocean made him realize just how foul-smelling it had been in the apartment. He sucked the saltwater air in greedily.

He left without saying goodbye to Elaine. She had the stars, and his twenty dollars, to keep her company.

He cursed at a skateboarder who nearly hit him. The skateboarder missed his obscenity as Walkman blasted sweet nothings into her ears.

A pretty girl, her bare feet black as she walked on the pavement, strode by. She had long blond hair and the same shape as Fifi. He hurried ahead and studied her face. It wasn't Fifi. She gave him a cold look and walked briskly away.

He ambled down to one of the brackish canals, and spent a few minutes tossing pebbles into the water. He had lots of pieces, but the puzzle just wasn't coming together.

The hairs on the back of his neck were tingling. He felt like he was being watched, but there was no one in sight.

He started walking back to his car, convinced he was being followed. But there were none of Rocco's goons in sight. The only person keeping pace was a Japanese tourist, capturing the buildings and the freaks with his Nikon.

As Diamond neared the run-down bungalows, he was alone on the street with the smiling tourist. They were in front of an alleyway when the man approached him.

"Excuse please, do you know the way to San José?"

"What?"

"Now that I have your attention," the man said in a guttural growl, taking out a very unsmiling automatic, "do you know what this is?"

"A Beretta, I'd guess."

"Very good. Please take a few steps backward."

The man was about four feet away, just out of reach. His movements were calm and professional. Diamond backed up into the alley.

"Thank you," the man said, putting the gun back into his belt.

Diamond lunged, and caught a knife hand thrust in his abdomen. The fresh seabreezes left his lungs in a whoosh.

The man took his time. There was no sadistic glee, no heavy breathing. Just strong, painful blows that made Diamond hurt in ways he didn't think possible. Diamond gave up fighting back as a veil of red agony slipped over his brain.

"Please mind your own business," the man said just before the callused side of his hand connected with Diamond's temple.

As the black curtain signaling the end of the show came down, Diamond noticed his assailant was missing part of his right pinkie.

He awoke to the feel of a slender hand in his back pocket. He was lying on his stomach. Two feral teenagers were standing over him. They didn't notice his eyes open.

"He looks good for a bum. Bet we can get five bucks for the shoes," the skinnier one, who was reaching for Diamond's wallet, said.

"Hope he's got more than just chump change," said the other, a buck-toothed youth who was holding a steak knife.

There were tears in his eyes from the pain, but Diamond made his hand grab the gun from his waist. He struggled to a sitting position, and put the gun to Skinny's head.

"Help me up, Boy Scout, or I blow your brains out."

"Sure. Sure," Skinny said. Buck Tooth took off down the alley, his sneakers kicking up debris as he tried to break the three-minute mile.

Diamond got shakily to his feet. He looked at his watch to see how long he'd been out. The watch was gone.

He put his arm over the youth's shoulder, and tucked his gun into the pocket nearest the teenager. He jabbed it as hard as he could into the young man's side.

"Gimme my watch back."

"Sure. Sure," Skinny said, taking the watch out and handing it to Diamond. "Mister, we was just—"

"Don't try to flimflam me, punk. I paid my dues in New York, on the toughest streets in the world. Just shut up and keep walking."

They were an incongruous pair, the tall man, looking like he was one step away from Forest Lawn, leaning heavily on the obviously reluctant good Samaritan.

But Venice was full of the unusual, and the pair drew little attention.

They made it to Diamond's car, he took his arm off the youth and poked Skinny with the gun in his pocket.

"Scram."

Skinny needed no prodding. He was a half-block away by the time Diamond had the car door open.

The ride to his motel took every ounce of discipline Diamond possessed. You deserve to die, he thought to himself, getting set up like that. One little guy, beating you to a pulp, then a couple of juvenile Jesse Jameses getting ready to strip you down to your skivvies. Red Diamond, victim.

He squinted his eyes, clenched his teeth, and kept driving.

The Jap was good. He'd suckered Diamond like a kid at a shell game. It wasn't like Rocco to use a Jap. That's what had thrown him off balance, Diamond decided. And that little guy packed a hell of a wallop. Diamond had gone toe to toe with heavyweights and not felt that kind of kick.

And he was still sore from his run-in with Tony. Of course, that was Rocco's style. Kick a guy while he's down, that was Rocco's game. Toy with the mouse before eating it.

But this mouse was carrying a .38, and the slugs had Rocco's name on them, Diamond thought.

27

A nap, a hot bath and two cups of coffee laced with bourbon later, Diamond dressed, and headed out to the address on the back of Tanaka's business card.

He had no doubt he could force his way into Tanaka's office. There'd been the time when Rocco's men holed up in a bank vault. A couple of feet of concrete and steel, and a half-dozen trigger-happy gunmen with Thompsons. Red Diamond had forced his way in there, when the entire Kansas City Police Department waited helplessly outside.

But there was something about catching a guy at home that made him more vulnerable. Put the war on his homefront. Catch him by surprise. Make it personal.

He took the Ventura, to the San Diego, to the Santa Monica Freeway. The freeway ended as Glenn Miller finished "The Anvil Chorus" on the radio, and Freddy Martin's crew launched into "April in Paris."

He hummed along, the Pacific on his left, a row of palms on his right, and trouble up ahead.

The front yard of the Tanaka home was filled with neatly trimmed plants and multicolored stones. The back yard was the Pacific Ocean. In between was a two-story white house with a nautical theme; small, circular windows, a deck circling the second floor and a fog horn spout used as the chimney. It looked like a ferry that had run aground.

Red leaned on the bell, and heard the first few bars of

"Anchors Aweigh" echoing inside. He was about to go for a second chorus when the door was thrown open so violently, he reached for his gun.

But he let the hand drop to his side when he saw the woman. She was middle-aged, with bleached blond hair that was beginning to show brown at the roots. She might have been pretty, if she took care of herself. She might have been pretty, if she smiled. She might have been pretty, many bottles of liquor ago.

"Whaddayou want?" she said, sending a cloud of alcoholic hatred in Diamond's direction.

"Is Kenino around?"

"No. He's with one of his tramps, the rat bastard."

"My name's Red Diamond. I'm a private investigator."

"Whoopie do," she said, beginning to close the door.

Diamond stopped it with his foot.

"You don't get your foot outta there I'm gonna call a cop," she slurred.

"It concerns your husband."

"Then it don't concern me," she said, leaning hard against the door.

"I think he's having an affair with my client's wife."

The scowl on her face lessened and she stopped putting pressure on the door. "I've been trying to nail that Jap bastard for years. You got any proof?"

"One of my associates is tailing him right now. Can I come in?"

She swayed like a small craft on the high seas as she led him down the hall to a large living room that looked out on the ocean. She retrieved her drink from a table made from a hatch cover and sat down on the blue green sofa.

"I hate him. I hate the ocean. I hate this Disneyland house. I hate fish. I hate his sailboat. I hate not having a maid. Now, whaddayou want?"

"Background information. About your husband."

"Why?"

"Because we believe he's having an affair with my client's wife."

"Do you have proof?"

"Some."

"What kind?"

"Well, I didn't bring the photos with me."

"Photos?"

Diamond nodded. For the first time, the woman smiled. She drained her glass and refilled it, without offering Diamond any.

"I want the photos," she said.

"You don't need them for a divorce out here. It's pretty easy to get."

"I know the laws. But I want to nail his ass to the wall. Send copies to every newspaper in this country. And his beloved Japan. I want to ruin him." The hate in her words was as strong as the liquor on her breath. "I want those pictures," she said, taking a determined swig of her Scotch.

"I don't think it would be ethical for me to do that," Diamond said, putting a little hesitancy into his tone.

"I'd pay quite well."

"I'd have to check with my client."

"Do that."

"I know he'd be a lot more receptive if you could help me with some information."

"What do you need?"

"Did your husband have any business dealings with a guy named James Randall?"

"What does that have to do with anything?"

"Randall is a pimp."

"My husband is too cheap to pay for sex. He's always hired obliging secretaries. But he has talked to this Randall. He got a call from him last night."

"Did you hear what was said?"

"It wasn't about any woman. Something about art and money. I think Randall had some art my husband wanted to buy. But Kenino got very mad. Which isn't like him. Usually he just has that silly, half-assed smile on his face, even when I call him names."

"You ever seen a Japanese guy, about five feet six inches, well built, missing a pinkie finger?"

"That's Katana. My husband's driver, bodyguard, right-hand man. He gives me the willies."

She stood up, swaying and trembling like a sapling in a storm. "My husband told me if I screw him up, he'll sic Katana on me. I believe it. It better not say any more. You better go." She took a strong belt of Scotch.

"Why don't you lay off the booze, and tell me—"

"Don't tell me what to do, buster," she shrieked. "Get out. Get out. Leave me alone." She sat down and wandered off into her own bitter world. She paid no attention as Diamond let himself out.

The governess grabbed him as soon as he stepped into the Manfred mansion.

"Thank goodness you're here," she said. "Mr. Manfred has gone off. Gwen is in the main hall, hysterical. I can't calm her down. Please do something."

There was a vaguely musty smell about the main hall, as if the room hadn't been used for quite a while. It was the kind of room where King Arthur could've thrown a quiet, sit-down feast for a hundred. Only the table wasn't round, it was long and bare.

And sitting at one end, sobbing, was Gwen. Oil paintings of the past ten generations or so of Manfreds stared down disapprovingly from the walls. But the girl was indifferent to their somber looks. She didn't even notice when Diamond came in.

"Why so glum, kid?"

Gwen lifted her head, jumped up and ran to Diamond. She threw her arms around him with a grip that, if she had been stronger, would've crushed the life right out of him.

It took a few minutes of soft words and stroking Gwen's head before he could get the story.

Alison had called about fifteen minutes earlier. Rosalie had come to where she was hiding out with Randall. Randall was going to clinch the deal on the hot art, then go off with the two women. Alison didn't go for the *ménage à trois,* and wanted Manfred to come get her.

Gwen hadn't been able to garner any more with her eavesdropping.

"I only did it because I wanted to be a private eye," she sniffled. "I tried stopping Daddy when he ran out, but he just pushed past me. I don't know where he went."

"Where was he when he took the call?"

"In his den."

"Let's go there," Diamond said, keeping his arm around the girl as they began walking briskly.

"I'm scared, Red."

"Kid, you wanted lessons on how to be tough?"

She nodded, and wiped her eyes with a handkerchief.

"Well, the first thing is to be scared."

"Really?"

"You read Superman comics?"

"Not anymore. But I used to. Why?"

"Was Superman tough when bullets were bouncing off him?"

She pondered the question. "I guess."

"No, he wasn't. Bullets just bounce off him. He's tough

when he's facing kryptonite. Something that can hurt him. Something that he's scared of. Like, would I be tough if I picked a fight with you?"

She smiled. "No, but you wouldn't do that."

"I wouldn't. That wouldn't be tough either. Because I'm bigger and meaner. But if you picked a fight with me, that would be tough. Understand?"

"You're not mean." She clutched him. "Stay with me."

"I can't, kid. I got a job to do. You got to be tough without me. Without anybody. When you're facing the big sleep, you're all alone anyway."

The door to the den was ajar. Gwen watched as Diamond looked over the papers on Manfred's desk. There was a small notepad next to the phone, but the top sheet was blank.

Diamond held up the sheet to the light. Manfred pressed hard when he wrote, and the impression was clear. "Randall, armed, Rosalie, Topanga and Happy Trail." The address, however, was illegible.

Ignoring her demands to be brought along, Diamond gave Gwen a farewell pat on the cheek. As he hurried out, he noticed that one of the automatics was missing from its place on the wall.

He ran to the car and jumped in, pausing just long enough to find Happy Trail and Topanga Canyon Boulevard in his Thomas Bros. map book.

He was doing sixty by the time he hit the Foothill Freeway, and seventy-five by the time it changed into the Ventura Freeway. The car began to protest when the speedometer climbed over eighty miles an hour, but he ignored it, and kept his pedal to the metal.

Then he was making a screeching exit onto Topanga Canyon Boulevard. The first mile-and-a-half was straight, through a pleasant, tree-lined residential area. Then he was out of the city of Los Angeles, on county land, and the road turned into a snaky, treacherous beast. There were few lights and fewer cars. Just trees, hidden little side roads, and dry arroyos. And more curves than a Vegas chorus line.

The road climbed, and the drop off the unfenced side grew more treacherous, but still he maintained his break-neck speed. He ignored speed limit signs that restricted him to half his chosen pace. He crunched over stones, oblivious to the falling rock warnings. He was Red Diamond, on the way to Fifi at last.

29

He heard the big booms as he made the sharp turn near Santa Maria Road, and he knew Manfred's automatic was near.

But the note had said Randall was armed, and there'd been those shell casings in the carton in Venice.

Randall was a dangerous ferret, with more enemies than Will Rogers had friends. And Manfred was a deter-mined old man, blinded by rage, and probably out of shape. Rosalie was treacherous and deceitful. And Fifi was caught in the middle.

Diamond leapt from the car after pulling off on the shoulder near Happy Trail. He ran to the nearest house, a wood-shingled affair that had seen better days, and pounded on the door. His .38 was in his hand.

There was no answer, so he kicked it open. Finding no one, he ran to the next house, and repeated the routine. It too was empty.

Lights were on in the third house. He pounded the door, and a stocky, bearded young man, smiling in a cloud of marijuana smoke, answered.

"What's happening?" the young man asked.

"You hear the shots."

"Like, yeah, but people are always letting off steam around here."

"Where'd they come from?"

"I dunno." He had an idiotic grin on his face. "I've got to go back to the TV. They got 'Dragnet' reruns on."

"Wait a minute," Diamond said, fumbling in his jacket. "You seen this girl around?" He held up the picture of Manfred's daughter.

"Like I said, we mind our own business here in the canyon. It's bad karma to go putting your nose where it don't belong."

The man noticed the gun for the first time when Diamond shoved it into his navel.

"Think any of your neighbors would give a damn if I gave you another bellybutton? Tell me where the girl lives, or you don't get to find out if Jack Webb gets his man."

"Three houses up. The converted trailer."

Diamond left him standing in the doorway as he bounded up the road. There was an orange glow coming from the trailer, like a cozy fireplace gone berserk. It didn't make Diamond feel very cozy.

There were flames visible through the windows as he hit the door at top speed. He crashed to the floor, swinging his gun to cover any movement.

Three bodies lay there. Two men, and a woman. Arms and legs twined together. One great beast, leaking blood as red as the flames onto the floor.

Diamond froze, oblivious to the flames that gave the scene a hellish lighting. Two men and a woman. Dead. Bodies on the floor.

He started flashing back. The hotel. Closet, darkness, gunshots, bodies, helpless, Simon, Milly, whore.

The girl's scream snapped him out of it. She was tied to a chair. Fifi. The fire about to turn her into Joan of Arc. Fifi!

Loaded with adrenalin, he stepped into the flames, lifted the chair with the girl in it, and carried it outside.

He untied the knots that bound her as his pants cuffs smoldered. The girl stood up, and fainted.

A propane fuel tank in the trailer exploded, and the flames began to play across the roof of the building. Diamond lifted her in his arms and carried her to the car. He had the glazed eyes and stiff movements of a zombie, and limbs that quivered with hormonal shakes.

Got to get out of the boonies, Diamond thought as he got behind the wheel, the girl on the seat next to him. Can't get any fares out here in the country. Get back to midtown.

What's she doing in the front seat? No fares up front, can't you read the sign, lady? No sign. Milly? No, a blonde. Milly. The books. Red Diamond. Who was he? He, him. Rocco. Long Island. Melonie. Fifi.

Fifi!

She stirred, and slowly sat up. Her shoulder-length blond hair fell across the top of a soiled white peasant blouse. She wasn't wearing a bra, and her breasts moved freely as the car swerved down the road. One eye was blackened and puffy, the other a dazed blue. Her feet were bare, with red nail polish on eight of her toes. She smelled of smoke and her skin-tight jeans were charred.

"Where am I?" said the voice he'd waited so long to hear. "Who am I? Who are you?"

"I'm Red Diamond, private eye. You're Fifi La Roche, my long-lost girlfriend. And we're on the road into Los Angeles. You're safe now, dollface."

"Fifi La what?"

"La Roche."

"That doesn't sound right. I don't know." She nibbled the long nail on her index finger. It had been painted the same color red as her toenails.

"It's okay. You're in shock. Can you recall what happened back there?"

The car ate up a few more miles as she continued gnawing her nail.

"I was with someone. A guy."

"James Randall. Jimmy the Geek."

"That sounds right. Kind of cute, and a real sharpie."

"Go on," Diamond said jealously. "Your memory ain't too good."

"Then this woman came. Rose, I think. A tramp."

"And she and the sharpie hit it off."

"They had stolen something together. And she wanted her money. He said he hadn't gotten it yet. She was mad. Then he told her she could come with us. Him and me, that is. I got mad. We were all yelling."

Diamond flipped on the radio as the girl paused to sort out her confusion. They continued to head south, with Glenn Miller playing "At Last."

"I called someone. Told him to come get me."

"Your father, Edward Manfred."

"I thought you said my name was La Roche."

"Just go on."

"So he came. And he got mad when he saw this," she said, pointing to her puffy eye. "Then Jimmy and Rose, Rosalie, jumped him. They said they were in trouble. Needed money. That was before they jumped him. Then they were fighting. Jimmy had a gun. So did the old man. Then, then . . ."

She began to cry.

"Was there any talk about paintings?"

"Yes. Yes. The old man, Manfred you said, said 'You stole my daughter and my artwork.' "

"What did Randall say?"

"He said Manfred could buy the paintings back, for a million dollars. Otherwise, he was going to sell to the highest bidder."

Diamond mulled over what she said, while the girl tried to sort out her memories.

"You sure my name is Fifi? It just don't sound right."

He nodded and they rode again without talking, the big bands on the radio the only sound competing with the road noise.

"I'm going to get us a room near the airport, so we can

blow this town quick when I'm done. I've just about got it figured out. What I need is Rocco's connection with this deal. And you've got to help me with that."

"I don't know anyone named Rocco," she said hesitantly.

"That's okay, babe, for now. You're still shook up over what happened. I don't blame you. We'll settle in tonight, and tomorrow I wrap this case up."

The neatly coiffed desk clerk, wearing a supercilious smile and a blue blazer with the motel chain's logo on it, studied Diamond carefully before deigning to pass him a registration card.

While he filled it out, he caught the young clerk taking stock of Fifi. Pale, black-eyed, bedraggled and smelling like the leftovers at a fire sale, she still was quite a woman.

Diamond guided her to their room, and sat her down on the bed. She stared straight ahead, silent, as tears trickled down sooty cheeks. Then the words began to flow.

"My name's not Fifi. It's Alison Manfred. My father is Edward Manfred. And he's dead. Him and Jimmy just killed each other. And that horrible woman, Rosalie, who used to be our maid. And I nearly got killed. And now they're all gone. It was horrible. They all died. Killed. The fire then, after the shots, and then . . ."

Diamond hugged her as she began to sob.

"It's gonna be okay," he said. "You're in shock. Just take it easy. It'll be okay."

After a few minutes of consoling words, Diamond convinced her to take a shower.

He could hear her crying as she shut the bathroom door and turned on the water.

Vargas and Tony, and Tanaka and Katana, were still on the loose. And Rocco, most of all Rocco. He'd let the small fry go free if only he could get his hands on the big man.

There'd be a lot more tears shed if he didn't take his devilishly clever enemy off the streets.

He toyed with the idea of just running away. Take Fifi and find a place where the cops were underworked, and everyone died from natural causes.

Why should Red Diamond persist where the police agencies of the world had failed? He was one man. One tired man.

Soon Fifi came out of the bathroom. She had regained most of her color, and smelled of the perfumed soap. He laid her down on the bed, tucked her in, and then drew himself a hot bath.

What a dame, he thought, envisioning what was under the damp towel that had wrapped her torso. And soon she'd be his alone. It was time for Red Diamond to settle down. A little domestic bliss would be welcome after so many shoot-outs.

It would be a hell of a wedding. He'd invite all the guys to it. The hard-boiled affair of the century. Marlowe, Spade, Nick and Nora Charles, Race Williams, Lester Leith, Lew Archer, Shell Scott. The guys from the Continental Op agency. Jo Gar from the Islands. Simon Templar and Bulldog Drummond from jolly old England. Mike Hammer and Matt Scudder from the Big Apple. Spenser from Boston. Chester Drum from D.C. Harry Stoner from god-forsaken Cincinnati. Max Latin could cater it. Casey or Kennedy could take the pictures.

It would be a bash as talked about as a good case. Make everyone check their heaters at the door. Some of the guys were sort of hot-headed, but they were a great crew anyway. There'd be booze, broads and a damn good time. With Red Diamond and his blushing bride the center of attention.

He'd have his hands full, keeping that horny bunch from making off with his lady. But he was as tough as any hombre.

He dozed, and was imagining himself in a tuxedo—with Fifi in a gown that showed off her charms and was still proper—when two gentle hands began kneading his shoulders.

He thanked her with a kiss. While she was toweling him dry, he noticed the can of soda sitting on the counter by the sink.

"Where'd you get that?" he asked.

"They have a machine in the lobby. I went out." She giggled. "That clerk is cute. He thought you gave me the shiner. Offered to help me get away from you. I told him you were my hero." She kissed him.

Diamond exploded. "Don't ever go out without my permission. It's a dangerous world out there, until I take care of Rocco." He held her hard. "Do you understand, Fifi?"

"My name's not Fifi. It's Alison Manfred. I found my driver's license in my pants pocket."

"Fake ID. Don't play games with me. Your name is Fifi La Roche."

"No it's not." She stamped her foot on the tile bathroom floor. "It's Alison Manfred. Don't try and confuse me. I know who I am."

"And I bet you never sang in that nightclub in Vegas? Or worked as a cocktail waitress in Chicago? Or married that rich guy in Boston? Or worked at Mange Chez Joseph in New York?"

"Where'd you get that from? I never did any of that stuff."

He kissed her again. "You gotta face reality, angel. It's a tough world, but don't blot it out."

"You're crazy."

"Crazy about you. I know all about it. I don't care about the other guys. I know about the time Rocco's boys gangbanged you in the back of that Frisco pool hall. It's okay.

210

Don't forget, I was the one blasted you out of that Nevada whorehouse. I love you, angel. We're gonna be married once Rocco is taken care of."

She stared at him, wide-eyed. "I just met you."

He grabbed her and clamped his mouth to hers. The towel fell away from his body. He lifted her up and carried her to the bed.

Her clothes fell away like autumn leaves. And he was on her and in her and there was no one else in the world.

He dreamed of a house on Long Island. Red Diamond, puttering around the workshop, Fifi in the kitchen. A boy named Sean, a girl named Melonie. A happy, domestic scene, until a woman named Milly came to the door with a man named Rocco. Then there were guns exploding, and two piles of bodies on the floor. Six bodies. Three to a pile. And blood on the carpet that couldn't be cleaned.

He awoke with a start, calling out "Milly."

"I thought you thought my name was Fifi?"

He looked at the woman next to him, and the nightmare world faded away. "Just premarriage jitters," he said, throwing an arm over the naked woman, and returning to sleep. It took her a lot longer to relax.

They slept most of the next day away.

He awoke as the door to the motel room was opening. He grabbed the gun under his pillow and pointed it at the entering figure, trying to squint away the somnolent haze.

"What're you doing?" Fifi demanded from the doorway. "You could've killed me!"

"I told you not to go out without me," Diamond barked, setting the gun down on the night table and sitting up.

"I'm a big girl," she said, shutting the door behind her. "It's way after lunch. I got myself something to eat. Do I need your permission to do that?"

"Yes. It's a jungle out there."

He got up and began getting dressed.

"Don't ever, ever do that again, Fifi," he said, like a parent who'd caught his child playing in traffic.

"You keep calling me Fifi. And you said the name 'Milly' a couple of times last night. Who are these women?"

Diamond scratched his head. "Milly? I must've meant Fifi. Your name is Fifi."

"Is not!"

"Is too!"

"Is not. It's Alison Manfred."

A plane rumbled overhead, shaking the motel like the San Andreas fault was coming unzipped. "Listen babe, soon we'll be on one of those big birds heading out of this crazy burg. Right after the wedding. And then you'll be Mrs. Red Diamond."

He sat down on the bed, oblivious to her befuddled look, and called the Sheriff's Special Homicide Unit. Diamond tried to get Browning's help, but the cop insisted that Diamond come in for questioning. Diamond hung up on Browning before the call could be traced.

"I knew I couldn't count on them," he growled. "It's just me and you against the world, doll."

"I don't even have any clothes."

"I'll go out and get you some, but I want you to stay here. If you don't give me your word, I'll have to chain you to the bed."

She gave him her word, and a list of items with her size.

He had trouble explaining what he wanted to the salesgirl at Bullock's. He didn't want to get Fifi the rather typical items she'd listed: jeans, sneakers, blouses. She had to look like Red Diamond's girl.

At last he found a common ground with the salesgirl. He ordered one dress like Veronica Lake had in *This Gun for Hire,* another like Lauren Bacall had in *The Big Sleep,* and another outfit like Mary Astor's in *The Maltese Falcon.* By the time he was done picking up a pair of high-heeled pumps in the shoe department, he was out about six hundred dollars.

But he happily hummed a medley of Artie Shaw tunes as he headed back to the motel. The idea for how to clear up the case had come to him, and Fifi was waiting.

He threw open the motel room door and yelled "Surprise!" his face covered by the stack of boxes he was carrying.

His gleeful shout echoed in the empty room. He dropped the boxes, and frantically searched. In vain.

He picked up the room phone and dialed the front office.

"Desk," a cranky, elderly male voice said.

"This is Diamond in one-oh-nine. Did you see my wife go out?"

"No, but I can tell you when she did. Exactly. It was five o'clock. You want to know why I say exactly? 'Cause she went off with my desk clerk. Gone. And the till is empty. That no good bum cleaned me out. I get my hands on him, I'm going to—"

Diamond hung up on the ranting motel owner.

Diamond called Browning again. The cop said he couldn't help unless Diamond came in. He promised Diamond wouldn't be arrested. He sounded as sincere as a politician making a campaign speech.

Diamond didn't believe Fifi had just run off. She wouldn't do that. Rocco! It had to be his handiwork. Fifi had gone to the punk at the desk, and he'd set her up. Rocco had put the snatch on her. That was it. It smelled of Rocco, stealing Fifi right out from under his nose.

He took his .38 from the night table where he'd left it for Fifi's protection. He checked the cylinder. It sounded like a roulette wheel as he spun it, each click coming up double zero.

Rocco was everywhere. Red had let his guard down briefly, but it was too long. No more Mr. Nice Guy. It was time for the showdown.

Anders hung up on Diamond when he called.

So he took a ride out to Anders's house.

"I will fix it so that you never cruise Westwood for nookie again," Diamond promised. He was deceptively calm, and Anders began to complain.

"You got me in trouble with Vinnie. I got beat up. And he's not going to invite me to screenings any more. And he threw me out of his house. I don't want anything more to do with you. Go away."

"You're concerned about survival, right?"

Anders nodded.

"Well then, you're going to give me Vargas's unlisted number. Or I am going to take you apart piece by piece, and then take the pieces apart."

Anders realized that Red was on the edge. The mad gleam he had missed in Diamond's eyes was suddenly a vital, and violent, presence in the room. Anders knew that even if he could get to his gun, he would not be able to stop the primal beast that faced him. He gave Diamond the number.

"Now, you can call Vargas and tell him I was here. It don't matter to me one way or another," Diamond said, before leaving the trembling professor.

He went to a pay phone, and called Vargas's house.

"Put Vinnie on the line," Diamond said when Tony picked up.

"Who's this?"

"Red Diamond. I got what he wants."

Vargas came on quickly. "I heard about Randall. So you did that?"

"I got what you want."

"How much?"

"Come to Coldwater Canyon Park. Nine tonight. Just you alone, and we work out a deal."

"Gimme some idea what—"

Diamond hung up, and dialed Tanaka's office. He identified himself to the secretary, and Tanaka picked up.

"I understand you talked with my wife," Tanaka hissed. "I don't like that."

"And I don't like you or your Yakuza friend. But you're going to do business with me anyway."

"Is that so?"

"Did you hear what happened to Randall?"

"Yes. Did you do that?"

"I got what you want."

"How do I know that?"

"Come to Coldwater Canyon Park. Tonight. Nine o'-clock. I'll show you what I got."

"How much are you asking?"

He hung up again, then called Browning.

"I'll meet you tonight, ten o'clock, Coldwater Canyon Park. We'll talk. No tricks. I'll be watching. I see anyone else, goodbye Charlie."

"Diamond, listen why can't we just—"

Again Red ended the conversation. He had a couple of hours to kill before the sun would go down. He'd baited the trap. Rocco would have to come. He could feel it. The final act. Then Browning could sweep up the pieces. His only regret was that he didn't get to say farewell, my lovely, to Fifi.

He put seventy miles on the car, cruising from the run-down houses in Watts, out to the Malibu mansions along the Pacific. Then into Pacific Palisades on Sunset, through West Los Angeles, and over to Hollywood Boulevard.

A couple of hookers were out, but not much street action. The low riders were crawling along, their hot pink cars going up and down as they yelled their love to haughty women on the sidewalks.

Tourists, armed with Instamatics and gawky grins—bending over to read the prints in Graumann's cement and buying postcards and gewgaws—roamed starstruck.

He went back to Sunset, passing the front gates of the mansions and hotels the tourists were dreaming about. He had the feeling he wouldn't be seeing the sights for quite some time.

The time was nearing, and he made the right onto Coldwater. The fog was beginning to creep in, softening the sharp edges on the stately palms that lined his way.

The fog turned from a thin broth to a thick stew as he drove into the hills. At first the facades of the multimillion-dollar homes, set back from the roadway, were visible. As the fog grew thicker, only the outlines of the thick-trunked palms nearest the curb could be seen.

Soon even they were gone, and he had to slow to ten miles an hour as he plowed into the billowing white.

He crawled to the crest of the Santa Monica Mountains, to where Mulholland Drive cut through the greenery like a giant paved scar. The drive was a favorite trysting spot, where couples could look down on the lights of Los Angeles while making cramped love in sports cars.

It reminded him of Fifi, and he clenched his teeth. There'd be no love for Diamond on lovers' lane when he and Rocco met up.

He pulled his car off onto the shoulder, a couple thousand feet from the nearest amorously indifferent couple. He shut the ignition and rolled down his window.

Sound carried further in the fog. He'd learned that in London, working on that caper with Bulldog Drummond,

216

Diamond recalled. It would give him an advantage over any group that sought to outmaneuver him.

He wanted to listen to the radio, but could not risk the sound. He slumped down in his seat, and allowed himself a cigarette.

Strange how nature balanced things out, Diamond thought. Like a blind man that could hear real good, what you couldn't see in the fog, you could hear. Red Diamond, philosopher.

He ground his cigarette out in the packed ashtray, and exhaled the last cloud of blue nicotine smoke. He took a few deep breaths of the pepper-tree scented air, then glanced at his watch.

It was a few minutes after eight. The half-dozen cars that had passed had continued on their way, hillside dwellers returning to their stilted homes.

Diamond got out of his car and walked the several hundred feet to the park. The stone fence was waist high in its tallest spots, and he climbed it easily.

Leaves crunched underfoot as he walked to a clump of ramrod straight coast redwoods. He stood between two, his front and back protected by the thick, hard wood.

Cars whooshing by on the misted road sounded like a waterfall. The air was filled with a rich, organic perfume. The damp breeze felt soothing.

Rocco and his buddies should be along soon, he thought. They'd want to get there early, set up an ambush, get the drop on Red Diamond.

But he'd beaten them to the punch. All he had to do was be patient.

He didn't have to wait very long.

He heard the tires snickering on the roadway, then a crunching sound as they pulled onto the dirt shoulder. Four car doors slammed.

"Spread out that way and wait 'til I give the signal," said a voice Diamond recognized as Vargas's.

"Got you, boss," Tony said. "I hope we get this piece of work done quick. This fog is hurtin' my bones."

"Just take Bruno and Buddy and get in place," Vargas said. Red heard the three hoods moving off to his right.

They had traveled about twenty yards when Vargas shouted, "Get down! Someone's coming."

More car noises, and then Tanaka's guttural hiss. Katana said, *"Hai, oya-bun."* Another man echoed his words.

Diamond picked up a fist-sized rock and tossed it to where he guessed Tony was.

"Who's there?" Tanaka yelled. "Diamond?"

"Tanaka?" Vargas said.

"Who are you?" Tanaka asked.

Diamond cupped his hands to distort where his voice was coming from. "He's the guy that was supposed to get the paintings you were supposed to get."

"Diamond?" Vargas and Tanaka said simultaneously.

"Where's Fifi?" he answered.

"Who?" Vargas said.

"Do you have the paintings?" Tanaka asked.

"I'll only deal directly with Rocco. After I see the girl."

"What the hell are you talking about?" Vargas said.

"Where are you?" Tanaka shouted toward Vargas.

Vargas ignored the question. "Diamond, I want the paintings. I'm prepared to pay."

"You will," Diamond said ominously.

"Who will pay?" Tanaka said. He was about thirty-five feet from Vargas, but they were invisible to each other in the thick fog. "I'll pay more."

"I want the girl and I want Rocco, and you two can split the paintings. Right down the middle, for all I care."

During a quiet moment, Diamond heard Tony, Katana and the other henchmen creeping through the underbrush. They were no further apart than their bosses.

"We're going to have an auction," he said, shifting position slightly and listening as the two teams of killers came closer to each other.

"Double crosser!" Vargas shouted, before launching a bunch of obscenities in Diamond's direction.

"I thought it was just between you and me, Diamond," Tanaka said. He definitely had moved closer to Vargas.

"Listen, both of you. I didn't bring the half-dozen goons who are sneaking around the woods here with guns in their hands and murder in their hearts."

Diamond thought he could hear the sudden intake of air as everybody froze.

"So nobody blow a fuse," he said. "You'll both get what you wanted. Just give me the girl, and tell me where Rocco is hiding."

The strongarms began skulking, more slowly now.

"I don't know what you're talking about," Vargas said.

"You both front for him. I know it, so don't play me for a chump," Diamond said.

"Ki-chigai. You're crazy," Tanaka said.

"I want the paintings," Vargas said. "Let's make a deal. I don't know nothing about no girl."

There was a long pause. Gravel crunched under Tanaka's foot, then a shplit sound, and a curse from Vargas.

"Tony, I been shot!" he screamed.

Tony's gun barked, and was answered by shplit sounds from Katana's silenced weapon. Bruno and Buddy cut loose. One had a machine gun that thumped a couple dozen bullets into the trees in the space of a breath.

Katana's silenced gun sounded like a whisper after the automatic weapon, but the gasp of pain from Tony made it clear the Japanese bodyguard knew what he was doing.

Red moved over a few trees when the angry swarm of bullets in the air was momentarily stilled. In the silence, he heard Tony's dying gurgle and gasp.

Tanaka shouted something in Japanese, and Katana answered. Diamond couldn't understand what was said, but he aimed his .38 at the direction from which he guessed Katana would be coming.

He saw the Yakuza moving crablike through the underbrush. It was a silly sight, a grown man in a three-piece suit crawling like a kid in the dirt, Diamond thought as he squeezed off two shots.

Before Katana died, he put four slugs into the redwood next to Diamond's head.

Bruno, or Buddy, cut loose with the machine gun. Diamond crouched low, and moved to another thick tree five yards away.

When the chopper chatter stopped, Diamond stood upright, listening to the sound of Bruno and Buddy charging through the brush toward him.

Diamond turned to change his position, and a figure in black came flying through the air at him.

"*Aiiie,*" the second Japanese hood screamed.

The flying side kick and *kiai* caught Diamond by surprise. One calloused foot hit his hand, and his shot went wild. The kung fu master's follow-up knife-hand slice knocked a stunned Diamond to the ground.

The blow saved Diamond's life as the machine gun filled the air with noise and lead again. The kung fu expert, poised to give Diamond a coup de grace kick to the temple, froze in midair as the bullets stitched across his chest.

He smiled, sighed, and collapsed in a lifeless heap.

Still woozy, Red crawled frantically around the forest floor, looking for his lost .38 like a nearsighted librarian in search of a missing contact lense.

Bruno and Buddy were coming closer, letting off short bursts from an automatic weapon. They both had machine guns, Diamond decided, hearing slightly different burst patterns.

He grabbed the .38 that was lying on a small pile of leaves. Not daring to stand up, he rolled down the hill as bullets buried themselves in trees all around him. Diamond tumbled into a dry arroyo.

After catching his breath, he peeled off his sullied jacket. When there was a let-up in the shooting, he scrambled to a nearby bush, and draped his jacket over it.

"Split up," one of the hoods barked. "Outflank the son-of-a-bitch."

They separated and came closer.

Diamond picked up a rock, and tossed it by the jacket-clad bush. When something works, you stick with it, he thought with a grim smile.

A figure came charging forward, his Thompson spewing bullets into the unfortunate foliage. The muzzle flash gave Diamond a clear target. He fired two shots, and the Thompson was stilled.

"Buddy? Buddy?" the surviving hood shouted.

"Listen, Bruno, this is Diamond. Let's talk."

Bruno answered with a burst from his gun.

Diamond felt safe, protected by the dirt in his natural bunker. But he ached all over, he had one shot left, and despite the ringing in his ears, he could hear the faint sound of approaching sirens.

"We can make a deal. There's three more Japanese guys roaming around here," Diamond lied. "Let's you and me team up."

Silence. The siren's scream was weak, but growing stronger.

"Okay," Bruno said. "C'mon out."

"How can I trust you? Throw your chopper down."

"How can I trust you?" Bruno responded.

"I'm Red Diamond, private eye. I never shot an unarmed man."

A Schmeisser came sailing through the air, and landed about ten feet from Diamond. Red estimated that Bruno was about twenty feet away as he climbed cautiously out of the gully. He had his .38 in one hand, and a rock in the other.

"What about you?" Bruno said. "You throw down your gun."

"Okay," Diamond said, tossing the stone off into the brush. He had a renewed respect for rocks and the trick the Continental Op had taught him over beers in that San Francisco bar. Diamond had thrown more stones in the last ten minutes than a Neanderthal on his first mammoth hunt.

Diamond and Bruno approached each other slowly, like two wild animals not sure whether to attack. Diamond held the gun pressed to his chest, his left hand on top of his right, so it looked like he was clutching a wound.

"You got a gun?" Bruno asked, his hulking shape looming up in the fog.

"No. Can't you see? I been shot."

"Too bad," Bruno said, suddenly jerking a .32 out of a shoulder holster. They were four feet apart.

Before he had it leveled, Diamond put his last bullet through Bruno's aorta.

Diamond knelt over the body and retrieved the .32. He wiped the butt of the .38 on his pants, then dropped it on the floor near the body. He took a few steps toward the road, then leaned against a tree and listened.

The sirens were closer, only a couple of minutes away.

"Vargas! Tanaka! Your muscle is gone. We can talk

straight now. No more games. I want the girl and I want Rocco."

There was no answer, just the sound of the siren getting louder.

He could barely see his feet as he walked quietly through the brush.

"Vargas! Tanaka! Answer me. I want the girl and Rocco, and you can get away."

"I don't know what you're talking about," Vargas said. His voice was weak, like it hurt him to talk.

Diamond moved closer.

"We're the only ones left," Vargas said. "The Jap is dead. We can make a deal. I want the paintings."

"Where's the girl?"

"First the paintings."

Diamond guessed he was no more than twenty feet from Vargas. "You need help, Vargas. Where's the girl?"

"Okay, she's . . ." Vargas spoke too softly for Diamond to hear.

There wouldn't be much time to get away, Diamond thought. He'd have to slip off in the fog, go cross country. By the time he was done explaining to the cops just who killed who, Rocco would be in Bogota, or Marseilles, or any one of a half-dozen hideouts.

"What did you say?" Diamond asked, hurrying forward.

"The girl is . . ."

His words were drowned out by the siren.

"Where," Diamond asked. He saw the outline of Vargas's body. "Tell me, quick, where is she?"

"Right here," Vargas said, lifting his gun and firing.

Diamond felt the kick of a mule on his chest. He squeezed off two shots from the .32, then joined Vargas on the dirt roadway. It was more comfortable than it looked, he thought, as he went to sleep.

It was dark in his Flatiron Building office, the failing evening light slanting in through ancient venetian blinds. The bottle of Scotch on his desk was as empty as a church on Saturday night.

The woman's name was Milly and she had a problem. Her husband had disappeared. The way she told it, he wasn't much, but he was all she had. She didn't have any money. She offered to pay with her body or some books.

She was an easy-on-the-eyes brunette, with a peculiar, not unattractive, antiseptic smell. But Red Diamond was not the kind of guy who'd take advantage of an abandoned wife. He chose the books, but they crumbled when she handed them to him.

Then a knockout blonde burst through the door, and both women began pounding his chest, tearing at him with fingernails that grew longer with each gouge. The light slanting in grew brighter.

"He's coming around," a man said.

Diamond opened his eyes. He was in a hospital. Everything was white, except for the black bars on the window. And the dressing on his chest, which was an uneven red.

"What's up Doc?" he said to the bushy-eyebrowed elderly man who was bent over him.

"We thought we'd lost you," the doctor said. "The bullet nicked your aorta. You're a very lucky man."

"If I was so lucky, he would've missed completely," Diamond said, lifting his head from the pillow. "Did he make it?"

"If you mean Mr. Vargas, no. There were four men dead at the scene when the police arrived. They'd like to talk to you."

"I bet." His head was too heavy to support, and he slumped back onto the pillow.

"Rest up now," the doctor said. "I don't think you're quite ready for them."

"You're the doctor."

For the next three days, Diamond drifted in and out of consciousness. He had a recurring dream of being chased by a yellow cab whose hood opened and closed like a mechanical mouth.

His skin became covered with punctures, from IVs, transfusions and megadoses of antibiotics. Each time he woke, though, the gauze pads on his chest got smaller and smaller.

When it was down to the size of a paperback book, the doctor allowed the police to visit.

Diamond sat up in his bed as Browning walked in. Another homicide cop and a court stenographer trailed the lieutenant.

"The doctor says you're going to live. Congratulations," Browning said.

"Thanks. You come here to deliver a get-well card?"

The stenographer, a homely middle-aged woman who chewed gum diligently, clicked open her machine.

"Ready?" Browning asked her.

She cracked her gum and nodded.

"Okay, Mr. Diamond, let me advise you of your rights," Browning began, going through the Miranda warning without bothering to use a card. "So what happened?" he asked after Diamond had waived his rights.

"Manfred had business problems. If you go to the library, there's a nice old lady who'll try and explain what it all means, but apparently this company led by Tanaka was going to take it over. These corporate takeover deals can be as vicious as a bare-knuckles barroom brawl, I was told."

Diamond pressed a button, and the bed folded up to give him a backrest. He leaned back.

"You got a cigarette?" Diamond asked.

"Not for you, doctor's orders," Browning said. "Go on."

"During some negotiations, I'd guess, Manfred decides to buy off Tanaka with this art he's got. Real valuable stuff Manfred heisted out of Japan when he served there during World War Two. Am I going too fast?" Diamond asked the stenographer.

She cracked her gum, and shook her head again.

"Does she speak English?" Diamond asked in a stage-whispered aside to Browning.

The stenographer took the words down impassively.

"No wisecracking. Just keep going," Browning said.

"Manfred starts shopping for an insurance company to cover the art. Then he's going to have it stolen by Tanaka. He'd get Tanaka off his back, and some easy cash.

"Meanwhile, back at the ranch, Manfred gets a couple of real lulus as servants. You might want to check if Tanaka put the fix in with the referral agency. Todd, Rosalie and Randall. Was Rosalie ever in the service?"

"How'd you guess that?"

"I figured she was the only one that could've shot Todd. She chose a military rifle, and was a damn good shot with it."

"She had a bunch of prostitution arrests by age sixteen. The last one, the judge gave her the choice of jail or the WACS. She was dishonorably discharged."

Diamond smiled. "Randall finds out about the art deal, and decides to cut himself in on the action. Rosalie goes along with him. Todd does too, reluctantly. That's what Todd was beginning to tell me when he got shot."

"You should've told me that," Browning said.

"Maybe," Diamond said with a shrug. "Tanaka's man, Katana, and Todd pull the heist, and deliver the paintings to Randall to hold. Then Randall decides to double-cross Tanaka, and fence the art to Vinnie Vargas. He also takes Fifi with him."

"Fifi?"

"Manfred's daughter Alison. She's a helluva broad. We're going to be married. I been following that dame for ages."

"I see," Browning said skeptically. "Go on."

"Randall owes Vargas. He's going to clean the slate by working out this art deal. But he don't trust Vargas, and he hides out in Topanga Canyon. With Fifi. Then Rosalie comes, and there's a dispute. Manfred goes out there. Three wind up dead."

Diamond shifted in his bed.

"What happened that night in Coldwater Canyon?" Browning asked.

"I guess I better think about that before answering," Diamond said. "You got any other questions?"

"Where are the paintings?"

"Rocco's probably got them."

"Who's he?"

"The guy behind it. The guy that's playing me for a chump. Vargas worked for him. Tanaka too. You must have him in your intelligence files."

"How much of this do you know, and how much are you guessing? And how many people did you personally kill?"

Diamond lay back in the bed as the room began to spin.

"What's Rocco's last name?" Browning asked.

"Rico. Rocco Rico. Born in 1900. He's about fifty years old."

"Wait. If he's born in 1900, he's got to be about eighty-four by now."

"No. He's about fifty, built like a pit bull, with greasy black hair. He, he . . ."

Diamond was very pale. He tried talking, but his lips wouldn't move.

"That's it for now," Browning said, gesturing for the stenographer to halt. "A court-appointed psychiatrist will be by to see you tomorrow. See you."

Diamond tried to wave, but he was too weak to lift his hand. He eased back into the comforting darkness.

"Mr. Jaffe? Simon Jaffe?"

The middle-aged man speaking the strange name was leaning over Diamond's bed. His smiling face loomed large. Diamond could see the long dark hairs in his nose. He had a lay-away merchant's smile. The elderly doctor stood, frowning, in the background.

"He is not well," the doctor said. "I want you to know I don't approve of this."

The middle-aged man kept his smile. "But the administration does. This is important. Do you hear me, Mr. Jaffe?"

"I think you got the wrong patient, buddy. My name's Red Diamond."

"That's not what your fingerprints say. Allow me to introduce myself. I'm Doctor Charles Mandelbaum. My patients call me Charlie."

"You're a shrink, right?"

The elderly physician smirked.

"A psychiatrist, yes," Mandelbaum said. "What makes you say that?"

"I'm a detective. I make my living playing hunches."

"Not according to your fingerprints."

Diamond sat up. "Yeah?"

"I must object strenuously," the physician interrupted. "This is too sudden, it should be done—"

"Doctor, you stick to the body. I handle the mind," the psychiatrist said with an unctuous smile.

The physician stalked out of the room, and Mandelbaum returned his attention to Diamond.

"Now, Mr. Jaffe, the police have matched up your fingerprints. You are Simon Jaffe, a cab driver who disappeared in New York a couple of weeks ago. Does that sound familiar?"

The psychiatrist's tone was as soothing as a dab of warm vaseline. He wisely stroked his chin. His face was unlined, and Diamond couldn't guess his age. He had a full head of dark hair, and dark, probing eyes.

"You have a wife named Milly," Mandelbaum continued. "A son named Sean. A daughter named Melonie. You live on Long Island. Does that help?"

"You got your files screwed up," Diamond said after a moment's hesitation. "My name is Red Diamond. I'm a private dick. I been on my own the past few years. Chasing a dame and a punk named Rocco Rico."

"The police checked out that name. The only criminal anywhere near your description died five years ago."

Diamond chuckled. "Just like Rocco to cover his tracks. He's probably holding Fifi hostage somewhere. Laughing his head off."

"Fifi?"

"My gal. I been finding her and losing her these past few years. It's been hell."

"Hmmm," Mandelbaum said, making a few quick notes on a piece of paper. "Would you mind looking at a few cards?"

"Suit yourself."

Mandelbaum took a deck of Rorschach cards out of his pocket. "What does this look like?" he said, holding one up.

Diamond studied it.

"Say the first thing that comes into your mind," the psychiatrist said.

"My chest hurts."

"No. About the card. What does it look like?"

"A blob of ink."

"Try using your imagination. Now, quickly, what does it look like?"

"Two guys fighting over a gun. Like the time me and Rocco were on top of the Empire State Building. He had his roscoe out, and—"

"When you say 'roscoe,' do you mean penis?"

"What do you think I am, sick or something? A roscoe is a rod. A piece. A shooting iron. Where you been, Doc?"

"What about this one?" the psychiatrist said, holding out another card.

"That's easy. Me and Fifi, holding each other, when we

hid in the closet in that bootlegger's shack in Kentucky. They were going to burn the place down, until—"

"And this one?"

"A puddle of blood. Like the time I caught up with Rocco's boys near Fisherman's Wharf in Frisco. I emptied both barrels into the big guy before he went down, made a puddle just like—"

"That's enough, Mandelbaum," a bespectacled young man said angrily from the doorway. The doctor stood behind the young man, who frowned and added, "You want to speak to my client, you get a court order."

"Roberts, I was doing it with his consent," Mandelbaum said. "Besides, I had the permission of—"

"Irrelevant. Get out. I wish to confer with my client. And don't think I won't report this."

Mandelbaum packed up his deck and left, glaring at the physician as he passed him. The doctor smiled, and closed the door on Diamond and Roberts.

The lawyer was about thirty-five, lean, well dressed, with a confident stride as he walked to Diamond and extended his hand. He squeezed just hard enough to demonstrate sincerity.

"I'm Alvin Roberts. Your attorney." He set his monogrammed leather briefcase down on the bed.

"You a public defender?" Diamond asked.

"No. My services, which don't come cheaply, have been taken care of. Don't worry."

"Who's my fairy godfather?"

"Godmother. I don't know how Gwen Manfred convinced the guardian of her father's estate to authorize it, but payment has been taken care of. Enough about that. Now, your case. We should be able to get some mileage out of self-defense. Obviously, the prosecutor is anticipating an insanity defense, or he wouldn't have sent a quack like Mandelbaum here. Mandelbaum is the kind who'd certify the psychos at Camarillo as heads of state if he thought he'd get paid."

"I'm not crazy anyway."

"Of course. But I've got a doctor who can counterbalance Mandelbaum. Leave our options open. My man will stamp you as a paranoid schizophrenic, with multiple personalities, as soon as he gets his check."

Diamond frowned. "I don't like that."

"Not to worry. We'll make you a manic depressive. With delusions of grandeur. Whatever you want."

"I don't like this whole bughouse bit."

"Listen my friend, they've got you dead to rights. Browning is trying to close the books on a half-dozen cases with you. And I hear New York wants you for a few more. We're not talking jaywalking here. We're talking the big M. Murder. Understand, Mr. Jaffe?"

"My name's not Jaffe. It's Diamond. Red Diamond."

"Good. That's the spirit. Multiple personality. I have to be back in court. But keep it up. And don't talk to anyone."

Roberts picked up his briefcase and made for the door.

"Hey, you know what happened to Fifi?"

"She's a potential witness on your behalf?" Roberts said, turning.

"Yeah. She's my girl."

"I'll find out. I'll let you know at the arraignment tomorrow."

Although Diamond was able to move around on his own, albeit slowly, Roberts insisted he appear at the hearing in a wheelchair. A sheriff's deputy pushed the wheelchair into the hearing room.

Diamond didn't realize how weak he was until he got into court. The noise, the television cameras, the questions, made him sag into the wheelchair. Roberts gave him a wink, and beamed.

Browning read an affidavit that accused him of the murder of virtually every person he had met since he came to Los Angeles. Browning referred to him as Simon Jaffe, a.k.a. Red Diamond.

The prosecutor, a petite young woman with a friendly manner and a razor-sharp tongue, insisted on calling him Mr. Jaffe as she cut him to shreds.

Diamond complained out loud, and the judge promised to hold him in contempt if he didn't remain quiet.

Diamond blew the prosecutor a kiss as she made him sound like a cross between Charles Manson and Richard Speck, with a little Attila the Hun thrown in for laughs.

Roberts's description of Diamond was so glowing that he looked around the courtroom to see who the attorney was talking about. Roberts, who referred to him only as 'my poor client,' said that even if Red wasn't as wonderful as he made him sound, then he was crazy. And besides that, everything the police had done was illegal.

After Roberts's impassioned address, the judge harrumphed and ordered Diamond held without bail.

Roberts vowed to file a ream of motions for violation of civil rights, discovery of police material, suppression of unfavorable evidence, dismissal of charges for prosecutorial overreaching and prejudicial pretrial publicity.

The judge harrumphed again, and ordered Diamond back to the court the next day for an extradition hearing.

He was wheeled from the courtroom. As he and Roberts had a moment alone, he asked about Fifi.

"She ran off with a motel clerk, Browning told me," the lawyer said. "They headed east. He thinks she's in New York. They want her as a material witness. I retained a private investigator to get to her first."

"Who?"

"Golden Investigations. A very good outfit."

"You should've checked with me. My buddy Phil Marlowe would've done it."

"*The* Philip Marlowe?" Roberts said, his eyebrows flying up like a skyrocket.

"Who else?"

Roberts stared at Diamond as the deputy wheeled him away.

Roberts began an eloquent oration at the extradition hearing, but Diamond interrupted him.

"Your honor, I'd like to address the bench," Diamond said, rising from his wheelchair.

The court buffs stopped their murmuring and the news people began scribbling. Roberts was left with his mouth hanging open.

"Go ahead," the judge said, leaning into his high-backed chair and idly fingering his nose.

"I just did what I had to do," Diamond said in uncharacteristically soft tones. "I guess I've worn out my welcome here. I'd like to go back to New York."

Roberts was tugging at Diamond's arm, trying to get him to sit down.

"Your honor, my poor client doesn't—"

"Mr. Roberts is a fine attorney, but I disagree with him," Diamond said. "I'm going to waive extradition and go back to New York."

The news people ran from the court. Roberts sat back in dejection. The prosecutor grinned as the judge ordered that Diamond be returned to New York to face additional murder charges.

The paperwork took two days to be processed. Red was moved from the jail ward at County–USC Medical Center to the infirmary at the jail on Bauchet Street. He spent both days staring at the wall, refusing to eat.

Rocco had beaten him, he kept thinking. The system didn't work. All his life, he'd been skeptical, cynical, pessimistic. But deep down, there'd been a certain faith, a basic belief in the decency of people and the efficiency of civilization. But Diamond was sitting in jail while Rocco was free to go about his business. The fact that good guys don't always win hit him harder than Vargas's shot.

And Fifi had disappeared under strange circumstances. Was it really possible she'd run off with the clerk? It hadn't been like he'd hoped with her. Nothing had worked out the way he'd planned. Maybe he'd find some answers in New York.

He sank into a depressed morass as sticky and deep as the La Brea tar pits. He stopped talking to his jailers. And swapping insults with the other inmates. And even refused to talk to Roberts.

He skipped lunch and supper, and spent the night staring at the obscene graffiti on the wall, never really reading what it said.

Breakfast, lunch and dinner passed again. Roberts visited, but Diamond said nothing.

"Tomorrow morning, you go back to New York. A detective is coming to pick you up. Good luck," Roberts said, as the door slammed behind him and Diamond was alone again.

Diamond hadn't moved as the morning light forced its way into the jail.

He heard two sets of footsteps walking down the hall. He recognized the tread of the fat deputy. And with the deputy was a familiar-looking man with an unlit cigar drooping from his lips.

"Hello. Remember me?" Detective Pete Anglich said.

Diamond looked at him through blank, bloodshot eyes.

Diamond stuck out his wrists to be handcuffed. Anglich pushed them down.

"We can do this the easy way, or the hard way," the cop said. His gravelly New York tones sounded soothing and sincere. "I can fold you up in a box and ship you back. I can knock you over the head and carry you on. I can cuff you and walk you on. Or we can get on the plane like two normal human beings."

The cop's speech didn't sound rehearsed. It was smooth, confident. Red felt in safe hands.

"I won't make any trouble," he said softly.

"I'll take your word for that."

The deputy looked on skeptically as the two men walked out, Anglich with a cocky waddle, Diamond stooped over slightly, a broken man.

They were chauffeured to the airport by a deputy in an unmarked car.

"Helluva town," Anglich said as they neared LAX.

"Yeah."

"Nice weather. I went to Disneyland about six years ago with my first wife. Midwinter, and I'm walking around in a T-shirt. All these cute little blondes in short shorts. My wife kept giving me the elbow to keep my eyes in my head."

"Yeah."

"Everything's so damn far apart though. Twenty-minute drive just to go to the john." Anglich smiled and waited for a reaction to his joke.

"Yeah."

They got out at LAX and boarded a 747. Anglich had to buckle Diamond in, as he just sat with his arms limply at his sides when the warning light came on.

They climbed to thirty-five thousand feet and the Seatbelts–No Smoking lights blinked off. Anglich left him strapped in, and offered him a cigarette. He took it and he and Anglich lit up. The cop pretended to be casual.

"You know, that Hollywood homicide guy Browning told me about what you said, about Rocco Rico and Fifi and all of that."

Diamond nodded and puffed on his cigarette.

"When I first met you, I thought that name Red Diamond sounded vaguely familiar. I ran it by a couple of old dicks back in New York. They knew of Red Diamond."

A small smile creased Diamond's lips. "I used to be quite a guy, I guess."

"Well, the Red Diamond they knew of used to be in the

pulps. And the dime novels. A tough private dick. I found one guy, he's gonna retire in a month or so, who was saying he's looking forward to rereading all of them. He was talking about Race Williams, the Continental Op, Philip Marlowe, the way younger guys talk about chicks."

Diamond gazed out the window. The plane was surrounded by clouds. It reminded him of the night in Coldwater Canyon Park.

"So I asked him about Red Diamond," Anglich continued. "He told me about Diamond and Rocco and Fifi. He said there were about twenty-five short stories in *Black Mask,* and then a half-dozen novels, all about Diamond."

Red gave what he hoped was a humble smile, and crushed the cigarette out in the ashtray recessed in the arm of his seat. "Yeah, they used to write about me pretty good back then."

"How old are you?"

"Forty-three."

"Well, I twisted this guy's arm and he loaned me a bunch of his pulps. I had to handle them with kid gloves. They were about to fall apart."

Anglich had Diamond's full attention. He extinguished his own cigarette, then tucked an unlit cigar in his muzzle.

"Anyway, the stories appeared in the thirties and the forties. A couple came out in the early fifties," Anglich said, like it was the punchline to a long joke.

"So?"

"That means when they appeared, you either weren't even a gleam in your father's eye, or were just out of diapers."

There was a roar inside Diamond's head that didn't come from the jet engines. Anglich lit another cigarette and pretended not to watch him.

"It can't be. I know it. I remember the cases so clearly. Like the one where they were running illegals across the

236

border, and I was working for the agency then, and I went to this town, and there were these guys, and . . ." Diamond began sputtering.

"I think you picked up details from other stories, like, was this town you went to called Corkscrew?"

"Yeah, that was it, Corkscrew," Diamond said confidently. "How'd you know?"

"That was a story by Dashiell Hammett. His Continental Op. I read a bunch of them. Pretty good stuff. A lot better than the crap nowadays."

"What about the time with Trimmer Waltz, one of Rocco's front men, when Fifi was tricked into making the pickup on that street. I was working undercover, and just happened to be in Tough Town when it went down. It was on Noon Street. I remember it real clearly."

"Pickup on Noon Street. By Raymond Chandler."

Diamond began to quiver. He rattled off a half-dozen more of his adventures, and Anglich supplied a title and author for each one.

"But, but they were about me," Diamond shouted. "I did it all. They stole it. Hammett, Chandler, Daly, Nebel, Gardner, Dent. Just a bunch of thieves. It's my life. My story!"

Passengers around them began to gawk. Diamond burbled, then lapsed into silence. His lips moved soundlessly. Anglich kept his hand on his lap. He was playing with mental dynamite, and he knew it.

A perky stewardess, her inquisitive face as Irish as a leprechaun perched on the Blarney Stone, came over and asked if everything was all right.

Anglich winked at her and explained Diamond was a famous method actor rehearsing his next part. She asked that he do it quietly, and took their meal order.

The food came and Anglich wound up eating his prisoner's untouched portion. Diamond just stared out at the clouds as the plane passed over the Rockies and America's flat belly.

"You know, I really did enjoy those pulp stories," Anglich said, trying to draw Diamond out of his shell after the trays had been cleared away.

Red just grunted.

Anglich had the stewardess pick him up a copy of *Sports Illustrated*, explaining that he couldn't leave his seat because of an old war injury. He flirted with her a bit when she came back, took the magazine and read it cover to cover.

Diamond mumbled and stared out the window. Anglich leaned over and eavesdropped on his solo conversation, but he couldn't understand what was being said.

As they passed over New Jersey, Anglich tried unsuccessfully to wangle the home phone number of the red-headed stewardess. He pretended to pay no attention to Diamond. Diamond paid no attention to him.

"She's a real cutie," Anglich said as the Seatbelts–Cigarettes Out light flashed on, and the stewardess made her way down the aisle, checking that all was as it should be.

Diamond said nothing.

A few bumps, a change in the engines' drone, and they were solidly on the tarmac at JFK.

The aisle was clogged with people shoving their way off the plane. As Diamond and Anglich waited for the crowd to thin out, Diamond turned to the cop and whispered, "If I'm not Red Diamond, then who am I?"

Anglich opened his notebook. "According to your prints, you're Simon Jaffe, age forty-three, a cabbie who lives on the Island. You've been married nineteen years to a woman named Mildred. Two kids. No arrests, two speeding violations. I interviewed Mildred. She seems like a nice lady."

"What does she look like?"

"I got a picture right here," Anglich said, taking out a snapshot of a man, a woman, a boy and a girl, in front of a plain-looking tract house. "She said the picture was about five years old."

He studied it. The man in the photo could be him. The jaw was weaker, the eyes seemed softer, and the man held himself in a limp kind of way, but it could be him. The woman wasn't bad. The kids seemed okay.

His hands began to tremble. He gripped the arms of the chair to keep them still.

"Time to go," the stewardess said, giving the two men a professional smile.

"One second," Anglich said, all business again. "Can you walk, Simon?"

"I . . . am . . . not . . . Simon . . . Jaffe," Diamond said. "I . . . am . . . Red Diamond, private eye." Each word was a strain.

The stewardess watched nervously, not sure what exactly was going on.

"I . . . am . . . Red, ready, right to get." Diamond began sputtering.

Anglich took an arm and lifted him up. "Let's go." His voice was firm. He was in command. Diamond obeyed.

"No more talk about it," Anglich said.

"Nothing to talk about. I am . . . Red Diamond," he said, forcing as much conviction as he could muster into his tone.

They walked out and through the baggage-claim area. Anglich hadn't brought any, and Diamond's needs were going to be taken care of by the state.

The chill of the evening air struck them as they waited at the curb for a cab to pull up. Anglich adjusted his wristwatch. With time-zone changes and travel time, it was already four-thirty P.M.

But the District Attorney had wanted him to bring Diamond right to his office. There was no time to settle in. There were headlines to be made, live feeds to be filmed for the six o'clock news.

The cab pulled up and they climbed in.

Anglich told the cabbie to take them to the District Attorney's office in Manhattan. The driver grunted, and stepped on the gas.

"Feeling better?" Anglich asked.

"Sure." There was a time when he wouldn't have given a homicide cop taking him in the time of day. But that time was past. The game was over.

"We got a little session with the D.A.," Anglich said. "He's a good guy to talk to. Then I'll check you in at Bellevue."

Diamond nodded. He knew what Bellevue meant. It was for bedbugs, loonies, wackos, psychos. Underneath Anglich's talk, that was the bottom line. Diamond felt too tired to protest.

"You still have that photo?" he asked.

"Yeah," Anglich said, fishing it out and handing it to him.

Diamond tried to imagine the lives of the people in the picture. The boy looked smart. The girl looked like she needed a spanking. The woman looked like someone he wouldn't mind knowing. Someone he had known. He was drowning in a thick sea of déjà vu, unsure where the shoreline of reality began.

"Don't take the Van Wyck," Diamond said suddenly to the cabbie. "The meter'll run and we'll sit in traffic. Take city streets. We're not a couple of hicks, you know."

The words came out reflexively. The cabbie checked him in his mirror, then turned off the highway.

"Hey buddy, I know you," the cabbie said. "You was

hacking. Remember me? Flitcraft. Charlie Flitcraft. You drove me from Forty-second to Fourteenth Street."

The driver's face didn't register until Diamond studied the license photo tacked to the back of the front seat.

Flitcraft's face was familiar. It swam at him in the confusing sea of faces that blurred his vision. A fare? Big tipper? Red Diamond? No, Flitcraft. Charlie no face. The faceless man. The loser. Just like me.

Diamond disassembled, shaking like a '64 Chevy with a bad suspension. Words exploded from his mouth, climbing over each other, fighting for position, falling down, slurring each other.

"In the garbage, no help, pulp, gone, pulp help, Milly don't, sold, alone, cab, city, hooker, trick tricked . . ."

Anglich let him babble, while the amazed cabbie watched in the rearview mirror.

"Hooker hooked, pimp, shoot, blood, blood, bodies and blood, pulp closet hero dark, help, need help . . ."

"Take it easy," Anglich said, worried as Diamond began to whimper. He squeezed his arm reassuringly.

"Maybe we ought to stop at a hospital?" Flitcraft asked. "He ain't gonna throw up in my cab, is he?"

"Just keep driving," Anglich ordered.

Diamond babbled less and less intelligibly. He sounded like a baby struggling to put together its first sentence. A frustrated baby with a man's voice and vocabulary.

"I think we better get him to a doctor," Flitcraft said.

Anglich took out his shield and flashed it. "This is official police business. Get us to the D.A.'s office and don't worry about getting stopped."

Flitcraft pressed the gas and grinned.

"Boy oh boy, wait till I tell the guys in the garage. This is just like Kojak. You really a cop?"

Anglich didn't say anything. Diamond didn't shut up, but he was talking a language that was his alone. The words were the same as Anglich spoke, but they came out in no particular order.

Horns blared and cars swerved as they barreled up Flatbush Avenue.

"Don't get us killed, ace," Anglich said. "Just keep us moving. To the D.A.'s office on Leonard Street. You know where it is?"

"Sure. Right near the Tombs. Just sit back, I'll handle everything." Flitcraft talked fast, beeping the horn and jumping a red light.

"No more of that," Anglich barked, as a bus jumped the curb to avoid totaling them.

The clearly disappointed driver slowed down, but picked up speed again after they were through downtown Brooklyn and onto the approach of the Manhattan Bridge.

"Cruise fares, all's fair, don't pick up no one you don't like, screw the commission, Fifi at the curb, Rocco in back, pay the bills, private eyes watching." Diamond's staccato babble increased with the higher speed.

"We're now in Manhattan," Flitcraft said proudly as they passed the midpoint on the bridge. "A record half-hour. In this traffic. What a day! Better than 'Colombo.' Better than 'Adam-12.'"

The streets were crowded as he sped from Chinatown to the Civic Center. Dozens of pedestrians used to jay-walking with impunity were forced to jump back as Flit-craft weaved through traffic.

A dignified matron angrily gave them the finger, a gesture that was repeated by numerous others. Anglich couldn't hear what they were shouting, but he had a fair idea it wasn't complimentary.

Flitcraft jammed on the brakes.

"Where are we?" Anglich's prisoner asked. His voice was different, less assertive, less confident. "What am I doing in the back seat? And who put a bulletproof partition in my cab?"

An excited Anglich offered Flitcraft a twenty-dollar bill.

"I don't need no tip, buddy," Flitcraft said. "It's not often I get this much fun."

"Keep it," Anglich said, taking the man born as Simon Jaffe by one arm and helping him out of the cab.

Simon stood wobbling, as office workers flowing out of the building breezed by him. Two men squabbled over Flitcraft's cab. Using an attaché case as a barrier, the taller of the two made it in. Flitcraft pulled away as the shorter man stood cursing on the curb.

"Relax pal, my cab's just up the block," Simon said.

"Not now," Anglich said. "You've got a date with the man upstairs."

He tugged Simon's arm and they entered the granite-based, limestone building. Anglich flashed his shield to the cop on duty at the desk, and was waved past.

"You remember anything?" Anglich said casually to Diamond as they waited by the bank of three elevators.

"It was raining, I thought," Simon began. "Milly threw out my stuff. All of it." He had a pained expression on his face. "I came into the city. I don't know, I guess I just wanted to get some air. It was raining. Ran out of gas. First time in all these years I ever ran out of gas. Then this hooker . . ."

Simon paused, ashamed. "I'm not the kind of guy that does that, you know. I just, sort of, went along."

"Sure, I understand," Anglich said soothingly. "It happens to the best of us."

"She knew someone I was searching for," Simon said. "I wouldn't have gone along otherwise."

An elevator opened and a dozen bodies piled out like clowns from a funny car. Anglich and his prisoner stepped in. Anglich pushed the button for the eighth floor, and eased Simon to the back of the car. Four people got in, pushed buttons for their destinations, and the elevator rose.

Simon stared at the graffiti-marked wall, oblivious to the people around him.

"She was a hooker," he said loudly. "I went with her to the hotel."

Anglich looked embarrassed as only a homicide cop can look. The other passengers pretended to be watching for their floors.

"She began to touch me," Simon said. "It felt good. I never did it before. Not with a hooker. I guess I was mad at Milly for throwing my stuff out. The hooker took control. Took advantage."

At the sixth floor the door opened and closed, with the dapper man who had pushed the button ignoring his chance to leave.

"Then there was the knock at the door," Simon continued. "I hid in the closet. She helped me to hide. Noises, scary noises. It was dark. When I came out it was quiet. I don't know how much later. Everything was gone. She'd played me for a sucker."

At the seventh floor the door opened and closed. The obese cleaning lady who'd originally pushed the button decided not to get off.

"I guess I got a little crazy," Simon said, unaware of the ten other ears that were taking in his tale. "I ran around. I got sick. I didn't know what to do. I had nowhere to go. So I went back into the closet. It seemed like days."

Simon was heaving and gasping for air as the memories forced their way out.

"I heard noises again. Another prostitute and a man. Then the pimp again. And shouts. And shots. And I came out and they were there. All dead."

Simon was wide-eyed and talking fast. "I didn't know what to do. Blood and bodies and my clothes were gone. Things got blurry, and then, then . . ."

The door opened on eight, and Anglich took Simon's arm. "Our floor," he said gently.

The other passengers stared as the cop and his prisoner got off. Anglich led Simon down a long corridor.

"There were more bodies. Black men, white men.

244

Women, more men. More dead." Simon began to cry. Anglich handed him a soiled handkerchief, which Simon rubbed across his eyes.

"Just sit here a second," Anglich said, easing Simon into a soft chair in the District Attorney's outer office. "I won't be a minute."

Anglich signaled to a uniformed cop at the far side of the room, pointed to Simon and mouthed the words "Watch him." The uniformed cop nodded.

Anglich barged into the District Attorney's inner office. Simon could hear his excited voice, and the reasonant sounds of a man accustomed to public speaking. Their words were obscured by the sound of the D.A.'s secretary, who sat typing at a desk a few feet from Simon.

Simon lifted his head and noticed the young woman. Ashamed of his tears, he tucked Anglich's handkerchief into his pocket. He stifled his sniffles. She gave him an understanding smile, like she'd seen a lot of sad people going into the prosecutor's office.

Her long blond hair fell over the shoulders of a tight-fitting red dress. Her body was wrapped just enough to be discreet, but she looked like the kind of secretary who didn't need to know how to type. The make-up she wore added to the fullness of her lips, and the depth of her warm blue eyes.

She smiled again, amused by his stare.

"Fifi?" he asked.

"My name's Fiona," she said in a voice as theatrically female as her boss's was male. "But my friends call me Fifi."

Anglich hurried out of the inner office, followed by a patrician-looking man in a dark gray suit.

Anglich knew something was wrong when his prisoner rose confidently from the chair and stuck out his hand to the District Attorney.

"The name's Diamond," he said. "Red Diamond. I wanna talk to my lawyer."

EPILOGUE

Cabbie Shamus Cleared in Multiple Slayings

Simon Jaffe, the cab driver who gained national fame as private investigator Red Diamond, was cleared by a state court jury of five counts of murder yesterday following a three-week trial.

Jaffe, forty-three, who apparently believes he is a 1940s tough-guy private eye, was found innocent by a seven-man, five-woman jury which deliberated four hours.

At the same time, California officials announced they would not be prosecuting him for the half-dozen homicides on the West Coast that he had been suspected of.

"In the interest of justice, we move to dismiss the indictment," Los Angeles District Attorney Frank Candida said. "Further investigation has shown that Mr. Jaffe, also known as Red Diamond, was just not culpable."

Jaffe had gone on trial for five murders. In the first incident, a pimp, a prostitute and her customer were found shot to death in the Lido Hotel in Times Square eight months ago.

Police also linked Jaffe to a double homicide on West 96th Street which occurred less than a week later. Two men, both with alleged ties to black organized crime, were found murdered in the apartment of one of the victims.

Jaffe's bicoastal defense team included a constitutional law scholar from Harvard Law School, an insanity defense expert based in New York and a leading criminal

246

trial lawyer from Los Angeles.

Just who was footing the hefty legal bill only adds to the mystery surrounding the case.

The New York trial went badly for District Attorney Timothy LoVallo. Defense lawyers were able to get key evidence and admissions suppressed in the deluge of motions they filed even before the case came to trial.

Self-defense and insanity arguments further set back the prosecution.

"I drove a cab for three years, and it's enough to make anyone crazy," said juror Edward Wait, 48.

Benjamin Dover, another juror, said, "It sounded like all the people he was accused of killing deserved to die. And those that didn't, he didn't really have a hand in. He was just in the wrong places at the wrong times."

Officials at the House of Detention for Men on Riker's Island, where Jaffe was held, said they've received hundreds of letters addressed to him. According to officials, and Jaffe's lawyers, the let-ters included requests to hire Jaffe, marriage proposals, and fan letters.

His wife, Mildred, who has remained in the family home on Long Island, filed for divorce shortly after Jaffe's disappearance. She could not be reached for comment on the verdict.

The courtroom had been packed each day by a crowd that seemed to support the defendant. Spectators identified themselves as cab drivers, former neighbors and avid readers of pulp novels.

As Jaffe walked from the courtroom a free man, the audience cheered. Judge Marcy Norton only smiled at the display of emotion in her courtroom.

Jaffe, who was pounded on the back and embraced by dozens of supporters, commented, "It's really great to be out. I'm gonna hole up somewhere with a bottle and unwind. Then I'm going to get Fifi back.

"I'm putting Rocco on notice," he added. "Red Diamond's back in action."